Frances Heasm[...]
to school in Dulwich, London, and [...]
universities of Oxford and Bristol. Since graduating she
has worked in television and films.

FRANCES HEASMAN

Blind Justice

Based on the TV series by
Helena Kennedy and Peter Flannery

PENGUIN BOOKS

PENGUIN BOOKS

Published by the Penguin Group
27 Wrights Lane, London w8 5tz, England
Viking Penguin Inc., 40 West 23rd Street, New York, New York 10010, USA
Penguin Books Australia Ltd, Ringwood, Victoria, Australia
Penguin Books Canada Ltd, 2801 John Street, Markham, Ontario, Canada l3r 1b4
Penguin Books (NZ) Ltd, 182–190 Wairau Road, Auckland 10, New Zealand

Penguin Books Ltd, Registered Offices: Harmondsworth, Middlesex, England

First published 1988
10 9 8 7 6 5 4 3 2 1

Filmset in Linotron Sabon by Centracet, Cambridge
Made and printed in Great Britain by
Cox & Wyman, Reading

PART I

CHAPTER ONE

Isn't English weather wonderful? Bright sunshine this morning, and now London's in the grip of some kind of non-tropical typhoon. Here I am, a reasonably respected member of the Bar, famous for my powers of organization, feared for my inability to suffer fools gladly; and every single one of my three umbrellas is at home. As a result, I am soaked through, miserable as sin, and going to shelter under this tree until the worst of this bloody rain is over.

Huddled damply under its branches, she cast a critical eye over two male members of her Chambers, as they passed by some distance away. Henry and Edmund hadn't got umbrellas; but the rain didn't seem to affect them at all. Laughing away. Pissed probably, she thought. Typical.

Well, she thought, leaning heavily against the trunk, at least it's dry under here. She looked up at the leaves above her head. What was this one called? She tried to remember. Her father would have known, tireless self-educator that he was. Probably a plane tree.

Sod it, she thought, as a gust of wind blew a cascade of huge drops on to her face. It's probably acid rain, too, she thought, as dampness trickled down her neck and inside her best white linen shirt.

She sniffed, and felt angry with herself when tears came to her eyes. Bloody judges. She knew she shouldn't be surprised any more at them but Judge Langtry today had more than lived up to his brutish reputation. Not only had he not shown the least interest in Katherine's defence: he had succeeded in talking through most of it.

Katherine sniffed again. She wiped her face. Were those tears or raindrops? Pull yourself together, Katherine Hughes, she thought.

Why had this particular case got to her? Patricia was guilty, after all. Transparently so. Shoplifting in Marks and Spencer's, Oxford Street, with such wild incompetence that store detectives had been queueing up to arrest her. Guilty, of course, but just as guilty – in Langtry's eyes at least – of being black, working-class and a young un-married mother-to-be.

A short sharp shock, Judge Langtry had ordered. Borstal, where no doubt Patricia would learn to be a more efficient shoplifter. Small wonder that British prisons were overflowing. So bloody unnecessary. She blew her nose. Did male lawyers cry about their cases?

'Turned out nice again!'

A sardonic male voice made her jump. It came from the neighbouring tree. Katherine smiled wanly. In Lincoln's Inn Fields, even the trees were articulate.

A familiar figure was peering at her. Katherine hoped she didn't look too rain-sodden, and then wondered why she cared. After all, Frank Cartwright had seen her in all sorts of situations. They were old friends. Mind you, she'd never allowed him to see her cry. She averted her face and dabbed away at it with her handkerchief. Turning round, she found Frank beside her, but fortunately he looked even more drenched than she did.

4

He looked at her like a sympathetic spaniel. Katherine knew that he knew she had been weeping.

'I'm having a bad day,' she said, defiantly.

He nodded. Katherine saw him looking at her shrewdly, the way he always did when he was leading up to something.

'Busy?' he asked, with elaborate carelessness.

Katherine bit back a caustic reply. She was always busy, for God's sake.

'Well, you know me, Frank!' she said instead. 'Anything for a bit of money!'

Frank laughed, knowingly. A wave of affection suddenly came over Katherine. She put her arms round Frank and hugged him.

'Great,' she said. 'You finally made it!'

'Yeah,' he agreed, with his usual attractive mixture of modesty and conceit. 'I've signed the lease. Fetter Court. Drop in. Right across from the Bailey.'

'Your own Chambers. It's wonderful!'

Katherine beamed with delight at her old friend's achievement.

'It's a democracy,' he scolded her.

'Well, it would be!'

Katherine grinned. She knew that she and Frank would never be able to agree on how a Chambers should be run. That was one of the many reasons why she knew they'd never be able to consummate a professional relationship. She liked him too much.

She hadn't noticed that the rain had stopped. Frank seized her by the arm and propelled her into the open.

'Come on and have a look,' he said.

She felt herself stiffen. Excuses began to form in her mind.

'Oh, I dunno,' she said doubtfully. 'I . . .'

She looked at his face, all boyish excitement and

expectation. Katherine felt Frank's enthusiasm rub off on her. Her black mood began to lift. Hell, she thought, why not?

Without seeming to think about it, Frank linked arms with Katherine, just as he had done on their first demo together. God, was it really twenty years ago?

As the two of them avoided the puddles down Chancery Lane, Katherine remembered her university days, when she had shared a flat with Claudia and Annie. They had been inseparable, a trio united by the revolutionary ideals of the time. Those days had vanished, of course; but Claudia and Annie remained Katherine's closest friends.

Claudia had gone into journalism and then broadcasting. Now she was a producer at the BBC, and Katherine hadn't 'seen her for months. She made a mental note to invite her to have lunch, or go to the theatre or something. God knows when she'd be able to manage it, though.

Annie had always been the prettiest; and it was through Annie that Katherine had met Frank. During the seventies, while Katherine was getting married and then unmarried, Frank and Annie had lived together in a small basement flat in Finsbury Park. After about seven years, the exotically named Alethea had come along (supposedly by accident, though Katherine never could see how, since she knew Annie was on the pill). The baby had necessitated a move to a two-bedroom, third-floor flat in Highbury.

Frank's increasing success as a barrister resulted in a move to a bigger house in Barnsbury, and Katherine had known that middle-class respectability had won out when Frank and Annie sneaked off to a registry office, a month before John was born. Katherine was out of the country at the time, and had been quite hurt that she had missed her friend's wedding.

Annie still looked good and amazingly thin, although three children and fifteen years of social work had given her an expression of perpetual anxiety. Even now, Annie was the most ardent feminist of them all — unless you counted Frank, whose feminism was conceptual rather than practical. Katherine had been unable to stop teasing them when she discovered that Frank now expected Annie to iron his shirts.

Katherine looked at Frank. He smiled back. Not the slim young man he used to be, she thought critically. It's all those restaurant meals, booze, cosy domesticity. Greying hair, more lines on his face . . . Still, he looked happier than she had seen him for ages. Over the last decade, Frank and she had had many a drunken evening, during which they had poured out their professional problems to one another. Annie would usually fall asleep, or go up to bed and leave them to it.

Katherine knew that Frank had been going through a bad patch, professionally, for about five years. His financial situation was improving; but, untypically for someone of his generation, he still managed to cling to most of his early beliefs and principles. Like Katherine, Frank was the token progressive in a very conservative Chambers. Unlike Katherine, Frank found the situation intolerable. For years, he had talked of breaking free and setting up his own radical Chambers. It would be a big risk, especially for a family man with three children; but now, at last, it was a reality.

Frank escorted Katherine round the back of the Old Bailey. She knew that Frank had chosen the new Chambers because they were convenient for the law courts, but not actually inside any of the old Inns of Court. Well, she thought, at least the entrance is impressive: rather like an Oxford college, in fact, with its huge wooden gate and a smaller door set inside it.

Frank opened the door, and she stepped through. Although the name 'Fetter Court' had sounded impressive when Frank had mentioned it, Katherine was disappointed to see that it was really no more than a derelict warehouse. And yet, as she knew from Annie, leasing the top floor was going to cost Frank a fortune.

They walked up five flights of metal stairs, and Katherine wished that she was fitter, and that she wasn't wearing high heels. Both of them were breathless by the time they reached the top, although Frank pretended not to be.

In front of them was a vast door of black steel. Frank unlocked it, and the door slid smoothly aside on rollers. He walked proudly into his new domain, Katherine following. It was certainly a gigantic space. Thick iron pillars and sturdy girders supported an impressive, unnecessarily ornate dome of Victorian glass. Birds were hopping around the floor, drinking from puddles which the rain had left. Katherine decided that the dome was more beautiful than it was functional.

'Good, isn't it?' said Frank, more as an expression of faith than as a question.

Katherine could see that he imagined the place already as a thriving law practice. She hoped that he was right.

'Is this a Chambers, or are you thinking of racing a few pigeons?' she asked, smiling.

'No. It'll be great!' Frank beamed, then looked hard at her. ''Course it all depends on who comes in with me.'

Katherine sighed. She had been through this umpteen times before. The rain began again, making a fearful racket on the glass dome.

'Don't be pissed off with me,' she said. 'It's boring.'

'I'm not!' Frank said defensively.

'You are. I've given you my reasons.'

'You haven't, actually. All you said, and I admit you were paralytic, but all you actually said was: you didn't want to sit around drinking Maxwell House, listening to half a dozen second-rate barristers banging on about Nicaragua.'

Katherine felt unrepentant. She remembered how she had argued, more or less coherently, that their job was to fight from within the establishment, not to set themselves up in a ghetto. Many bottles of *Fitou* later, Annie had excused herself and left Frank and Katherine to continue their ideological struggle in the basement kitchen. Alethea, now a sulky thirteen, had come all the way down from her garret to complain about the noise the grown-ups were making.

'Who's in so far?' Katherine asked, watching the rain cascade through the biggest hole in the roof.

'Well, a lot of first-rate young barristers. The sort of people who get crapped on in straight Chambers,' said Frank. 'Tessa Parks, Alison Rye, David Milner.'

Katherine looked hard at Frank. She knew all these people. They were bright, dedicated but very inexperienced.

'How are you going to pay the rent,' she asked, 'if you're the only one earning any money?'

'No, no,' Frank protested. 'Ken Gordon, Michael Kahn . . .'

He hesitated, and then continued.

'James Bingham.'

'Oh the radical toff himself,' Katherine remarked, wrinkling her nose. Not surprisingly, the whole place smelt damp. She hoped that Frank had had a proper survey done.

'James is excellent,' insisted Frank. 'But what I need is a heavyweight woman. Someone with a good practice in crime and political stuff.'

'Why not ask Margaret Wharton?' enquired Katherine.

'Because I want a stayer. A genuine lawyer. Not someone passing through on her way to a safe Labour seat.'

'Who's clerking for you?' asked Katherine, changing the subject. 'Whoever it is had better be good.'

'She is. And she's on a salary. No ten per cent for the clerk.'

'Very egalitarian. But it might have been cheaper to put her on ten per cent,' Katherine said, before she could stop herself.

She saw that her air of superiority was beginning to irritate Frank. After all, he knew that she was far from happy at her own Chambers.

'So that's the big attraction of Grimshaw's, is it?' Frank said, trying to rile her. 'The company of other big earners? Or is it that you love the clerking there so much? They carve you up, you know.'

'Grimshaw's is no worse than most,' Katherine said, annoyed to be on the defensive. Trust Frank to pick on her weakest point. She should have known better than to tell him any of her problems.

'I know where I stand there because Grimshaw supports me,' she said, affecting to ignore Frank's expression of disbelief. 'Sort of. He believes trouble-makers like me should be allowed a corner to live in because he thinks he believes in making room for the dissenting voice, blah, blah. But really because it makes him look good, makes him look broad-minded, you know. So I'm left in peace and I don't have to deal with people who think they're radicals. People like . . .'

'James!' said Frank, hurriedly.

James Bingham was the name she was about to utter. Fortunately, Frank had seen him first, Katherine turned round. James was undeniably tall, dark and handsome, but in a very obvious, boyish kind of way. Despite his radical pretensions, Katherine had never seen him when he wasn't wearing an expensive, hand-made suit, of which he seemed to have a great many. Today was no exception.

'James!'

Frank greeted the newcomer with apparent enthusiasm,

although Katherine thought she detected a certain irritation in Frank's voice. Had he seriously thought he could drag her up here and persuade her to join him?

'Hi,' said James, as he shook out his umbrella. 'Katherine, hello.'

'Hello, James.'

Katherine shook the hand which James offered. The threesome stood around awkwardly. Katherine was secretly pleased at James's arrival. At least it would make Frank realize there was no love lost between James and herself, and that she'd never want to join any Chambers of which James was a member. She decided it was time to be going.

'Well, look . . . Good luck,' she said, more to Frank than to James. 'Really. Fingers crossed.'

As she left, she glanced back and waved. James was already strolling around, inspecting the new premises; but Katherine noticed that Frank was still looking at her, an exasperated expression on his face.

CHAPTER TWO

The rain was still pouring down as Katherine left Fetter Court. Needless to say, there were no taxis; so she decided to walk. She tried to take her mind off the weather by counting her blessings.

At least meeting Frank like that had put the Patricia Swales case into some kind of perspective. Okay, Patricia was a victim of discrimination and injustice; but then the whole system is loaded against ordinary people. That's no reason for you to behave like Frank, she thought, and cut yourself off from the establishment.

Besides, Katherine reminded herself, working in a traditional Chambers is good for me. It keeps me constantly aware of my own humble beginnings. I only have to look around me to see all the things which I came into the law to change. What could be worse than having to work with a number of like-minded individuals? It would be far too cosy, self-indulgent, defeatist.

Katherine walked up the wooden staircase to the first-floor office which she shared with another barrister.

'Sorry,' she muttered, backing out again. Alan Ackroyd was having a case conference with three barristers from other Chambers.

She fetched a towel from the lavatory and walked into the clerk's room. She sat, rubbing her hair dry in front of the radiator. Tom, the clerk of the Chambers, and his new junior, Edward, bustled in.

'Miss Hughes, how did your case go?' Tom enquired. He was a thin-lipped man in his late thirties, and always reminded Katherine of a more than usually untrustworthy weasel. Deferential to the point of grovelling towards male barristers, his attitude towards Katherine verged on superciliousness.

'She got Borstal,' Katherine replied. 'Still, Langtry had a chance to act out his sadistic fantasies. That's the main thing. That's what we're here for.'

'Lily up to her tricks again?' Tom asked.

He winked at Edward, who laughed dutifully.

'Lily?' asked Katherine.

'Langtry,' explained Tom, flapping his wrist in an effeminate manner. Again, Edward laughed over-enthusiastically.

'You should have seen his face, Edward,' said Katherine. 'The way he enjoyed it. That's the business you're coming into.'

'Who's this?' asked Alan Ackroyd, who had just finished his conference and came in accompanied by the three barristers.

'Oh, he's an absolute swine!' Alan groaned, when Edward told him.

'Poofs are all the same,' said Tom, comfortably. 'They're the worst in my view. They're all a bit vicious, aren't they?'

'For God's sake,' Katherine muttered into her towel.

She got up and wandered over to the clerks' desks.

'Is this for me?' she asked, picking up a brief. Both Tom and Edward ignored her, as the other barristers chimed in with their reminiscences about Langtry. Katherine waved her brief at all of them in farewell, and left the room.

Back in her office, Katherine sat down in her large leather chair by the window and gazed at the greyness outside. Everything at Grimshaw's was a contrast to Frank's vision of Fetter Court. The company at Grimshaw's might not be so congenial, but the accommodation was definitely superior. There were no puddles on the wall-to-wall Wilton, which toned perfectly with the rich velvet curtains. Handmade bookcases filled with law books occupied the two walls that weren't covered with rather good English watercolours.

Sitting at her desk, she picked up a little toy that had been with her ever since she had been a pupil. It was a monkey sitting on two sticks and wearing a judge's full-bottomed wig. She clenched the wooden sticks and made the monkey turn a spectacular, undignified somersault. For some reason, doing that always made her feel better.

CHAPTER THREE

'A nun?' asked Harris.

'Yes,' said Holland. 'A nun. Remember, stay as close to her as possible. We don't know where she might take it. We've got to know exactly who she talks to at any given moment until she disposes of her consignment.'

The tannoy at Heathrow airport announced the arrival of the Air India flight from Bombay and Delhi.

'OK,' said Holland to his subordinate. 'Let's get cracking.'

Harris accompanied Holland past a row of men who had just come off a flight from Lagos. Most of them were black. All of them were handcuffed and sitting on lavatory pans. Each was suspected of swallowing drugs in order to smuggle them into the country. Harris was glad that other Customs officers were having to supervise them.

Holland and Harris made their way along airport corridors to Holland's favourite vantage point for watching passenger arrivals.

Arrivals from the Air India plane were already beginning to trickle out from passport control and along the passage-way to the green and red exit points. A grey-haired, dumpy nun of the Franciscan order came into view, wheeling her trolley serenely towards the green channel.

'Are you sure that's her?' said Harris, who among other things was a devout Roman Catholic.

'Of course I'm sure,' snapped Holland.

She didn't look much like an international drugs smuggler to Harris; but he decided to shut up, or he might soon be back studying Nigerian bowel movements.

The nun discovered that the green channel was closed, and redirected herself into the red channel. She stood in line, and smiled kindly at the customs officer when he asked her to put her luggage on the bench for inspection. Holland signalled for others in his team to position themselves near the nun when she came through.

'Sorry, love,' apologized the customs man, when he had rummaged through everything and found nothing.

'Thank you,' said the nun politely, doing up her bags, 'and God bless you.'

She picked up her luggage and began to make her way out to the arrival area.

'Good,' said Holland. 'All according to . . .'

Holland and his men watched with horror as two men stepped in front of the nun.

'Cora Davis?' shouted one of them, so that the entire concourse could have heard what was going on. 'We're police officers. We're arresting you. This is the arrest warrant.'

'Who the hell are they?' raged Holland to his subordinate, as an irreligious oath escaped the lips of the nun.

'Search me,' said Harris.

*

'Search me?' said Cora, as she was frogmarched into a waiting police car.

16

'Yeah. You're nicked, sweetheart,' said Detective Sergeant McCabe.

'I think you're making a mistake, officer,' said Cora. 'My Mother Superior's going to want a very good explanation for this.'

McCabe and Simpson sat on either side of her as the car sped off towards central London.

'Why don't you just tell me what you want?' she pleaded. 'Can't you see this is a mistake?'

Simpson emptied her bags, but failed to find what he was looking for. He glanced across to McCabe, who looked hard at the woman.

'Where is it?' he demanded.

Cora looked at him, in apparent bafflement.

'I don't understand,' she said. 'I'm sorry. Could you please tell me what you want from me?'

McCabe took a knife from his pocket and ripped out the linings of her bags. Cora saw the police driver watching anxiously in his rear-view mirror as the two officers ripped her luggage to pieces.

'For Heaven's sake!' she cried, closing her eyes as if in prayer.

McCabe looked inside a brown paper bag and held up an unused sanitary towel.

'If you were a customs man looking for naughty substances, would you search a nun?' he asked his colleague.

'I might,' replied Simpson.

'If you were a customs man looking for naughty substances,' McCabe continued, 'would you search a nun if you thought she might be having her period?'

'Oh, leave it out,' Simpson muttered in disgust.

'Exactly,' said McCabe, looking at Cora.

'I don't think you're a policeman,' she said defiantly.

'I don't think you're a nun,' retorted McCabe.

Cora suddenly seemed to regain her confidence. She leant forward and tapped on the driver's shoulder.

'You seem like a decent man,' she said. 'If you have any Christian feelings, stop this car.'

'Keep your eyes on the road, driver,' snapped McCabe.

'Get in the fast lane and put your foot down,' ordered Simpson.

'Anorak!' McCabe snapped.

Reluctantly, the woman unzipped the jacket which covered her Franciscan habit.

'Skirt,' he continued.

'I refuse,' cried out Cora.

'You take it off or I do it for you,' McCabe threatened.

'I am not removing my underwear. Have you got no feelings? What sort of men are you?'

'Look, I'll give you three seconds to get those drawers off, starting now. One!'

'Bloody Hell,' gulped the driver, trying to concentrate on the road.

'Two! Three!' McCabe counted down as Cora shrank feebly back into the car seat.

Simpson restrained her arms, as McCabe leant over and grabbed her capacious, elasticated knickers.

'Get your filthy hands off me, you bastard!' roared Cora, with surprising strength.

*

'And all of us at Christian Heritage Holidays sincerely trust,' said the courier, 'that you will thoroughly enjoy your visit to Britain.'

There was a ripple of applause from the coachload of elderly American tourists.

'I hear that nowadays London is nearly as dangerous as New York,' whispered Mrs Dwight E. Stonehampton III. 'Dorothy, we live in Godless times.'

'Don't be so foolish,' said her sister, who had visited England before, and had lived for a long time on the Upper East side of Manhattan.

'Do you think I should be wearing my jewellery? There's so much violence in the world.'

'I shouldn't think too many tourists are mugged in Westminster Abbey or St Paul's Cathedral,' said her sister. 'Besides, everyone always says the British police are wonderful.'

Dorothy's voice trailed away, as she looked down from their coach. A police car raced past with its lights flashing. Oddly enough, she thought she caught sight of an elderly, half-naked nun in the back seat, screaming and waving her legs in the air as she was interfered with by two men.

No, decided Dorothy firmly, she must have been imagining things. Maybe her sister was right, and she had been living in Manhattan for too long.

CHAPTER FOUR

Katherine finally gave up all hope of being able to concentrate on *Marxism Today*. She laid the magazine on one side, and watched with growing incredulity as Alan Ackroyd struggled through his defence speech for the fourth time.

Of all the barristers in her Chambers, there were perhaps two or three who were more stupid than Alan. There might even have been one or two who were more disorganized than Alan. But there was undoubtedly no one who could compete with Alan when it came to lack of speaking ability.

There he was, twitching, sweating and looking as if it was he, and not his client, who had been accused of murder. For the past half hour she had tried to sympathize with his misery; but finally she could bear it no longer.

'Alan, screw it! It's only another case,' she said.

'Why, do I look nervous?' he asked, anxiously gathering up his papers, in preparation for court.

'It'll only be submissions,' Katherine said, doing her best to be supportive. 'You've got good briefs handling the other defendants. Just do what they do.'

'I think I can handle it, actually,' he said stiffly. 'Thanks all the same.'

Patronizing, sexist, elitist, incompetent git, thought Katherine, as he closed the door. And I haven't even got a case at the moment. She decided to make herself a cup of coffee, and went through to the clerk's room.

'Look, why did you get him briefed?' she asked Tom, pouring herself a coffee from the filter machine. 'He can't do it.'

Tom merely grunted non-committally.

'He's not a barrister,' said Katherine. 'He makes serious speeches that make the jury *laugh*! Just because his grand-father was a barrister and his father was a barrister, why does *he* have to be a barrister? Why can't he sell soft toys or something?'

'Have you finished?' Tom asked, wearily.

Katherine noticed that he had a brief in his hand. He held it out to her as if it was beneath contempt, and therefore might just conceivably be good enough for her.

'Would you like a granny who smuggled half a million quid's worth of heroin into Heathrow?' asked Tom. 'Pleading to it. Not a lot for you to do.'

Katherine took the brief.

'Yes,' she said. 'Anything else for me?'

'No,' replied Tom curtly.

'Any money?' Katherine kept pushing.

But Tom was already performing his usual trick of pretending not to hear her. Knowing when she was beaten, Katherine returned to her office. She glanced at the title on the front of her brief: R. v. *Cora Davis*.

*

Katherine's current lover, Robert, was a set designer ten years younger than herself. Under oath in a court of law, she would have had to confess that she had fallen for his looks, rather than his intellect. Nevertheless, she found his infatuation for her distinctly touching. And he had a lovely body.

Katherine had always felt Claudia was mean for nick-naming him Brief Encounter (the film which they saw first together) and for dismissing him out of hand as a dumb brunette. He was, in fact, quite a good conversationalist; and since Katherine had been sleeping with him for six months, the encounter was turning out to be far from brief. Katherine was uncertain whether the cause was passion, or simply inertia; but anyway she was disinclined to find anyone else at the moment. And it was all very well for Claudia to accuse Katherine of having a toyboy, but every attractive man of Katherine's own age seemed to be gay or married or both.

Like every other actor she had met, Robert seemed to be almost permanently out of work. This was bad luck for him, but good news for Katherine, since it meant he did most of the cooking and had plenty of energy left over for sex. In the bedroom at least, he was a notable performer.

Tonight, he was staying over at Katherine's flat in Notting Hill, which was fine by her and a considerable improvement on the squalid, unheated flat he shared with three other actors in Tooting. Katherine had never quite been able to bring herself to sleep there, for some reason. It reminded her of all the worst things about being a student. No wonder Marcuse had thought students would be in the vanguard of any revolution: they had nothing to lose.

They had been in such a hurry to get to bed that all the dinner things were still waiting to be washed up. Never mind, thought Katherine, they will still be there in the morning. Disconcertingly, Robert tended to want to do the washing up as soon as they had stopped making love. Katherine preferred to talk, and then maybe make love again. She wondered if she could interest him in her new brief. She picked it up from where she had left it, at the side of the bed.

'Sixty-year-old woman here,' she said, 'charged with bringing in half a kilo of heroin stuffed inside her knickers!'

'Mm?' said Robert.

'Know what she says?' asked Katherine.

'Mm,' said Robert, meaning no.

Katherine continued. She decided to act oblivious to the fact that Robert was biting her neck.

'She says she's got lots of Asian shops near her house and she's always wanted to go to India!'

Katherine giggled as Robert began to nibble her ear. She felt him moving his body rhythmically against her back. Surely this wasn't turning him on?

'She says she dressed up as a nun so the Indians wouldn't pester her!'

Roaring with laughter, Katherine lay on her back, ready to receive Robert. Instead Robert looked at her reproachfully, climbed out of bed and slouched out of the room. Maybe he wanted to go to the loo.

Katherine lay back, folded her hands behind her head and inspected the ceiling.

'You're for the high jump, granny,' she said.

Suddenly, Katherine heard the sound of pots and pans being angrily washed up in the kitchen.

'Robert! Come on!' she called out. Oh God, she thought, did he think I was laughing at him? Men are so moody sometimes.

'Come and see me for a minute!' she pleaded.

Robert, rather sulkily, wandered back into the bedroom and sat on the edge of the bed. She ran a hand over his shoulder and gave him a quick kiss.

'Mmm. Come on,' she murmured. 'Come on . . .'

She felt the muscles in Robert's shoulder relax. As he crawled back under the duvet, Katherine removed the papers from the bed. Bending down to place them carefully on the floor, she felt Robert slide himself against her. What bliss, she thought, and a new position. All thoughts of Cora Davis were beginning to fade when the phone rang, again and again.

Oh, sod it, thought Katherine after the fifth ring. I haven't left the answering machine on.

'No, no, just ignore it,' she murmured, trying to do so herself.

Nevertheless, the insistent ringing irritated Robert. Or maybe he just felt the tension in Katherine's body. Anyway, he stretched across her and picked up the receiver. He listened for a few moments and then passed it over.

'Hello?' she said. 'Who? Oh, right, right. Yeah, I've got it in front of me, actually.'

It was Frankland, the instructing solicitor on the Cora Davis case, on the other end of the line. Katherine's mind clicked into action, and she bent down to pick the papers up from the floor.

'I wondered what your first impressions were,' said Frankland.

'Well, I think it's as well she's pleading guilty. There isn't a lot here in terms of a defence.'

Frankland laughed in agreement.

'Nothing whatever, I'm afraid. Extraordinary woman. She seems more concerned about the imminent birth of her fourth grandchild, than she is about being charged with smuggling heroin. So we'll be looking for something elegant in the way of mitigation.'

'Well,' mused Katherine. 'I can talk about how she needed the money. Beyond that though, there is no mitigation in cases of drug smuggling. I'll do my best, but I think she's facing a long stretch.'

'Perhaps you'd like to meet her?'

'Yes, I think I'd better. Get your clerk to ring my clerk, will you?'

'She's a jolly old dear. I'm sure you'll enjoy her.'

'Oh, just one thing: has she given you any clue about who she was running for?' Katherine asked.

'No, I'm afraid she's not interested in talking about that.'

Katherine put the phone down just as she heard her front door slam. She called out to Robert, gave a long sigh and lay back, thinking.

Unfortunately her acclaimed rapport with clients never seemed to find an equivalent in her personal relationships. Like so many career women she knew, she found it much easier to hold down a job than a life-partner.

Why did men always think that her dedication to work, and to her clients' interests, meant that she didn't care about anything else? Men were so demanding. What was it her ex-husband had said? Something about her being prepared to care for the whole world but being totally unprepared to care for him. Selfish bastards, men.

CHAPTER FIVE

'Well, I don't know what to say. You're an arsehole, that's obvious, but it's not a full explanation of a cockup of this dimension.'

Commander Stanton of the Robbery Squad glared at the balding, ferret-faced man who was literally on the carpet in front of him. The man in question, Detective Sergeant McCabe, studied his shoes with intense concentration.

'You find out about a major heroin-smuggling operation, so you just swan out to Heathrow and arrest this old woman. Didn't it occur to you to ask anybody?'

Stanton brought his fist down on the table so hard that the coffee mugs rattled.

'Didn't it occur to you that other people might've been interested in seeing where she was going? How did you know about her?'

'Information received, sir,' came the standard evasive reply.

'Don't give me information received, sir. I want to know where is the bleeding paperwork? I've got this bugger Holland from Customs and Excise going apeshit in the DAC's office. Bananas are being gone on the tenth floor and there's not a piece of paper in here that tells anybody how you knew. I want it on my desk by four o'clock today or I'll put you in a room with the Customs and Excise and you can explain it to them yourself. Now get out!'

Outside, McCabe punched the wall. Violence often seemed to clear his mind; and it worked again on this occasion. Of course, he thought. McCabe made his way down to the canteen to confer with Simpson.

*

The most noticeable thing about Henry Griffiths was the constant look of surprise on his face. He was surprised that anyone could conceive of a life without ganja; surprised at the way police kept stopping him and searching him and his friends; and surprised at being charged with drug-dealing, when he had had only a small amount of dope on him, and that for his own use.

Nor was this the point at which the surprises ended. He was puzzled when the police kept objecting to him being given bail. Am I a public menace, or what? he asked his mother, when she came to visit him. Do they think I'm going to skip the country? His mother, who had had similar problems with Henry's older brothers, told him that the police were just doing their job.

The biggest surprise had come this morning, when Henry found himself released before he came to trial. The police had dropped their objections to bail. Just like that. Henry couldn't work it out. Maybe his friends were right. Maybe he really was the least streetwise guy in South London.

He stood at the top of the court steps, breathing in the damp London air and relishing his freedom. No sooner had he relaxed, than he was surprised again: this time at the sight of Sergeant McCabe beckoning him from across the road. Wearily, Henry walked down the steps and got into the police car where McCabe sat waiting for him. Simpson pulled the black Granada out into the passing traffic as McCabe started to have his little chat.

'Well,' said McCabe, 'don't say thank you. You can go back any time you like. All I have to do is pick you up for doing your gas meter or whatever, and you've broken your bail, haven't you?'

Henry gawped at McCabe.

'We ain't got gas,' he said. 'We're all electric.'

McCabe shook his head.

'Oh, Henry,' he said, 'you are a pitifully stupid specimen. Let's keep it simple, shall we? Did you like it in Brixton?'

'No,' came Henry's instantaneous reply.

McCabe laughed.

'No, it's awful, isn't it? Totally out of order, what the scum have to put up with. I've written to my MP about it, but he doesn't give a toss. Would you like to stay out, then?'

Henry had no doubts about this one, either.

'Yes,' he said.

'Yes,' repeated McCabe.

McCabe passed Henry a piece of paper and a pen.

'What's this?' asked the lad.

'It's a statement you forgot to sign. Don't read it. Just sign it.'

'I don't know a woman called Cora Davis. Oh, no, no,' Henry protested and tried to give back the paper to McCabe. 'I ain't signing this.'

McCabe sighed deeply.

'Let's start again, shall we? Did you like it in Brixton?'

Henry squirmed in his seat. He took the biro. What was the alternative?

'You won't have to give evidence,' McCabe said soothingly. 'She's pleading guilty, anyway. It's just a bit of paper-work.'

Henry signed. Simpson slowed down the car, and McCabe leant across Henry and opened the door. The next thing Henry knew, the Granada was speeding away and he was on the pavement. Henry scratched his head. This was all very puzzling and a bit frightening. He wondered where he could get help. Suddenly he thought of that bloke on the telly.

CHAPTER SIX

Katherine sat waiting for Cora, in one of the interview cubicles at Holloway prison. Sitting next to Katherine was Miranda, a clerk from Frankland's office. Katherine couldn't work out why it was that she took an immediate dislike to Miranda. She was a pleasant-looking girl, with shiny, shoulder-length, blonde hair held back in an alice band.

'What made you join a solicitor's, Miranda?' Katherine asked.

'Oh, no, I just help out,' twittered Miranda. 'It's a bit of pin-money for me. Actually, I've just started an acting training course.'

'Oh, I see,' said Katherine, trying hard to overcome her initial prejudice.

'My Uncle David's a partner. David Frankland.'

'Oh, right,' said Katherine. 'So you're not really interested in the law?'

'Oh, yah, I mean yah.'

'But not as a career,' said Katherine.

'Erm . . . no. I mean I know there's a lot of money in it and everything. But,' Miranda wrinkled her attractive nose, 'I dunno . . . it's a bit of a slog. If you're a woman, I bet.'

'Women can slog,' retorted Katherine.

'Oh, yah, I mean I'm not saying that,' said Miranda, hurriedly examining her cuticles.

A thought struck Miranda.

'One thing that fascinates me,' she said. 'When a barrister gets somebody off, when you know they're guilty . . . I mean . . .'

Miranda looked meaningfully at Katherine.

'So? What's the question?' asked Katherine, knowing full well what was coming.

'How do you cope?'

'Cope?'

Katherine snorted incredulously and looked at Miranda. Did she come from a different planet?

'I don't need to cope,' said Katherine. 'I'm too busy celebrating.'

The door of the cubicle was opened by a female prison warder. Cora Davis walked in. Katherine tried to imagine her in a nun's habit, but couldn't. She was dressed in an ordinary blouse and skirt with a cardigan. Katherine had never seen anyone who looked less like an international drugs smuggler. Still, presumably that was why whoever-it-was had employed her.

Cora sat down on the other side of the table. She had a coarse, rosy complexion, mousy hair and a perm, which had more or less grown out. She was clutching a packet of cigarettes. She was obviously nervous, but trying to put a brave face on the situation. She looked across at the elegant Miranda apprehensively. Katherine smiled warmly to try and put the older woman at her ease.

'Cora,' Katherine started off, 'I'm just going to ask you some things and talk a bit about the case. OK?'

Cora nodded.

'Damn,' said Miranda. 'This felt-tip doesn't work.'

Katherine lent her a felt-tip pen which worked; and Miranda began to make notes on the conversation.

'Now,' continued Katherine, 'your statements to the police and to Mr Frankland admit that you brought in the heroin. You *knew* you were a courier?'

'Yes.'

Cora sat bolt upright, her hands in front of her on the table, clutching her cigarettes. The presence of Miranda taking notes clearly inhibited her.

'OK,' said Katherine. 'Take a minute to think about this. Did you know for certain *what* you were carrying?'

A cagey expression came over Cora's face.

'Well . . .'

Katherine interrupted before Cora could continue.

'I mean, could it be that you might've been told it was jewellery, say?'

'Well,' repeated Cora. 'I thought it might be cannabis.'

Katherine nodded sympathetically. Cora was obviously lying.

'A little Indian bloke,' said Cora.

'He didn't introduce himself? OK. You concealed the stuff in your underwear before boarding a flight back to London.'

'Well . . .' said Cora, hesitantly.

'What?'

'*He* did it, as a matter of fact,' said Cora. 'They didn't tell me *that*.'

Ah, thought Katherine. Now we're getting somewhere.

'Who?' she asked.

'Who what?'

'Who didn't tell you?'

'Tell me what?'

Katherine looked hard at Cora. She couldn't be that thick.

'Who didn't tell you before you went that you'd have to open your legs to a little Indian feller so he could tape the stuff to you?'

'Nobody. That's what I'm saying. Nobody told me.'

'OK,' said Katherine, recognizing that she would get no further right now. 'And you wore this stuff all the way back like that?'

Cora was evidently suspicious. She merely nodded.

'I've been through all this with Mr Frankland,' she said.

Katherine felt puzzled.

'How many hours? Twelve hours? With all that polythene stuck to you, sitting on a plane? Must've been awful. I can't imagine it.' Katherine turned to Miranda. 'Can you imagine it, Miranda?'

Thank goodness, Miranda looked sympathetic rather than embarrassed.

'Must've been really uncomfortable,' said Miranda.

'It was shocking. When I think back! I dunno ... the things you do for money, eh?' Cora laughed and pursed her lips in an imitation of Frankie Howerd.

The three women laughed together.

'It's not the worst I've done for money, but it was the most uncomfortable,' said Cora, beginning to warm up. 'I can tell you: twelve hours or no twelve hours – I didn't move about much!'

'Not surprising,' said Miranda, 'with half a kilo of smack inside your undies.'

'Half a kilo?' Cora said, affronted. 'Three kilos, if you don't mind! Half a kilo? My shape, you wouldn't know half a kilo was there, love!'

Katherine joined in the laughter, but simultaneously checked through her papers.

'Cora,' she said gently. 'You're in enough trouble with half a kilo. And since we're on the subject: whereabouts exactly *did* you put it?'

Cora looked at Katherine blankly.

'Cora,' Katherine explained, 'you are charged with importing half a kilo of heroin.'

Cora shook her head vigorously.

'Three kilos,' she insisted.

'Let me get this right,' said Katherine, slowly. 'How many strips of polythene did the little Indian feller tape inside your drawers?'

'Six.'

'Did you remove any between Bombay and London?'

'No.'

'So how many did they find when you were searched?'

'What – the first time or the second time?'

'Whoa, hold it, I'm lost. Hang on.' Katherine speed-read the relevant passage in her brief. 'Yeah, according to the police you were searched at Lewisham police station where they found – this is the two women police officers, yeah? – they found one bag of heroin weighing half a kilo.'

'Yes,' said Cora patiently, 'but, the other two – the men, the ones who arrested me – they'd already found the six bags in the car on the motorway when they ripped my knickers off with all those people lookin' in on the bus. That's why we had to stop at Marks and Spencer's.'

Katherine and Miranda looked at each other in surprise.

'I'm sorry, Cora?' said Katherine.

'So they could get me some new ones. The old ones were in shreds. Then we parked near the station and they had some new sticky tape and they put one bag back on me because I had to be searched formally, they said. But they couldn't get it all in again they said, but they said that didn't matter though, and I got the new knickers on and in we went. And these two young lady police – they were lovely, actually, like nurses – they searched me properly. And there was the stuff. Surprise, surprise.'

'Were they surprised? The WPCs?'

34

'Very. I was still dressed like a nun, you see.'

Cora was in earnest; but Miranda burst out laughing.

'Miranda!' said Katherine sternly, before turning back to Cora. 'But not the two male detectives? Were they surprised when they found the stuff on you in the car?'

'Oh no, they were looking for it. Pigs!' Cora sniffed.

Katherine sat back in her chair and sighed. Her drug-running granny seemed to be in deeper trouble than she realized.

'Cora,' said Katherine, leaning forward and looking intently at her. 'It would be best if I just forget that I heard any of this. You're charged with a half a kilo. Let's forget the rest.'

'Well, where did it go?' Cora asked.

Yes, thought Katherine grimly, that's what I'd like to know.

'It's not our problem,' said Katherine.

'But surely, if we tell the judge . . .' Cora pressed on.

'I'm not going into that court and saying my client wishes it to be known that she didn't bring in a half a kilo of heroin, she brought in three kilos. No way,' said Katherine. 'Forget it. You're in deep enough trouble. I didn't hear it. OK? Nor did Miranda. Christ. Now, where were we?'

Katherine looked at Cora. For the first time, the older woman looked genuinely anxious.

'What do you mean deep enough trouble? You're giving me palpitations here,' said Cora. 'Mr Frankland says to me there's no reason for despair.'

'That's true, but . . .' Katherine thought for a moment, trying to think of the gentlest way to break the news. 'Maybe Mr Frankland didn't want to upset you too much. You're admitting to a very serious crime and you couldn't have picked a worse time. I promise you my level best with

35

the mitigation speech. But, Cora, you've got to realize that we're looking at . . . well, five years minimum.'

Cora slumped back in her chair. Her face seemed to crumple. Katherine lit one of Cora's cigarettes and passed it to Cora and Miranda asked if she could have one too. Cora sucked on hers like a baby on a bottle. Katherine could see that there was nothing more to gain from talking to her today.

Katherine and Miranda walked down a green painted corridor to the main gate, and waited for a prison warder to let them out. Katherine shook her head in frustration.

'Did I say *five* years? What we need here is a good account from Cora about Mr Big and his threats to her family if she names names, which I am sure is the truth of it. Blah, blah, blah. Mitigation. Tell your Uncle David, will you?'

'But I mean surely we should be doing something about those cops?' said Miranda.

'Like what?' asked Katherine.

'Well they've obviously taken five bags of heroin. God!'

'What I don't understand,' said Katherine, 'is if the police decided to help themselves, why didn't they take the lot? You know: half a kilo's worth a lot of money, right?'

'But . . .'

'What?'

'But they took it, didn't they? I mean God! Can't we do something?'

'What do you want me to do about it? Ask them to put it back in Cora's knickers and rewrite the charge-sheet?' Katherine said witheringly. 'And by the way, don't bum cigarettes off an old granny doing time!'

They walked out through the prison gates. Miranda was just about to get into her little Peugeot when Katherine stopped her.

'One more thing. Write this down,' she ordered. 'I want

you to ask your Uncle David; how come those detectives – who aren't even Drugs Squad – knew about Cora? How did they know? Do they hang around Heathrow Airport all day looking for suspicious old biddies, or what? There's nothing about it in the papers, but somebody must've tipped them off. Who?'

Miranda finished noting this down, and got into the driver's seat.

'Right. Yah. Can I give you a lift?' asked Miranda.

'No thanks,' said Katherine, brusquely. 'I want some time on my own. To think.'

'Oh. Right. Yah,' said Miranda. 'Bye.'

Something in Miranda's eyes, just as she drove off, made Katherine aware that the younger woman regarded her as offensive, hard and incomprehensible. Too bad, thought Katherine. And, sod it, she's gone off with my felt-tip pen.

CHAPTER SEVEN

Henry Griffiths was surprised at how crowded the Law Centre seemed to be. It reminded him a bit of *Hill Street Blues*, all kinds of people moving this way and that. He clutched a crumpled piece of paper, his eyes darting round the room. He was on edge. There was a black receptionist of about his age, but she was on the phone. A tall white woman, much older, placed a large brown envelope on the receptionist's desk, and looked at Henry.

'You want some help?' she asked, in a gentle voice.

Henry was slow to respond. He looked up at her and then down at the piece of paper in his hand. He was glad when the receptionist came off the phone.

'OK, Miriam,' she said to the older woman's departing back. 'Can I help you?'

Henry realized the receptionist was talking to him, and consulted his crumpled piece of paper.

'Alton Phillips,' he stated.

The receptionist picked up a telephone.

'Is he expecting you, Mr . . .?'

'I saw him on telly,' said Henry.

She put the phone down.

'OK. Well he's very tied up just now. He won't be long. You need legal advice of some kind, yeah?'

Henry nodded.

'I'm on a hell trip,' he muttered plaintively.

He started rocking backwards and forwards. His feet remained motionless, as if they were nailed to the floor. Tears welled up in his eyes and slowly rolled down his cheeks. He breathed deeply and wiped his eyes on his overcoat sleeve. The receptionist looked at him with obvious suspicion. Shit, he thought, I bet she thinks I'm some kind of addict, or something.

'Well, sit down a minute, eh?' she said. 'I'll get you a cup of coffee in a minute, OK?'

Henry wandered over to the row of chairs running along the wall which faced Angela's desk. He sat down, then stood up again and began pacing up and down. He watched as a smart black man in a three-piece suit burst out of an office and gave some papers to the receptionist. Henry recognized him at once, although he was a couple of inches smaller than he looked on the telly.

'Gentleman here wants a word, Alton,' said the receptionist.

'OK. Give me five minutes, right, and I'll be with you, Angie. This must get to Frank Cartwright before he goes to Bristol tonight.'

'I'll put it in a taxi,' Angela replied, already dialling.

Henry felt confused and spaced out. He'd never met anyone before who'd been on TV, and here was this guy walking up to him and smiling, like he'd known Henry all his life.

'Four minutes,' said Phillips. 'Would you like a coffee? Angie, get him a coffee, yeah?'

He spun on his heels and darted back into his office. Henry felt a bit reassured, until another smartly dressed

39

guy, an Indian or something, walked out of his office and practically collided with Henry.

'Pilecki?' asked the Indian-looking man. 'Is it Pilecki or . . .?'

Henry stared back at him in fright, then across to the receptionist.

'Hang on a sec, can you?' murmured Angela down the phone. 'Dilip, Mr Pilecki is a Hungarian.'

She returned to the phone.

'That's right,' she said, 'Fetter Court. It's near the Old Bailey.'

'You're not Mr Pilecki?' Dilip asked Henry, who shook his head.

'Pilecki's gone, Dilip,' said Angela. 'Miriam spoke to him.'

'I'll come back, I fink,' Henry said over his shoulder, making for the street door.

'No, look! He'll be free in a minute!' Angela called out.

'OK. Sorry,' said Alton, emerging from his office. 'Where is he?'

'Gone,' said Angela.

'Why?' asked Alton. He had sensed real fear coming off Henry.

'I dunno. I think he was on something. Man, he was weird.'

'What did he want?'

'He didn't say.'

'Did you ask him?'

'Not specifically. You said five minutes.'

'What was his name?'

Angela shrugged her shoulders. She had forgotten to ask.

'Well, we sorted him out, didn't we?' Alton said sharply.

'He said he'd come back,' Angela retorted.

'Oh yeah?' Alton returned to his office, exasperated.

*

It was getting dark as Alton left the Law Centre and walked down the road to his car. He saw a lonely figure crouched beneath a lamp post, and recognized him immediately as the youth who had disappeared from the Law Centre earlier in the afternoon. Alton squatted on his heels beside him. He put a comforting arm round the youth's shoulders. Although the evening wasn't cold, he was shivering.

'You're in big trouble, right?' said Alton. 'Shall we go back to the centre? Or I'll buy you a beer, if you like.'

Henry just stared out ahead of him, saying nothing.

'Are you hungry?' Alton continued.

Henry thought for a moment and then nodded his head.

Alton stood up and helped Henry to his feet. They walked off down the road to the local café, where Alton ordered a coffee for himself and a large hamburger and chips for Henry. Henry ate in intense silence. Finally, as he licked the last ketchupy crumbs from his lips, he seemed to gain enough confidence to talk.

'I ain't a choirboy, Alton. I ain't saying that.'

Alton nodded sagely.

'Well,' said the youth, 'ever come across a cop called George McCabe?'

Alton nodded.

'Friend of yours, is he?' asked Alton.

'Friend of mine? You must be jokin'!' The youth looked terrified. 'That bloke puts his fags out on your legs!'

'I've come across him once or twice,' said Alton coolly. 'He's not nice. How do you know him?'

'I know him 'cos he's sitting on my back, Alton. He's a

killagorilla. Even when I fink I've got bail, McCabe's got his fist down my throat.'

'What's he nicked you for?'

'Dealin'. But it ain't what I'm nicked for that's worrying me. It's the other thing. Cora Davis.'

The name didn't mean anything to Alton; but he began to take a closer interest as Henry began to explain about his car-ride with McCabe.

CHAPTER EIGHT

There was no sound in the interview cubicle except the noise of Miranda's teeth chewing the top of Katherine's felt-tip pen.

'Are you going to answer?' Katherine asked irritably.

She and Miranda had spent a futile afternoon trying to get information out of Cora. The elderly woman looked tired and beaten, but was not responding.

'Who were you running it to, Cora?' Katherine persisted.

Cora continued to say nothing.

'Well, maybe the judge will come to his own conclusions about that,' said Katherine. 'He'll maybe think you've got yourself a nice little business.'

Cora laughed disparagingly.

'Well, it's up to you,' Katherine continued. 'It seems that all you have to say is that you're guilty. So what? You're guilty. Great. Now tell me something interesting. Give me something to build a case on – or I can't help you.'

'Well, I'd better have another barrister then,' muttered Cora.

'Fine,' said Katherine. 'Is that what you want?'

'Well, you can't defend me, you say,' grumbled Cora. 'Over and over and over.'

'OK,' said Katherine, looking across at Miranda. 'You can get your solicitor to ask me to return the brief if you want. You've a perfect right to do that. If that's what you want.'

Cora nodded.

'I'll bugger off then, shall I?' asked Katherine.

'Yes. Do,' said Cora roughly. 'Bugger yourself while you're about it. I don't need you. I'll plead guilty.'

Katherine turned to Miranda, who was continuing to note down the conversation verbatim.

'Miranda, stop writing. Have you got any cigarettes?'

'Mm,' Miranda assented, continuing to chew the felt-tip pen.

'Well, get them out,' Katherine ordered.

'Oh, yah, sorry.' Miranda pulled a packet out of her coat pocket and handed it to Katherine. Katherine held it out to Cora who took a cigarette. Katherine placed another cigarette in her own mouth.

'I didn't know you smoked,' Cora said sharply.

'When I want to,' Katherine replied.

'So typical of your generation,' said Cora. 'What I want, when I want. No idea about sacrifice.'

Ah, thought Katherine. So I was right.

'Sacrifice?' said Katherine easily. 'OK, let's talk about sacrifice. Is Leoni being taken care of?'

Cora glared at Katherine.

'I hate people like you.'

'Let's leave me out of it,' said Katherine. 'I didn't walk through customs with a load of heroin stuck up my fanny.'

'I know you. I know all you're interested in is winning a case.'

'Thank your lucky stars.'

'I brought up that girl without a father, so don't take the piss out of me.'

'I'm sorry. OK.' Katherine stubbed her cigarette out in the tinfoil ashtray.

'I've never expected anything from life, so whatever happens to me doesn't matter.'

Katherine had heard a lot of this defeatist self-pity in her time; but it always drove her up the pole.

'I got myself into this mess,' said Cora stoically, 'so I'll have to pay the consequence.'

'Bollocks. How much are they giving Leoni?'

Katherine leant forward and glared at Cora, who glared back and stubbed out her cigarette.

'Is it a lump sum, a weekly allowance or what?' continued Katherine. 'I hope it's a lump sum in advance of the trial, because once you go down Leoni will never see them again.'

Cora tapped her fingers nervously on the table but said nothing.

'Well, I probably won't see you again until we get to court.'

Katherine handed back Miranda her cigarette packet and started to put her papers away in her brief case.

'Is there anything you need?' Katherine asked, more gently. This exasperating old woman seemed so vulnerable, so unaware of what lay ahead for her.

'No, thank you,' said Cora sanctimoniously. 'I have everything I need. We don't need much when it comes down to it.'

Katherine was fuming as she left the interview room.

'I don't know if Cora's all there or not, but I know one thing: she's driving me round the bend. Does she think she's really a nun?'

'Yah,' said Miranda, 'but I mean it's all to do with sacrifice. Like she said.'

'Well, if she wants to suffer for her sins,' said Katherine grimly, 'we've got a criminal justice system, that'll be happy to oblige her. I've done all I can.'

'Oh, right,' said Miranda. 'Would you like your pen back then?'

'Keep it,' said Katherine.

'Oh, right. Yah. Brilliant,' said Miranda.

CHAPTER NINE

Henry felt much more relaxed now that Alton was a personal friend of his. He even felt mellow about this huge office he was in, with the glass dome. The walls had recently been painted white and the metal pillars were black. There was a metal staircase in the centre of the room, leading up to a gallery which went round three sides of the area.

'Hey,' said Henry, 'this is what they call open plan, right?'

'That's right,' said Lorraine. 'The barristers share the main office area, and Hugh and I sit here in the middle.'

'Hey,' said Henry, who was feeling good in his red tab levis, American baseball boots, jacket and cap worn back to front.

He could see that Hugh and Lorraine had plenty of paperwork to do, but knew they were supposed to look after him while Alton and this barrister, Frank, discussed his situation. Right now, Henry felt he was the centre of attention, and he liked the buzz it gave him.

He wanted to chat, and perched on the edge of Hugh's desk. Henry was particularly curious about Hugh, who was the youngest black man he had ever seen in a suit. And it was a pinstripe.

'So like what goes on in here then?' Henry enquired.

Hugh looked up at him.

'Well this is the clerk's area. Really the nerve centre of the Chambers. All the work comes through here. We negotiate with solicitors and that, don't we Lorraine?'

'Yeah,' said Lorraine. 'Basically, we get work from people like Alton for people like Frank. And we negotiate their fees and make sure the right brief arrives in the right place at the right time.'

Hugh looked at Henry and smiled.

'We do all the hard work, basically,' said Hugh.

'Amazing,' said Henry. 'So you're sort of like judges and that.'

Hugh and Lorraine grinned at each other.

'No, not really,' Lorraine said.

'Oh right. What are you then?' Henry asked.

'Well, I'm a barrister's clerk and Hugh is a junior barrister's clerk.'

Henry looked sympathetically at Hugh.

'Oh, but still it's great,' said Henry. 'It's a job, innit? Do you have to have any bits of paper, Hugh?'

Henry noticed that Lorraine was making small, choking sounds. Suddenly, she seized a pile of papers from her desk and ran over to some pigeonholes behind Henry.

'Not really,' said Hugh.

'So I could apply,' added Henry, starting to plan a career on the other side of the law from his usual one.

'Yeah,' Hugh humoured him.

'Oh, brilliant!' said Henry. 'I'll get a form then.'

'Right.'

Henry leant down confidentially and whispered to Hugh.

'Fancy a spliff?'

Hugh hesitated for a moment and looked round the office.

'Yeah, all right.'

*

Meanwhile, Alton was not making the progress he had hoped to make with Frank.

'They've leaned really hard on this little man, Frank. He's done nothing to deserve this. They find him with a few grammes of grass, do a bit of agriculture and charge him with dealing, just to make their figures look good. They refuse him bail so whatever happens in his case, he's done a bit of time, you know, another nigger off the streets. And he could get five in front of the wrong judge. I mean he's just a nice little space cadet. If he wants to spend his Giro to stay spliffed out of his head all week, why should anybody care? He says reality is for people who can't handle drugs.'

'I can do something for him on the drugs thing when the time comes,' said Frank, 'but this other thing . . . Why not ring C4?'

'And say what? "One of our nice policemen is using the bail laws to blackmail my client" – and he isn't even my client – "into verballing some woman called Cora Davis. Please arrest him straightaway." There must be something better than that. Come on, Frank! I know this advice is free, but shit!'

'OK,' said Frank. 'Maybe we can give the legal process a helping hand.'

Alton called Henry over and introduced him to Frank.

Henry grasped Frank's hand and shook it furiously as if to congratulate him.

'Oh, fantastic, yeah.'

'Hello, Henry,' said Frank, showing Henry a seat. 'You've got a bad problem.'

'Oh yeah, it's a bummer. I'm having really bad dreams. I'm only twenty-two.'

Frank nodded sympathetically as if Henry was making sense.

'We've had a talk,' said Alton, 'and Frank wants to help.'

'Fantastic. I fink to myself I can't lose with two good people on my side. McCabe better watch out, eh? Wait till I tell my mother, eh?'

'Well, hang on,' said Frank. 'There's the slight problem that you already have a solicitor.'

Henry looked puzzled, and turned to Alton.

'What we're worried about,' continued Frank, 'is you leaving Fleming to go to Alton, McCabe finding out about that – and we have to presume that he would, I think – and coming down on you again. I mean the last thing we want is your bail to be rescinded.'

'Yeah, yeah,' said Henry, by now in a state of panic. 'But I mean: I can't go back to Fleming now, can I? I mean I need help, you know.'

'Calm down, Henry,' Alton said calmly.

'What you *can* do quite legitimately when the time comes is tell Fleming to brief me,' said Frank, 'and I will accept if I possibly can.'

Henry looked suspicious.

'I mean I will,' Frank assured him. 'If Fleming says "Why Frank Cartwright?" just say "Why not? I had a friend who had him and he got him off." OK?'

'When would I get Frank then?' Henry asked Alton.

'When they set a rough date for the trial, then we all jiggle with dates,' said Frank. 'Not that long I wouldn't think.'

'See, Frank, I'm not a dealer!'

'Frank's not allowed to talk to you about the actual case

yet,' said Alton quickly, seeing Frank's unease at the way things were going.

'Why?'

'It's just the rules. All that will happen later.'

'Sorry, Frank.'

'No, no,' said Frank. 'Let's try in the meantime to do something about this false statement. I know a man called Holland who works in Customs and Excise. Give me a day or two to get alongside him, OK? Let me see if he knows anything about Cora Davis and George McCabe.'

CHAPTER TEN

Parked round the corner from Holloway Prison, Pam Hollis looked at herself in her hand-mirror, and wondered if she had overdone the rouge. She patted a stray wisp of peroxide hair back into place, and looked across at her gentleman friend in the driver's seat.

George didn't seem himself today, especially since that meeting of his with his Italian business contacts. Normally, he liked giving her a lift in his shiny new BMW; but Pam could see he was out of sorts, sweating a lot, looking in his rear-view mirror, to see if he was being followed. And he nearly jumped out of his skin when that passing car backfired.

Probably, like her, he was worried about Cora Davis.

'What am I supposed to say to her?' Pam Hollis asked.

'She was your bright idea,' snapped McCabe. 'Tell her the baby'll end up in a Bolognese sauce if she opens her trap.'

'Oh, that'll really settle her nerves, won't it?' Pam retorted.

Pam watched McCabe anxiously, as he leant forward and rested his head on the steering wheel and thought for a few moments. He raised his head and straightened himself up. Beads of sweat glistened on the steering wheel.

'She's got to see sense. Tell her twenty-five grand is out of the question now. See if she'll take ten.'

'Where are you going to get ten grand?' said Pam.

'I dunno,' McCabe grunted, wiping his forehead.

Pam got out of the car and slammed the door. She tottered off on very high heels towards the prison entrance, where she waited with a large group of visitors.

As she sat, Pam puffed thoughtfully on her menthol cigarette. She was unsure how to make Cora keep silent.

'Oh my Gawd, Cora!' Pam gawped at Cora entering the cubicle. Pam was used to seeing the changes that prison brought about in people, but she wasn't prepared for the difference in Cora; all her old perkiness had disappeared and she had become a defeated, tired old woman.

'This place is a madhouse,' Cora said. 'A girl killed herself day before yesterday. Hung herself. I can't stand it. I just keep thinking about the money. Are they sorting it out?'

'Yeah,' said Pam evasively. 'Oh yeah. Only there's a little bit of a problem. You see, they say you didn't make the delivery so you shouldn't get the full whack.'

Cora looked at Pam with a steely expression.

'Those kids need that money. Without that money, all they've got in the world is Leoni and a father who's a half-wit doing seven years in Wormwood Scrubs.'

'But, Cora,' whined Pam, 'if you take me down with you it won't make any difference to what you get from the judge.'

'That's not what my barrister thinks, I can promise you that.'

'But naming me would be pointless. It wouldn't help them.'

Cora looked at Pam shrewdly.

'No, but it might make you try a bit harder, love. And I want some on account. Leoni needs money *now*.'

*

It was towards the end of afternoon visiting. The maternity ward was packed with proud dads, visiting grandparents and friends. Katherine wondered what she was doing there, visiting someone she had never met.

She supposed she wanted to know that Cora's daughter, Leoni, was all right. Giving birth was difficult enough without having your mum and your husband in prison. Impossible as Cora was, Katherine wanted to be able to reassure her about her daughter and grandchild.

She wandered down the ward, looking for a nurse to point her in the direction of Leoni. A sister pointed her in the direction of a bed in one corner of the ward. A small, waif-like girl was sitting up in bed with her baby sprawled across her open legs. There were no other visitors.

'Leoni?' asked Katherine, holding out a bouquet of roses.

The girl looked puzzled, suspicious of the posh stranger.

'Katherine Hughes,' said Katherine.

Leoni pulled herself up and smiled at Katherine, who noted, with a sinking feeling in her stomach, that it was the smile, just ever so slightly twisted, of a loser. Leoni, she knew at once, was a future client.

'Oh yeah,' said Leoni. 'Hello. Nice of you to come.'

Katherine looked down at the tiny baby.

'She's lovely,' Katherine said sincerely. 'Hello, little Cora.'

'You got any?' asked Leoni.

Katherine merely held out her bunch of flowers, hoping to avoid any further questions about an issue which she had been avoiding for years.

'I hope you like roses,' said Katherine.

'Oh lovely. Thanks. Really sweet of you. Mum says you've been ever so good to her.'

Katherine tried not to show surprise, and felt rather guilty.

'Did she say that?'

'She says you really care.'

Katherine did not reply.

'Will it be long for her?' Leoni asked.

'No, no, it won't be long now. I'll get a vase or something, shall I?'

Katherine walked down the ward to find a nurse, passing a hard-looking peroxide blonde of uncertain age, tottering along on ridiculously high heels. Katherine watched as the new arrival walked over to Leoni, bent and pecked her on the forehead.

'Hello. How's the little chicken? Oh, look at her! Leoni, I've just spoken to sister and she says if you have a good night's sleep tonight she'll let you come home to my place tomorrow, OK?'

Leoni frowned.

'I don't want to,' she said. 'I want to go home.'

'Now, Leoni,' said the woman. 'Don't complicate things now. You know the arrangements. After the trial you can do what you like. And you'll be able to afford to. That's settled, then.'

The new arrival patted Leoni's hand and sat down on the chair next to the bed. Katherine returned with a vase containing the roses, just in time to hear the threat in the woman's voice.

'Pam,' said Leoni, 'this is Katherine Hughes. Katherine, Pam Hollis.'

Katherine could see Pam quickly appraising the cost of her weekend outfit of designer jeans and cashmere pull-over. Pam's outfit had cost a bit too; but Katherine did not consider it money well spent. Pam might almost have been taking a correspondence course in How To Look Like A Gangster's Moll. She had also managed to drop food down the front of her lurex jumper.

'Katherine is mum's barrister,' Leoni explained.

'Oh. Nice,' Pam muttered.

'Not really,' replied Katherine, putting the vase down on the bedside cupboard. 'I don't like it when the wrong people go to prison.'

Pam didn't reply. Katherine bent down to put her finger in little Cora's chubby hand.

'She's adorable,' Katherine said, with genuine surprise.

'Did you say you had one?' asked Leoni.

Katherine let go of the perfect little hand and gazed down at the small baby for a brief moment. She shook her head.

'No.'

Katherine quickly made her farewells and left the hospital. Visiting maternity wards always produced contradictory emotions in Katherine. She had never resolved the conflict between career and motherhood. She always said that the one did not preclude the other. I'm the ideal aunt and godmother, she told herself, but motherhood? I could never make that commitment myself, although . . .

Katherine had no definite plans for the rest of the afternoon. After a nightmare tour round Sainsburys (during which she swore for the umpteenth time never again to go near a supermarket at the weekend), she dumped her shopping in the car and stopped on the off chance at her friend Claudia's house in Shepherd's Bush. She had just rung the bell for the second time, when she remembered that Claudia was away for a few weeks filming in South America. Katherine got back into the car and drove back to her flat in Notting Hill.

This was Katherine's favourite part of London. She loved Portobello market, the fruit and veg during the week and the stalls of dubious antiques on Saturdays. She loved the contrast of black reggae stores, cheek by jowl with bookshops devoted to nothing but food or travel. She loved the culture clash between All Saints Road, with dope dealers trading openly in the street, and the smart, fashionable restaurants in Kensington Park Road. Most of all, she loved the feeling in the air that something might be just about to happen. For her, it was the nearest that London could get to New York.

She had to park her car at some distance from her flat, and to walk along several streets with her shopping before she reached her front door. A wave of self-pity and broodiness overwhelmed her as she lugged her carrier bags of shopping up the stairs.

She had a first-floor flat in a stucco Regency terrace house which had long ago been divided into flats. There were three large, high-ceilinged rooms. The elegantly furnished sitting-room, which doubled as her study, had tall windows which overlooked several acres of communal gardens, giving an atmosphere of tranquillity in the centre of London.

Katherine unpacked her shopping and stashed it away in the high-tech kitchen which led off the living-room. Still feeling glum, she selected a good bottle of Burgundy from the wine rack and poured herself a glass. She turned on Radio Three, and settled down on her huge squashy leather sofa. But the combination of Mahler and nearly a whole bottle of Pommard only seemed to deepen her depression.

She had sunk to the floor in front of the sofa, and was leaning moodily on the glass coffee table, when Robert let himself in. Quickly summing up the situation, he threw his leather jacket across a chair and walked over to Katherine. He picked up the wine bottle and tried to remove the glass from her hand. She looked up at him, and brought his face gradually into focus.

'Don't do that please,' she mumbled.

He let go of the glass and replaced the bottle. Katherine watched him walk across the room and into the kitchen, take a loaf of bread from the bin and start to make himself a sandwich. She pulled herself up from the floor and staggered across to him.

'I'm sorry. I'm more than sorry. You deserve better than this,' she said, miserably.

Robert put down the bread knife and looked at her pityingly.

'I don't know if you can imagine,' Katherine continued. 'If I have any right to ask you to imagine, but . . . day after day, week after week, year after year: the same desperate people being sent down for the same desperate reasons. The same stories. The same fit-ups. Punishment, punishment. Slap them down, bang them up. Pass some more laws if these ones won't do. Catch more people in the net. Fill up the prisons till the roof blows off. And I'm in this. I do this for a living. I help process them through the machine.'

She swayed and leant against Robert for support.

'I look at these faces staring out at us from the docks and the jury boxes and the galleries, looking at us as if we're talking Latin. Which we are, half the time. While their lives get chopped into pieces. And do you know the question I always think they'll ask but never do? "How fucking dare you do this?" But do you know what they *do* ask? "Why the fancy dress?" And I say "Oh, it's part of the history of the Bar," blah, blah, but the real reason for the fancy dress is so that you can stop feeling like a real person because if you had to be yourself, you'd die.'

She swayed again. Robert put out his hands to hold her steady.

'How much have you had to drink?' he asked.

Katherine hung her head like a little girl; and he pulled

her towards him, hugging her tight. She wrapped her arms around his neck and started kissing him, first slowly and then, as he relented, more and more passionately. He eased himself away from her, and looked at her closely.

'How much have you had to drink?' he repeated, smiling.

'Just enough.' Katherine smiled hazily and resumed her embrace.

She laughed, as Robert put his hands up under her sweater, and began to caress her breasts. She began to relax, and was about to let him carry her to the sofa when the door-bell rang. Katherine's head cleared. She disengaged herself and pulled down her sweater.

'Oh, that'll be Frank,' she said, patting Robert affectionately on the chest.

'Frank!' said Robert.

Katherine looked at him sharply. She had never seen him more angry.

'It's nothing, just somebody he wants me to meet,' she shouted over her shoulder, as she went to the front door.

'Well sod that! And sod you!' shouted Robert. 'I'm going out!'

'No, please, please!' Katherine came back across the flat and kissed him passionately. 'It's a quickie.'

The door-bell rang again, and she darted off to let Frank in. Robert grimaced and went back into the kitchen.

Katherine ushered Frank in together with a distinguished-looking middle-aged man, whom Frank introduced as Mr Holland, an Investigations Officer from Customs and Excise.

Katherine smiled at Robert, as he uncorked a bottle of wine and set the glasses out on a tray. He was evidently surprised at Katherine's change in mood. She was no longer tearful and low. Instead, she was bubbly and amusing. She pulled him down next to her on the sofa and made ostentatious play of stroking the back of his neck as Frank explained his mission.

'I'm briefed for a guy called Henry Griffiths. He had a little bit of dope planted on him by George McCabe.'

'I know him,' Katherine murmured.

'I know you do. Is Cora Davis pleading to the heroin charge?'

Katherine laughed.

'Pleading? She's going beyond guilty. A totally new concept in self-flagellation. How do you know about Cora?'

'McCabe made my client sign a statement saying he tipped off McCabe about your client.'

'Why?'

'He needed a reason for arresting her.'

'You know he helped himself to most of the stuff?' said Katherine. 'He must be worth five million quid.'

'We think maybe he was running her.'

Katherine shook her head. 'No. I can tell you that's not on. I mean I've talked to her about the way he took the stuff off her in the car. I mean you couldn't invent that.'

Holland leant forward and joined in for the first time. He had been sitting back, quietly sizing up Katherine and her flat.

'Has she told you who was running her?'

'No,' said Katherine, aware that Robert was getting bored and therefore trying to bring the conversation to an end. 'Nor will she now. It'll be over for her in a week or two. Apart from five years inside.'

Both Frank and Holland looked disappointed, and studied the bottoms of their glasses. Frank poured some more wine. Robert jerked himself away from Katherine, and edged towards the other end of the sofa.

'Why don't you make some coffee, Robert?' asked Katherine.

Robert rose sulkily, and mooched across to the kitchen.

Frank looked at Holland.

'You're still convinced it's McCabe?'

'He's got all the credentials,' said Holland. 'He's been crooked for years. He's got woman trouble, he's got money trouble, he's got all sorts of trouble. He's in hock to everybody, trying to live like a stockbroker on policeman's pay.'

Picking his leather jacket off the chair where he had thrown it, Robert went over to Katherine and pecked her on the cheek.

'I'll see you later,' he mumbled.

Frank looked at the departing figure and then at Katherine, who took a large gulp of wine.

'What's his woman trouble?' asked Katherine quickly.

'He left his wife, he went back, he got chucked out, he went back, he left again,' said Holland. 'He lives half the time with her indoors and half the time with a piece on the side with a sweetshop in Acton. It's been going on for years. She also operates as his gofer into prisons to do deals for him with people on remand: "You plead to this and George'll see his way to dropping that." Pamela Hollis is her name.'

Katherine perked up.

'Say that again,' she said.

'Pamela Hollis,' repeated Holland.

Katherine clapped her hands.

'Oh, this is brilliant!' she chortled, remembering the woman at Leoni's bedside.

CHAPTER ELEVEN

The following morning, Katherine felt slightly the worse for warehouse wine. Nevertheless, to her the alka seltzer dissolving in a glass sounded like soft music. She was full of enthusiasm, and whistled to herself as she ground the coffee beans for breakfast.

Holland's information about McCabe meant that she could now, at long last, do something with Cora Davis's case. She poured out two mugs of coffee, leaving one by Robert, who was dead to the world after returning drunk at midnight.

He was still asleep when she had showered and dressed, and was ready to leave for Chambers. She kissed him gently on the forehead and looked at him. She remembered that they'd had one hell of an argument. She'd had to point out that Frank's wife saw even less of Frank than Robert did of her. Robert had said he wasn't Frank's wife, which Katherine had said was missing the point. Afterwards, there had been no tenderness in the way Robert had made love. Katherine wondered whether to wake him, then looked at her watch. Quickly, she gathered up her bits and pieces, and dashed to the tube.

She bounded up the stairs to Grimshaw's and into the clerk's room, where she grabbed hold of a telephone, while calling out to the junior.

'Edward, could you get hold of David Frankland? Tell him I'm going to do the business of Cora's knickers after all. Can he ring me? He'll know what I mean.'

There was no answer on the number that she had dialled.

'Oh come on,' she said.

Tom was posting mail in the lawyers' pigeonholes. He paused and looked across the room at Katherine.

'Oh my goodness, they'll be selling tickets for this one,' he said.

Katherine chose to ignore the jibe, and asked him whether Cora's case was listed. Tom merely continued posting the papers. It was Edward who paused from ringing Frankland for a moment to answer Katherine.

'Yes. Next Tuesday. Langtry it is.'

Katherine groaned.

'Oh, give me a break,' she said. 'Can you remember who's prosecuting? I've got to get a postponement.'

'Colin Campbell-Johnson,' said Edward.

'He's OK.'

Relieved, Katherine put the telephone down and looked up Campbell-Johnson's number. She tried not to be distracted by the arrival of other barristers, all chatting about their weekends and the cases they had on this week. She was still looking for Campbell-Johnson, when Tom came across and addressed her with his usual languid sarcasm.

'May I ask when you think you'll have time to defend this woman if you postpone it?'

This time, it was Katherine's turn to ignore Tom.

'Or are you aware,' continued Tom, 'that last week you asked us to try and have it brought forward, which was accomplished with no small difficulty?'

Katherine looked up from her address book.

'Oh, shut up, Tom!' she snapped.

The other barristers' chatter stopped. Katherine felt everyone looking at her. She returned to the telephone, and punched out Colin Campbell-Johnson's number.

'And she wonders why life doesn't run smoothly,' Tom said softly, but just loud enough for everyone to hear.

'Listen,' said Katherine leaning across the desk towards Tom. 'One more foolish, puerile remark from you, you ignorant, lazy, overpaid, overstuffed berk and I'll shove this telephone down your stupid throat.'

Katherine heard several sharp intakes of breath and one or two stifled giggles. Fortunately, at this point the telephone connected at the other end.

'Hello? Colin Campbell-Johnson? Katherine Hughes,' she said.

She smiled at the other barristers in the room, as if butter wouldn't melt in her mouth, as Tom returned to his pigeonholes.

Campbell-Johnson listened to Katherine and agreed to her suggestion of an adjournment. The idea of confronting Lily Langtry with Cora's knickers evidently amused him.

*

That afternoon, Katherine and Campbell-Johnson went to visit Judge Langtry in his Chambers at Knightsbridge. Without his wig, he looked like one of the more seedy drunks who passed in front of him in court. The wig was thrown over the back of a chair, and he wore an old cardigan over his robes. He sat with his feet on his desk, and a fag hanging out of the corner of his mouth.

'Mr Campbell-Johnson,' he drawled, not bothering to address Katherine, or remove the cigarette from the corner of his mouth.

Colin Campbell-Johnson shut the door behind Katherine and began to explain the desirability of an adjournment.

'There does seem to be a danger in proceeding too quickly, Judge. There's a strong element of doubt in my mind about the police evidence, and I understand the two detectives in question could even be subject to an internal police enquiry. There's a lot of concern about how they came to be on hand.'

Langtry removed the cigarette from his mouth with a flourish. He regarded Colin Campbell-Johnson and Katherine with great deliberation, as if pondering the problems of the world.

'Yes,' he said finally. 'But I fail to see how any such doubts would affect a case in which the defendant intends to plead guilty. Is that still the intention, Miss Hughes?'

'Even so, Judge,' said Katherine, 'I think we should all be extremely worried about this whole case.'

'Worry away, Miss Hughes,' sneered Judge Langtry. 'No doubt you are paid to worry. However, I still see no proper reason to keep this woman waiting. Surely the time approaches when the poor creature must be put out of her misery.'

He took another puff on his cigarette. Katherine darted a look at Campbell-Johnson, who responded hurriedly.

'Yes. Er ... Judge, there is also a very clear forensic difficulty which Miss Hughes has brought to my attention only today.'

'And what's that?'

'Well,' Campbell-Johnson shuffled his feet and looked a trifle embarrassed. 'Perhaps Miss Hughes would prefer to explain it herself.'

Katherine addressed the judge with great seriousness.

'Judge, it concerns my client's underwear.'

'Oh,' said Judge Langtry with distaste. 'Really?'

'I asked for her pants to be examined by Home Office forensic scientists and their findings make it clear that the garment in question must have been tampered with in some way after her arrest.'

Langtry removed his feet from his desk and sat up. He arched his eyebrows, in a passable impersonation of Edith Evans playing Lady Bracknell.

'Tampered with?' he asked. 'In what way?'

'Well,' continued Katherine, 'the panties she was wearing when she was searched by WPCs Kenton and Platt cannot be the ones she wore on her journey from Bombay to Lewisham police station.'

'Why not?' queried the Judge.

'Well, sir, how can I put it? The absence of debris strongly suggests this.'

'I'm sorry,' said Langtry. 'I don't follow you.'

Katherine looked the judge straight in the eye.

'To put it bluntly, if you wore a pair of knickers from Bombay to Lewisham there'd be certain tell-tale signs, however microscopic.'

Langtry pondered the point.

'Oh, I see,' he said. 'Well, why didn't you say so? We'll take the case out for a week or two. I'm very impressed, Miss Hughes.'

'Thank you, Judge.'

Langtry's face contorted itself into what Katherine supposed must be a smile.

'I must say,' said Langtry, 'if I'd been caught red-handed in possession of a large amount of heroin, the tell-tale signs in *my* underwear would be considerably more than microscopic!'

*

Katherine and Frankland went to Holloway to break the news to Cora. She was uncertain whether they would succeed in persuading Cora to change her plea, but she thought it was worth a try. Katherine was shocked when Cora shuffled into the interview cubicle. She seemed to have aged, even since their last meeting. The old woman tugged nervously at the bottom of her cardigan. Katherine wondered if Cora's mind was starting to wander.

'Hello,' mumbled Cora.

'Hello, Cora,' Katherine smiled reassuringly.

'Hello, dear,' said Frankland, in his best bedside manner. 'Now, did somebody let you know that your case was listed for Tuesday?'

Cora looked even more confused.

'Was?'

'We've been given an adjournment,' Frankland explained.

'I don't want an adjournment,' said Cora, aggressively.

'Let me finish, dear,' said Frankland. 'Now, Miss Hughes has a few things to say to you and then you're going to make a decision, so listen carefully. And remember the decision is yours.'

'Cora,' Katherine smiled at her client. 'Pamela Hollis.'

There was no response to the name.

'Your friend Pamela,' continued Katherine, 'who asked you to go to India and bring back some heroin.'

Cora stared intently at the table.

'Pamela Hollis is Sergeant McCabe's mistress,' said Katherine.

Cora looked up at Katherine, incredulously. So I was right, thought Katherine, she didn't have a clue.

'Pamela Hollis also works for her lover, running messages into and out of prisons to men waiting trial. Prisons like Wormwood Scrubs where your son-in-law Dennis is imprisoned.'

Katherine watched Cora starting to put the pieces together.

67

'That's where you met Pamela, didn't you? Sitting in the waiting room.'

Katherine paused. Cora nodded.

'And she befriended you? And heard all your money problems. And found a way to help you.'

Cora looked shattered.

'We don't possess corroborative evidence of any of this, Mrs Davis,' said Frankland, 'and so there's no hope of having the case thrown out. However, that hardly matters. Since we've given fairly clear warning of our intention to expose McCabe and Mrs Hollis in court, the police solicitor is very likely to instruct counsel to offer no evidence, rather than risk a complete fiasco.'

'I see. But I've pleaded guilty.'

Cora looked from Frankland to Katherine, confused.

'Not at all,' her solicitor continued. 'None of your previous statements now matter. What matters is what you say in court on the day.'

'Well,' said Cora, 'I shall be saying what I've always said, that I'm guilty.'

Frankland looked staggered.

'Are you saying that you still intend to plead guilty?'

'Yes.'

'You're sure about that?'

'Yes,' said Cora. 'I am guilty, remember.'

Frankland looked at Katherine in exasperation, and shook his head. Katherine, too, was beginning to get very irritated with Cora.

'What's guilt got to do with anything?' said Katherine. 'Guilty people go free all the time. Innocent people go to jail all the time. This is a lottery, not a confessional.'

Cora looked unimpressed.

'You've been given a winning ticket,' persisted Katherine. 'You mustn't get mixed up between the law and morality.

68

What you did was wrong – but the judge won't give you absolution, just a meaningless prison sentence.'

Katherine could hardly believe that Cora was prepared to sentence herself to prison.

'What's *right* about you going to prison while Hollis and McCabe and whoever's behind *them* stay free? What good would be done? Will you be an example? Is anybody going to be put off from being a courier? No, of course not. The dealers will just have to pay more for the greater risks, because there'll always be people who need the money like you did. It would be completely pointless, Cora. All you have to do is go along with it.'

The three of them sat in silence for some time. Cora pondered Katherine's arguments. Slowly, she raised her head and looked at the space between Katherine and Frankland.

'I won't say I'm not tempted,' said Cora. 'Thank you for all you've done, both of you.'

She got up from her seat, walked to the door and knocked to be let out. She looked hard at Katherine.

'I wish you hadn't told me about Pam,' said Cora. 'How could the bloody cow do that to me?'

'Why don't you ask her next time she pops in for a chat? Or has she already been in today?' snapped Katherine.

Cora paused at the door as it was opened. She looked back at Katherine as if she was almost sorry for her.

'It's a fantastic amount of money, Katherine,' she whispered.

'See you in court,' murmured Katherine, as Cora returned to her cell.

CHAPTER TWELVE

Henry sat on his favourite bench, in the marbled and tiled entrance to the Inner London Crown Court. He was waiting with Fleming, his solicitor, for Frank to arrive. Henry didn't recognize the man who came up to him, togged up in a gown and wig.

'OK, Henry?' asked the man, glancing round the entrance hall.

Slowly Henry realized that it *was* Frank.

'Henry's thinking,' Fleming told Frank. 'I dunno. Might he be better pleading, looking for a bit of leniency, not wasting the court's time?'

Henry saw Frank looking keenly at him.

'Is this your idea, Henry?' asked Frank. He looked and sounded displeased. 'I thought we were agreed to fight it.'

'Well,' said Henry, 'it's just Mr Fleming thinks I should be trying to get the best I can for myself.'

'I see.'

Frank pursed his lips. Before he could say anything, a woman came out of the courtroom and walked up to them.

'Mr Cartwright? Are you in Griffiths?'

'Yeah.'

'Is it contested?'

Henry saw Frank looking at him, hard.

'Let me get back to you,' Frank told the woman.

Henry felt a bit confused.

'That was the clerk of the court,' explained Frank.

'Yeah?' said Henry.

The clerk went back inside the court and Frank looked around the lobby again. Henry wondered who Frank was looking for. Two men in a huddle on the main staircase beckoned to him and then Frank turned back to Henry and Fleming.

'That's the prosecution. They want to talk,' said Frank.

'If they're offering a deal,' said Fleming enthusiastically, 'I think we should bite their hands off. Possession, yeah.'

'Let's see.'

Frank walked across the hall and up the stairs towards the two men. The prosecuting counsel nodded at Frank.

'Good morning, Cartwright.'

Frank greeted them, warily.

'I was wondering how you saw this case?' asked the prosecuting counsel.

Frank looked most serious.

'I'm looking forward to getting George McCabe into the box,' he said.

The prosecuting counsel smiled.

'We wondered whether it might not be in the general interest to drop the dealing charge.'

'I think it would,' Frank agreed.

'Well, we'd need something from you, of course.'

'You want him to plead to possession?' said Frank.

'I think that would allow us to proceed quickly.'

Frank looked across the throng of people waiting to go into court. He saw Henry and Fleming looking at him anxiously, wondering what was being proposed. Frank continued scanning the entrance lobby for new arrivals, but could see no sign of McCabe.

He decided to take the risk. He spun around on his heel and spoke to the prosecuting counsel.

'No, I think we'll take it into court and give it a run,' he said affably.

He walked back down the stairs to Henry and Fleming.

'What did they want?' asked Fleming.

'Just sit tight a minute,' said Frank. 'Henry, can you see McCabe anywhere?'

Henry was glad to have something to do. He got up, looked around, even peered outside the court. He returned to his lawyers and shook his head.

'Nah,' he said.

The clerk of the court was with Frank again.

'Mr Cartwright? Is it contested?' she asked.

'Yes,' said Frank.

The three men sat down on the bench and settled down to wait while the previous case came out through the doors.

'That's us next,' Frank explained to Henry.

The prosecuting counsel beckoned to Frank again. Frank got up and walked across to him.

'Well done, Cartwright. We won't offer any evidence. In the absence of our star witness.'

Frank smiled wryly and went back to tell Henry the news.

'You're free,' said Frank.

'What?' said Henry.

'You can walk out of here, an innocent man,' explained Fleming.

'What?' said Henry, unable to conceal his amazement.

*

72

PCs Hobbs and Sutcliffe got out of their motorway patrol car, to see if they could help the motorist who had broken down on the inside lane.

'You'd think he could have got his motor on to the hard shoulder,' said Hobbs.

'Look at him,' said Sutcliffe. 'He looks like he's seen a ghost.'

'What's the problem?' asked Hobbs, tapping on the driver's window.

The driver just shrugged his shoulders and continued staring into space.

'You can't just sit here, pal,' said Hobbs.

Sutcliffe looked hard at the man, who was sweating profusely.

'Get out, sir,' said Sutcliffe, 'and we'll push the vehicle on to the hard shoulder.'

McCabe got out of the car and stood to one side, as the policemen pushed.

'Well, sir,' said Hobbs, 'let's see if we can find out what's wrong.'

McCabe knew exactly what had gone wrong. First, his home had been torn apart by the Customs and Excise. Then his wife had said she never wanted to see him again. Finally, two heavies had frogmarched him out of the pub, and taken him to meet his Italian business contacts, who had told him to disappear. Or he'd be found dead under a bush.

The two policemen had managed to get the bonnet open.

'Try the starter, sir,' said one of them. 'Try the starter.'

But the driver had vanished. Hobbs and Sutcliffe looked in amazement as they saw the man running away from them across the neighbouring field, discarding his clothes piece by piece.

'Takes all sorts,' said Sutcliffe, shaking his head.

The pair of them stood and watched the naked man clear a ditch.

'Won't get far without his clothes,' said Hobbs.

'I wonder what he did for a living,' Sutcliffe added.

CHAPTER THIRTEEN

The evening before Cora's court case, Katherine went home to find two messages on her answering machine. One of them was from Robert. The other was from Frank, inviting her to join his party at the Field Club Ball.

'I know a Ball is not your usual idea of exciting entertainment,' said Frank's voice, 'but I've got this extra ticket, so why don't you come along and cheer us all up? If I don't hear from you, I'll see you tomorrow night. Bye.'

Katherine listened again to Robert's message, then went to look in her wardrobe for something to wear the next evening.

*

Deep below the courtroom, Katherine tried one last time to persuade her client to change her plea. Cora was having none of it. She sat still and composed, waiting for her trial to begin.

'Okay,' said Katherine. 'I'm going round to see the judge. I'm going to ask him for another adjournment.'

Cora shook her head vigorously.

'Don't worry,' Katherine assured Cora. 'He won't allow

it. It's just so I have something to bargain with. Assuming he refuses, and you then plead guilty, you'll be sentenced this morning. OK, Cora?'

Cora looked as if she couldn't care less. Katherine made her way through long corridors to Langtry's room.

'Judge,' said Katherine. 'I think this is now a very clear case. The evidence is overwhelming, albeit circumstantial evidence, that those policemen entrapped my client.'

'This may well be true,' said Langtry drily, 'though you clearly cannot establish it or we wouldn't be sitting here. But entrapment is not in any case a legitimate defence. Presumably she knew what she was being asked to do, and she jolly well went and did it.'

'Perhaps so, Judge. But you must admit, it's great mitigation. Another week or so might allow the full facts to emerge.'

Judge Langtry sighed deeply.

'But, Miss Hughes,' he said, 'these enquiries you wish me to await might go on a very long time and still never establish the exact role of the police in this affair.'

He twirled his glasses in the air, as he lectured Katherine.

'It is so often the case that the police are afterwards found to have behaved a little unwisely, but without the criminal wickedness so frequently imputed to them by defence counsel.'

He then came back with the final blow.

'Besides which,' he added, 'your client still intends to plead guilty.'

Katherine thought for a split second and decided to lie.

'My client is reconsidering her plea.'

Katherine returned to Cora's cell and explained the situation to her.

'He's determined to get the whole mess under the carpet as tidily as possible. He won't have anything to do with an adjournment. He doesn't want to sit in a case where there

76

might eventually be hard evidence of police involvement in drug smuggling. He won't be precise about sentence. If this was anybody else, I'd be expecting maybe eighteen months. You've done six. With remission, you'd be out in another six. But he won't say. I don't trust him. It's up to you, Cora.'

Cora looked up at Katherine.

'I expect he'll go easy on me, won't he, love? After all, I *am* a granny.'

Cora attempted a chuckle. Katherine could see that all the fight had gone from her. All she could do was throw herself on the mercy of Judge Langtry. Langtry of all people.

*

Regina v. *Cora Davis* lasted only a couple of hours. The courtroom was empty, except for the necessary court officers and a sprinkling of people in the public gallery. Katherine spotted Leoni snivelling into a tissue. Holland was also present, sitting on his own at the back of the courtroom.

'And therefore, your Honour,' said Katherine, beginning to wind up her mitigation speech, 'I respectfully suggest that an enlightened view of the whole circumstances of my client's case, including the role of the police, her age, and her five and a half months in prison on remand, will have convinced your Honour that the severity of the crime has in this case been uniquely diminished. Thank you.'

Katherine sat down on the bench, next to Miranda, and looked up at Langtry.

'Oh,' said Langtry. 'Have you finished?'

Katherine kept hold of her temper and stood up again.

'Yes, your Honour. Thank you,' she enunciated as she sat down again.

As Langtry began his sentencing he looked hard at Katherine.

'I must first of all,' he said, 'dispose of one very distasteful aspect of this affair. Matters have been raised with me concerning the conduct of the police officers in this case. It would not be appropriate for me to make any comment. Their conduct has not been a matter for this court. I intend to confine myself to matters on which I've heard the facts.'

He now looked at Cora, almost for the first time during the trial. She stood in the dock, gripping the rail. She was pathetic, grey-faced and trembling.

'Cora Davis,' he resumed, 'you are a very stupid old woman. The crime you've admitted committing is a disgraceful and despicable one. Despite this, however, I have been asked to show leniency and compassion. And I intend to show compassion.'

A sly smile crossed his face as he gazed at Cora, who smiled wanly but trustingly back at him. Katherine closed her eyes, knowing what was going to happen.

'Compassion, that is, for the community that you have polluted. I am sending you to prison for three years.'

Cora gawped up at him.

'Thank you,' she whispered.

Langtry looked at her in surprise.

'What?' he said.

'Thank you, sir.'

'You're very welcome,' said Langtry, sarcastically. 'Take her down, will you?'

A woman police officer led Cora away.

*

Afterwards, Holland was waiting for Katherine in the concourse outside the court.

'Pleased with your day's work?' he asked.

'Are you going to charge McCabe?' Katherine asked wearily.

'With what? You had the only witness,' said Holland. 'At least we got her.'

Katherine looked at him angrily.

'Well, for Christ's sake!' she said. 'It's just an old woman on her way to Styal Prison in the back of a van. I mean, what good is that doing anybody?'

'She'll be out in eighteen months.'

'That really annoys you,' said Katherine bitterly.

Holland leant closer to Katherine.

'I'd *hang* people who bring in heroin,' he said. 'It's our only chance of stopping it.'

'You're talking to the wrong person.'

'Yeah?' he said. 'Have you ever seen a twelve-year-old strung out on heroin?'

'No.'

'Want to see some photos?'

'No, thanks,' said Katherine.

Despite her reply, Holland took a photo out of a folder he was carrying, and pressed it into Katherine's hand. She ignored it and hurried towards the exit.

'Look at it! Go on!' he shouted out after her. 'Put it on your desk! Look at it next time you get asked to help a heroin dealer.'

'She wasn't a dealer,' Katherine called back.

'You know what twelve-year-olds do to get hold of the money to buy it? Twelve-year-old girls?' Holland pursued Katherine relentlessly.

She stopped and rounded on him.

'Talk to the people responsible! Talk to the people who made the world where twelve-year-olds *want* heroin! Talk to the people who protect the big dealers! Get them into court for a change!'

'Why?' Holland retaliated. 'So somebody like you can

do a deal with a bent judge and get them a fortnight in a holiday camp?'

'You do your job, I'll do mine.' Katherine resumed, walking away as fast as possible from Holland.

'You're bent, dear! Completely bent!' he shouted after her.

Katherine ripped up Holland's photograph and threw the pieces in his direction. She then turned around and strode away.

*

Later that evening, Katherine stood alone and thought about Cora. Katherine had turned down several offers to dance, preferring in her present mood to stand on the sidelines and breathe in some evening air. The dancing, in any case, was beginning to get dangerously energetic. Katherine's room-mate, Ackroyd, was trying to jive with Mrs Ackroyd, who was as drunk as she usually was on such occasions. Several well-known silks were attempting to do the hokey-cokey, with their own musical accompaniment. There was a sudden crash as Mrs Ackroyd collided with a waiter carrying a tray.

Frank came up to Katherine, pulled a bottle out of his dinner-jacket pocket, and topped up her empty glass.

'How's Richard?' he asked.

Katherine looked at Frank, surprised.

'Richard who?' she asked.

Frank groaned. He was always getting people's names mixed up.

'Robert, sorry,' he said.

'Packed his bags and gone home to mother,' she said, with a little laugh and a shrug of her shoulders.

'Sorry,' said Frank. 'I thought it was working out.'

'He said living with me was like being stuck in a lift with the Bride of Lammermoor. Can't say I blame him.'

Never one to let an opportunity pass him by, Frank homed in.

'You,' he said authoritatively, 'need the support of people who believe the same things as you do about this job.'

'Which is what, Frank?' Katherine asked hopelessly.

'That the law's a bulldozer being driven by vested interests. We can pull a few people clear of it. We can pull a few great strokes like you did for Cora Davis. But we can't make it make sense. If she'd got off it wouldn't have made sense. It isn't supposed to make sense. It's supposed to stop people at the bottom from thieving from people at the top, that's all. Any justice that gets dished out on the way is purely accidental.'

Katherine emerged from her reverie.

'How does lefties huddling together in Fetter Court change that?'

'It doesn't in the short term,' admitted Frank. 'But it says something. It says we have little faith in the system we're locked into, but we have a bit of faith in ourselves. We do what we can, while the band plays on.'

Frank looked at Katherine, and smiled. Katherine smiled back. She took Frank's glass and bottle, and deposited them on a nearby table. She then placed her hands in his and led him out on to the dance floor.

There are times, thought Katherine, when the only thing you can do is stop thinking, forget your troubles and dedicate a few hours of your life to serious and strenuous enjoyment. Meanwhile, the band played on.

PART II

CHAPTER ONE

Gavin Blinkho was on his way home when the nuisance started. A tall, fit man with a crew-cut, he stood out from the commuters on the train by virtue of his combat fatigues and a ten-day growth of stubble on his face. On his lap lay a large rucksack.

Although Blinkho was prepared for trouble, he wasn't expecting it. He was on an ordinary, early evening commuter train, travelling from Blackfriars through the amorphous sprawl of South London. The trouble was these black kids: four of them, male, drunk by the look of it, all making a nuisance of themselves.

Two of them were pretending to be horses, and the other two were riders. They were jousting with each other, down the narrow central aisle of the carriage. Blinkho reckoned they were well plastered. One of them looked half daft as well.

It was the daft one who fell off his 'horse' and trod on a woman passenger's feet. She looked too scared to object; but the bloke she was with muttered something. It sounded like 'bloody nuisance', but Blinkho couldn't be sure. The leader of the lads immediately went over to the bloke who had spoken up.

'What you say? You don't mind our fun, do you?'

The man didn't reply. Too scared, thought Blinkho, noticing that the other people in the compartment were looking anywhere except where the trouble was.

'Oi! Mate?' said the leader. 'Do you?'

'No,' said the man, nervously.

'Course you don't,' said another of the youths, ''cos you know you'll get your head kicked in, don't you!'

The lads all shrieked with laughter.

'You want your head kicked in?' said the daft one, sticking his face into that of the man. 'Are you looking for trouble?'

Blinkho watched impassively as the youths crowded round the man, pushing and shoving him.

'Just leave me alone, all right?' said the man. 'I've told you. Get off me!'

Blinkho was wondering whether to intervene on behalf of the silent majority, when an old man in a cap spoke up.

'Let him alone, you mental bastards!'

Good for him, thought Blinkho. Just the same, the mood of the lads changed right away, from drunken bravado to something a lot more menacing.

'Who said that?' asked the simple one. 'Who called me a mental bastard?'

'It was him, Paul,' said another of the youths, pointing at the old man.

'I'm warning you lot. I've got a pacemaker here,' said the old man, tapping his heart.

'You shouldn't have called me a mental bastard then, should you? Eh?' said Paul, knocking the old man's cap on to the floor.

As the old man bent down to retrieve his cap, Paul pushed him so that he doubled up.

'You're sorry, are you?' Paul shouted at the old man.

As the old man gasped for breath, the first man who had spoken rose to his feet and shouted through his tears.

'For God's sake, he's an old man!'

This seemed to tip the one called Paul over the edge. He left the old man and dashed back down the carriage to the first one.

'Right! I'll have you then! You've had it mate!' he screamed. 'What did you call me?'

The other youths gathered round Paul as he stood over the frightened man.

'I didn't call you anything,' mumbled the man.

'Oh, you've bloody had it, mate! You call me names, you've bloody had it!'

Blinkho watched as Paul grabbed the bloke by his tie and pulled him into the central aisle. The leader of the gang jumped on the man's back, while the other two lads cheered them on. The whole compartment looked on with horror. Still, no one wanted to get involved.

'Come on horsey, giddy up!' Paul chanted as the man fell to his knees. The leader of the gang got off and started laughing.

The woman whose feet Paul had trodden on stood up and called to everybody.

'For God's sake, somebody do something to help him!'

One or two people looked as though they might respond. Blinkho bided his time.

'Sit down!' yelled the leader. 'Everybody sit down and shut up, unless you want the same!'

'Hands on heads! Hands on heads! It's time you learnt some discipline!' chanted Paul. The other youths took up the chant.

Gradually, everyone in the carriage obeyed, except for Blinkho, who rose from his seat and began to walk slowly down the aisle towards the youths.

'What do you want?' jeered the one called Paul.

Blinkho didn't bother to reply. He just unsheathed his knife and held it up, so that they could all see it. Three of the youths backed off. Only the one called Paul stood his ground, but fear flickered across his face.

'I ain't scared,' he said.

Blinkho stopped, to give Paul a fair chance to retreat.

'Paul, come on,' said the leader of the gang. 'All over now, right?'

'No,' said Paul, without taking his eyes off Blinkho. 'I ain't scared.'

Instead of retreating, Paul began to walk up the aisle towards Blinkho.

'Stick it in the bastard,' yelled the old man. Others in the compartment muttered their agreement.

Blinkho rarely showed his emotions, but was genuinely amazed when the youth just kept on coming, as he raised his knife. The way the youth groaned and fell to the floor was just like they were acting in a Clint Eastwood movie; but the screams of the passengers and the blood which gushed out of the black kid's stomach were real enough.

CHAPTER TWO

Frank was on his way to have lunch with Katherine, when he saw that Tessa Parks was also on her way out of the Chambers. She was one of the brightest young barristers at Fetter Court, bringing in a reasonable amount of work; and yet she seemed to have been avoiding his eye a lot recently. He thought he knew why. He'd seen her talking to Michael Khan.

'Tessa,' said Frank, catching her up and falling into step beside her.

'Frank.' Sure enough, she wouldn't look at him.

This is ridiculous, thought Frank. I'm supposed to be running a radical Chambers, and at least two of our four black barristers are acting as if I'm some kind of racist.

'Talk to me some time about the Nola Marshall inquest,' he said.

'What's there to say?' said Tessa, quickly. 'She's a black woman dancing in the street. She's drunk. She falls over and bangs her head. Now she's in a fridge with her name on her toe.'

'Yeah,' said Frank, 'but I mean about me and Bingham being briefed in it.'

Tessa shrugged, as if she couldn't care less.

'The Marshall family hired Alton Phillips to do the job,' she said. 'He chose to brief you and Bingham.'

'No, come on,' said Frank. 'Michael Khan is angry about it. You're angry about it.'

Tessa stopped walking.

'What's Michael said?' she asked sharply.

'Michael Khan says there should be a black on it,' said Frank. 'You don't say anything, but I think you also think there should be no whites on it.'

Tessa didn't say anything. Frank ran his fingers through his hair, exasperated.

'I can't believe this is happening in our Chambers,' he said.

Tessa looked at the pavement.

'It's one of those issues, Frank. Sensible people go mad. It pushes people's buttons.'

Frank was irritated.

'Are your buttons being pushed?' he asked.

Tessa continued to avoid eye contact.

'If Alton Phillips wants to brief you and James, why not?' she said. 'I mean, you two are heavyweights. At least your taking it on shows that we mean business.'

'But the black community feels very strongly about this case, and James and I are white,' said Frank.

Tessa shrugged, and said nothing.

'Bingham's doing it for free, you know,' said Frank.

'I know, I know. You're heroes.'

'But you think that you or Michael Khan should have been briefed?' persisted Frank.

Tessa looked hard at Frank, for the first time in some days.

'There's pros and cons,' she said. 'Whoever does it is in a war with the police. If it was two black barristers, the press would use it. If it's two white barristers, Alton gets called an Uncle Tom. If he gets one of each, it's called the Black and White Minstrel Show. You're not going to win that argument. Don't try. Just get on with it, win the case. Get that result. "Unlawful killing". Because Nola Marshall's was . . .'

Tessa broke off, nearly in tears.

'Lorraine showed me the photographs,' she added.

Tessa looked up, and saw the anger on Frank's face.

'It's not Lorraine's fault,' Tessa said. 'She didn't know Nola and me were friends.'

Frank hadn't known it either. He handed Tessa a handkerchief.

'What was Nola's problem, then?' he asked. 'Why the booze?'

'Her problem was she was a black woman doctor,' said Tessa. 'She was a pioneer. People expected an awful lot from her. She was never allowed to forget what she represented.'

Tessa blew her nose. Sniffing, she patted Frank on the chest.

'Just nail them, Frank.'

He nodded.

'Because they can't be allowed to keep on getting away with this, OK?' said Tessa.

*

Katherine had been concentrating so hard on the brief in front of her that she hadn't noticed the time. She hurriedly collected up her things. She'd have to go straight on to court, after lunch with Frank.

Tom was answering the telephone when Katherine entered the clerk's office.

'Edward, can you arrange a conference with Rod Connor for late tomorrow, fiveish?' she asked the junior.

'Can do,' said Edward, making a note of it.

91

'I'm going out for lunch,' said Katherine. 'Then I'm in court, so unless Rod Connor needs to talk to me . . .'

Edward nodded, to show that he understood what she was saying.

'Hang on, Derek,' said Tom. 'I think she may be able to.'

Tom indicated to Katherine that she should hang on.

'I can ask her now.'

He covered the mouthpiece with one hand.

'Can you do a rape for Derek Harrison next week?' Tom asked. 'You seem to be free. It looks like a Wednesday/Thursday. It's straightforward, he says.'

'Ask him what's the defence,' said Katherine.

'Derek? She'd like a word.'

Tom put the phone down. Katherine walked across to pick it up.

'Hi, Derek.'

Katherine listened briefly.

'Um, is he admitting the sex? He is? OK. Well, I don't do that, Derek, OK? I don't do consent rapes. OK?'

She listened again, for a moment.

'No, sorry I can't help out,' she lied. 'Oh I'm fine. How are you? OK. Sorry. Bye.'

Tom was signalling to her, that she wasn't to put the phone down.

'Hang on. Tom would like you back.'

Katherine replaced the phone on the desk. She went across to the notice-board, where she saw some messages that Tom hadn't bothered to pass on to her.

'Oh, sorry, Miss Hughes,' said Edward.

'Derek, can I offer you Alan Ackroyd?' Tom was saying.

Katherine raised her eyes to the ceiling in disbelief.

'I'll have a word with him this afternoon,' continued Tom. 'Haven't you? He's a very, very good brief. A rising star.'

Katherine looked stupefied.

'And I'm sure he'd love to do it!' added Tom. 'OK, I will. Bye.'

There was silence as Tom put down the phone. Katherine was leaning on Edward's desk, writing a note in response to one of her messages.

'I take it,' said Tom with a sneer, 'you have no objection to other barristers earning a living even if you don't wish to?'

'No. Nor to earning one myself. And I don't want to argue with you, Tom,' said Katherine, 'because we both know from experience that you will not understand what I'm saying.'

'But surely the man has a right to a barrister,' Edward objected.

'Tom's fixing him up with one. Alan Ackroyd will, no doubt, do what's required in these cases. I wouldn't be able to. I do not attack rape victims.'

Katherine returned to her note. Out of the corner of her eye, she could see Tom preparing to needle her.

'Perhaps one day we might get a case where somebody has raped a policeman, or a judge.'

Tom winked at Edward. Katherine folded her note and put it in an envelope.

'No?' Tom asked. 'So in future then: no more rape cases for you?'

'If the defence is "I didn't do it" or "It wasn't me", I can do that,' replied Katherine.

'Well, it's outrageous, that's all,' said Tom. 'And it's asking for trouble, because it's a denial of one of the pillars of the legal system.'

Katherine rounded on Tom.

'Oh, don't give me pillars of the system,' she said. 'Where was your concern about everybody's right to a barrister when Alex Grimshaw – the head of this Chambers – turned down brief after brief, during the miners' strike?'

'No, no, no,' retorted Tom, 'he didn't turn down a single brief.'

'He did,' said Katherine.

'No, he didn't,' said Tom, with a smug expression on his face.

'He did.' Katherine stood her ground. 'If you say to a striking miner on remand in Armley prison on some trumped-up charge of obstruction "Yes, I'll defend you but it'll cost you 500 a day" and he says "All I've got is legal aid", then you're turning him down. Why is it all right to turn down a brief out of financial greed but not out of political conviction?'

Edward was baffled by the whole conversation.

'Politics?' he queried.

'Yes, politics,' said Katherine.

'Well, answer me this,' said Tom. 'Why is it all right to get an acquittal for a nutcase who bottles people when you know he is guilty, but not to try and do the same for a rapist?'

Edward looked at Katherine with a 'you hadn't thought of that one' expression.

'The answer is simple, but may be hard for you to understand,' answered Katherine. 'It's all to do with power.'

Edward looked dubious.

'Edward, let's have lunch one day. I'm late.'

Katherine picked up her briefcase and left the room. She leant against the wall, outside the clerk's office.

'Is this or is this not the most appalling hypocrite at the English Bar?' she heard Tom ask.

'She's mental,' commented Edward.

'You know who she's lunching with, don't you?' asked Tom.

Katherine knew that Tom couldn't wait to see the back of her. She did not wait to hear Edward's views on the subject.

*

'I thought James was supposed to be joining us,' said Katherine.

Frank and Katherine were in the middle of lunch. Katherine was tucking heartily into her salad. Although Frank was only toying with his food, he was making good progress with a bottle of claret on his own. Up to now, they had been making enjoyable small talk, but avoiding the real purpose of the lunch.

'Erm . . . It doesn't look as if James will be coming. I'm sorry,' said Frank. 'But the important thing is: he's very keen for you to come in.'

Katherine stopped sipping her mineral water and laughed incredulously.

'Frank,' she said, 'don't be ridiculous! It's the last thing he wants. He knows *you* want it, that's all!'

'You underestimate him. He's very much his own man,' said Frank, stabbing a sausage.

'He's an opportunist,' said Katherine. 'He's never done anything that wasn't calculated to get him one step closer to taking silk. His politics are a joke, really. He thinks you can still get away with being a radical toff. You can't. Except in places like this, or the Bar mess. This is where he's at home, where you can hear the authentic sound of timid careerists quacking like nervous ducks, worried they might have offended somebody in the Lord Chancellor's office. It's that particular combination that drives me round the bend: cowardice and ambition.'

Frank and Katherine stared at each other. Frank took another swig of wine.

'It drives you round the bend,' remarked Frank, 'but

you seem happy to stay in a Chambers built on precisely those virtues.'

Katherine hesitated.

'I didn't say I was happy,' she said.

'I think perhaps you are,' said Frank, pouring himself another glass of wine. 'Living in your corner. Pretending you're the only show in town. The only one with any real politics.'

Katherine refused to answer.

'Come on,' said Frank, 'there's a job to do. You can't go on being their pet monster. You make yourself look foolish.'

Katherine continued eating.

'Well, look,' said Frank. 'Margaret Wharton has been asking me out to lunch. I can't hang around waiting for you. If you change your mind in the next few days, let me know.'

'Right,' said Katherine. 'Sorry, I must go. I've got to be in court.'

'Fine,' said Frank gloomily. 'I'll pick up the bill.'

Frank's mood was not improved when seconds later James pushed his way through the lunch-time throng, clutching a plate of salad, a bottle of bubbly and three glasses.

'You're late,' said Frank.

'Sorry, I was held up,' said James. 'Has she gone?'

Frank nodded.

'She still says no, then?'

Frank nodded again.

James poured out a couple of glasses.

'What do we do?' asked James. 'Get down on our hands and knees?'

*

Twenty-four hours later, Frank and James welcomed three people into one of the conference rooms at Fetter Court. Alton Phillips looked as immaculate as ever, in a three-piece suit, but said little.

Alton left as much of the talking as possible to Nola Marshall's parents, Jo and Ivan. Both were in their sixties. Ivan had a shock of white hair, a white beard, and an air of deep depression. Jo looked the more resilient of the two, and was very obviously sizing up Frank and James.

'Nola was our only child,' said Ivan. 'When we came here, we didn't expect it to be easy. Ten hours a night stacking boxes in them walk-in fridges. I'm still there despite I've lost four of my toes. We pushed Nola through all the classes. She became a nurse to our pride. She could have gone anywhere. But she stayed where she was needed. She was the perfect daughter, Frank.'

Frank saw Jo Marshall look askance at her husband. She evidently realized that he was already rewriting history.

'Will this inquest tell me the point of this?' continued Ivan. 'I put up with all the talk about coons and about rivers of blood. Twenty-seven years I put up with it. Twenty-seven years later, where am I? Twenty-seven years after we come to start a new life, my lovely daughter Nola is kicked to death by . . .'

Ivan paused, choking back the tears.

Jo touched Ivan gently on the sleeve. She looked from Frank to James, awaiting their response. Frank cleared his throat.

'It's important from the outset,' said Frank, 'that we are able to speak plainly among ourselves. Because if we don't, they'll bury us.'

Ivan just sat staring into his lap, with tears rolling down his face. Jo patted his hand and looked up at Frank.

'Nola,' said Jo, 'was an alcoholic. We know that. Everybody knew that.'

Ivan glared at his wife.

'I don't want her name dragged through the mud,' he said.

Jo turned to her husband.

'Ivan,' she said sharply. 'Listen to me. It would be better if you sat in Alton's car.'

Ivan nodded slowly. As Ivan rose, James got up and offered him his hand.

'There's a waiting room,' said James, leading Ivan out of the conference room. 'I'll get you some tea.'

Jo watched her husband leave, then turned sharply to Frank.

'Mr Cartwright,' she said, 'you ask for plain speaking. Here's mine. Nothing will come of this. No Home Office action. No action at all by anybody. This is just another black person dead. If this had been a white doctor, the papers would be full of it every day.'

'That's true,' agreed Alton, 'but when the inquest starts –'

'Let me finish, Alton,' said Jo. 'We've been fools. Our generation was used to doing what it was told. Nola's generation won't do that, they're going to stand up for their rights.'

She turned to Frank.

'You've seen the photographs.'

Frank nodded.

'So you know what they did to her, and you know why. How many times, Alton, did Nola give statements about police brutality on blacks? She was marked down for this.'

Jo rose from her chair, as James returned to the room.

'It would be better if I sat with Ivan,' she said. 'Alton says you're good lawyers and good men. He says you'll do your best.'

'Mrs Marshall, just give me a second,' said Frank. 'If we can force the coroner's court to establish that what happened to Nola while she was in police custody amounted to unlawful killing, then the police will be under severe pressure to open their own criminal investigation.'

Jo shook her head.

'Mr Cartwright, I think the police already know what happened to Nola.'

Alton now spoke up.

'Jo, when we get a chance to show the world exactly what kind of shit is coming down here, we've got to take it. We can't shrug our shoulders and say "You win". The whole black community is looking to the outcome of this case.'

Jo studied him intently.

'The Association of Black Families is paying all your fees, not me. I'll shut my mouth. But if the day comes when blacks need real leaders, they better be careful who they choose.'

Alton looked at her with astonishment, then back at Frank. Frank suppressed a grin.

CHAPTER THREE

Katherine and Ackroyd were working at their desks when Tom bustled in.

'Michael Feingold has come on about an attempted murder.'

Katherine looked up from her paperwork and nodded.

'Fine,' she said.

'The thing is,' said Tom provocatively, 'am I to get you the brief or issue a questionnaire or . . .?'

'Well, what is it?' Katherine asked.

'A stabbing on a train at Lewisham.'

'I read about it,' said Katherine. 'They were black, and he was white, yeah?'

Tom sighed.

'I've no idea. His name is Bilko or something.'

Katherine tried to recall the news story, while Tom shifted from one foot to another.

'I think if you want to vet the brief for every political nuance,' said Tom acidly, 'I cannot really be of great assistance to you. You have Feingold's number. If you decide to take the brief, perhaps you could let me know.'

Tom slammed the door hard behind him. Katherine

picked up the phone and began to dial the solicitor's number. She looked up from the instrument and noticed Ackroyd gazing at her. He evidently had some terrible secret to divulge. She could guess what it was.

'I'm . . . doing that rape,' he murmured.

'Good luck,' Katherine replied brusquely.

'It was actually a pretty tepid thing,' said Ackroyd hurriedly. 'He didn't knock her about or anything.'

Katherine took a deep breath.

'I expect he'll get a medal then,' she said.

Ackroyd flinched, and returned to reading his papers.

'Hello?' Katherine had got through to her number. 'Katherine Hughes here. Can I have Michael Feingold?'

*

At the end of the day, Katherine met Feingold in a pub off Chancery Lane. It was full of legal and city types having a quick drink, ostensibly to avoid the commuter crush on the train home. Katherine bought herself an orange juice and joined Feingold, a small, grey-haired, bespectacled man who was nursing a fine malt.

Feingold filled Katherine in on the details of the case. He spoke with a faint German accent.

'I've met him three times since he was arrested, taken long statements from him, and looked meticulously at the way the police are handling it,' he said. 'It's all above board: it's really very interesting in fact, Katherine, because it's law and order. He's saying "I couldn't stand it any longer and I went for him with a knife", which he was carrying because he's been on a camping holiday and not because he's a psycho or anything.'

'What is he then?' asked Katherine.

'He's a very buttoned-up man. Lives alone. Steady job in a library. No nasty habits except voting Conservative. He's a man who reads all about the law and order crisis.

He believes there's a mugger round every corner; you put him in a situation where he's threatened and he's got a weapon and bam!'

Katherine felt uneasy.

'Is this what he says?'

Feingold shook his head.

'Well, he doesn't say much, to be fair. You'll need all your famous skills of rapport with your clients.'

Katherine smiled wryly.

'But the witnesses are all saying it loud and clear,' continued Feingold. 'And I think if Blinkho's got any sense he'll go along with it. I mean, it's a field day for you: you can blame anybody you like as far as I'm concerned: the *Sun, News of the World*, Thatcher, Tebbit . . .'

Katherine smiled again.

'Can I call them?'

'I think we may have a bit of trouble on that one,' laughed Feingold.

'Okay.' Katherine nodded her agreement.

Feingold looked delighted.

'Great. There's no money in it,' he added apologetically. 'He's on legal aid.'

'Why can't I defend *rich* psychos?' asked Katherine, with a sigh.

'Because they don't get caught,' said Feingold, picking up Katherine's glass. 'Same again?'

*

Katherine's drugs case in Oxford finished earlier than anticipated, and she decided to go straight home rather than via Pump Court. She flung her briefcase on to the floor and kicked off the high-heeled shoes she always wore in court. She flicked through the post, which contained nothing more interesting than the usual glossy come-ons from credit cards, urging her to spend more. As usual, she threw them straight into the waste-paper basket.

She went into the bedroom, took off the new bra which had been digging into her shoulders all day, and squeezed into some jeans and a sloppy sweater. She looked at herself in a full-length mirror. Not bad, she thought, although the jeans are getting a bit tight round the bum.

Re-entering the living-room, she noticed the red light of the answer machine winking at her. There was a message from Robert, suggesting a trip to the theatre for old time's sake. Another message from Peter Jones said that her order would be further delayed. Katherine grimaced. Her carefully chosen wedding present would now be three months, rather than one month, overdue. Finally, there was a curt message from Tom, saying that he had only just missed catching her at Oxford and would she come into the Chambers immediately. Something urgent had cropped up. Katherine groaned inwardly, and went to change back into her legal gear.

Grimshaw's never held an inviting atmosphere for her; so she did not notice anything that different, as she entered the clerks' room. Tom, Edward and a number of barristers from the set were standing around in silence, looking glum. Katherine looked expectantly at Tom.

'I got a message,' she said.

Before Tom could reply, Alex Grimshaw's door opened. One of the other barristers, Dick Smith, came out with a solemn expression on his face. Alex Grimshaw followed him out and indicated that Katherine should come into his room.

Katherine felt puzzled as she sat down opposite Alex, on the other side of his vast Victorian mahogony desk. Alex looked gravely at her.

'There's been a terrible accident,' he said. 'Alan Ackroyd

was taken to hospital last night, having unfortunately taken an overdose of sleeping pills.'

'You mean he tried to kill himself?' Katherine said.

Alex did not reply, since Tom had just entered the room, carrying the court diary.

'Shit,' she muttered. 'How's his family? Is he OK?'

'Well, he's going to survive,' Alex declared. 'Things had rather been building up. I was aware of it but not of the extent. The important thing is that we all rally round.'

Katherine nodded in agreement.

'Yes, of course.'

'Now,' said Alex, 'Tom thinks you're free on Thursday, and there's a rape case at the Old Bailey you could take over.'

'Ah, well.' Katherine flashed a dirty look at Tom. 'It would be better if someone else . . .'

'Katherine, there is nobody else,' Alex said sternly. 'We're all doing things we don't want to do. I'm the only one free to go to Swansea for three days next week to defend some appalling football fan, but there we are. We have to pull together. Everybody is mucking in.'

Katherine acknowledged defeat graciously.

'Yes, of course,' she said.

She looked up and saw a look of triumph on Tom's face.

CHAPTER FOUR

As Katherine had feared, the client in the rape case turned out to be a loathsome, reptilian creature. He reminded her more than a little of Tom; but Katherine knew she had to forget her personal feelings. A barrister has to win, she told herself; and so she duly marshalled her skills for the man's defence.

Katherine stood up in Court Number Four at the Old Bailey to address the plaintiff, a thin, once pretty blonde in her mid-thirties, dressed in a shabby suit.

'Mrs Welsh,' said Katherine sympathetically, 'you are aware, aren't you, of the seriousness of the charge you've brought against my client? That what you are claiming happened that afternoon carries the possibility of grave consequences for him?'

Mrs Welsh stared out of the witness box, as if she hadn't heard.

'Are you aware of that?' Katherine repeated.

'Yes,' replied Mrs Welsh, softly.

'Could you please speak up so that everybody can hear you?' Katherine said, beginning the necessary task of undermining the plaintiff's confidence. Mrs Welsh looked round the courtroom, as if this were all a bad dream.

'Yes,' she reiterated more loudly.

'Good. So you can see – can't you? – that all the relevant facts are bound to be laid before the jury.'

'Yes.'

'In fact you wouldn't want them to be concealed, would you?'

Mrs Welsh was not sure what Katherine was driving at.

'No,' she replied hesitantly.

'Good,' said Katherine. 'Now. We've heard you earlier describe, with enviable flair, the events of that afternoon. We've all heard you tell how you met my client in a public house, where you'd spent the afternoon drinking with friends; that my client and other men and women made their way back to your flat with you – though you do not now, apparently, remember issuing an invitation to any of them; that more drinking there ensued, during which music was – '

Mrs Welsh interrupted.

'I didn't say that.'

'I'm sorry?' said Katherine.

'I said I didn't say that. I didn't have anything else to drink.'

'I didn't say you had. I said there was further drinking. Are you now denying that?'

'No.'

'So there was drink.'

Katherine paused, while everybody made a note of that.

'There was music. There was dancing. By some time around 4.30 – you can't remember when, exactly, no doubt your head wasn't as clear as it might have been – the other guests left your impromptu party.'

Katherine noticed the prosecuting counsel glance at the judge, who frowned but did not intercede.

'It wasn't a party,' protested Mrs Welsh.

The prosecuting counsel looked again at the Judge, who

nodded for the cross-examination to continue. Katherine decided to press on.

'And you found yourself alone with my client. Which you claim was not something you welcomed.'

'Why should I welcome it? I hardly knew him,' retorted Mrs Welsh.

'Mrs Welsh,' said Katherine with a patient smile, 'you are of course a married woman?'

'Separated.'

'How long is it since your husband left home?'

'Um . . . it's a bit less . . . nearly a year.'

'Do you work?'

'No.'

Katherine paused for a moment and looked at the jury, comprised of three men and nine women.

'So then, for nearly a year you've lived alone in your apartment in Hampstead and you don't work.'

Mrs Welsh looked guilty, and glanced at the jury.

'Who pays the mortgage?' asked Katherine.

'My husband. Well, actually the business. It's complicated because I was owed.'

'Yes,' said Katherine impatiently. 'Just answer the question please. The answer is your husband pays the mortgage.'

'Yes.'

'Thank you.'

Katherine waited again, while everybody wrote this down. Then she continued.

'And so what do you do with yourself, Mrs Welsh?'

'Well, I . . .' Mrs Welsh looked confused. 'Sorry, you'll have to be more specific.'

'Well, what time do you get up in the morning?'

Mrs Welsh thought for a moment.

'Usually?' probed Katherine.

'About 10.'

Katherine looked hard at Mrs Welsh and then at the jury.

'10 o'clock?' Katherine repeated, as if in astonishment. She could see some of the jury thinking, 'Lazy cow.'

'There's not much point in me getting up early,' rejoined Mrs Welsh.

'And then what? Do you dress for breakfast?'

'No, I just sit and have a coffee.'

'What time is it by the time you manage to dress?'

'About 11.30.'

Katherine looked incredulous. Judge Meredith had finally had enough, and intervened.

'Miss Hughes, fascinating though all this is . . .'

'I think my point is about to become clear, your Honour.'

Meredith nodded. Katherine proceeded.

'So at around 11.30, you dress – and then what?'

'Well, shopping or . . .' The woman's voice faded away.

'Or what? What other sorts of things?' Katherine paused. 'Let me help you. How often would you say you went to the pub at lunchtime?'

'I didn't know it was a crime to go to the pub,' Mrs Welsh said defiantly.

'Nobody's suggesting that.'

'Well.'

'Not every day?'

'No.'

'Once a month?' asked Katherine.

'No.'

'Shall we settle on two or three times a week?'

'I really don't see the relevance of this,' said Mrs Welsh, beginning to get flustered.

'You must answer counsel's questions,' said the Judge.

'Would it be fair to suggest,' said Katherine, 'that things had gone on the slide a bit since your husband left?'

This finally forced the prosecuting counsel to his feet.

'Your Honour,' he objected.

'Miss Hughes,' Judge Meredith reprimanded Katherine. 'Perhaps you could confine yourself more closely to the issue.'

Katherine prepared for the kill.

'Mrs Welsh, on the two or three occasions per week that you go drinking at lunchtime, how do you dress? As you are now?'

Mrs Welsh thought for a moment and then decided to tell the truth.

'No,' she admitted.

'How, then?' asked Katherine.

'Casually.'

'Does that mean skirts and cardigans?'

'No. Jeans and a shirt or – '

Before Mrs Welsh could continue, Katherine continued.

'Is that what you were wearing on the day you met my client in the pub?'

'Yes.'

'Jeans and a shirt,' repeated Katherine. 'Tight jeans?'

Katherine paused. Mrs Welsh's misery was plain to see, as she felt herself being scrutinized and mentally undressed by every male in the courtroom.

'Yes. I suppose so.'

Mrs Welsh looked a broken woman. She no longer addressed her replies to Katherine but spoke to the space a few yards in front of her on the floor.

'A heavy shirt? Or a thin shirt?'

'Not particularly thin.'

'Not particularly thin,' said Katherine. 'Do you normally wear a bra, Mrs Welsh?'

The prosecuting counsel was up on his feet again.

'Your Honour.'

Judge Meredith chewed over the objection for a few moments and then pronounced on the matter.

'No, it's a reasonable question in the circumstances.'

Katherine noticed tiny smiles playing on the lips of the judge, the prosecuting counsel and some of the jury. They had all picked up Katherine's innuendo about Mrs Welsh's breasts. Katherine felt a twinge of nausea, as her client looked across at her and winked.

'No,' muttered Mrs Welsh. 'I don't.'

'And you weren't wearing a bra on the day in question.'

'No.' Mrs Welsh looked up, in a last show of defiance. 'Nor do I think it would have made any difference if I'd been in a suit of armour.'

Katherine gazed steadily at the woman.

'Why this particular pub, Mrs Welsh?'

'There are sometimes people there that I know vaguely...' said Mrs Welsh. 'Well enough to have a conversation ... you see ... You lose your friends when your marriage goes ...'

Katherine let the poor woman ramble on.

'You get desperate,' said the woman, sobbing. 'You want ... you just want ...'

Katherine glanced at the prosecuting counsel. He had the air of a man who knew he had already lost his case.

*

Afterwards, Katherine tried to make her way out of the courtroom as quickly as possible. She felt no pleasure in her success, even though the defendant was jubilant and kept on shaking her by the hand. Not surprisingly, he couldn't believe his luck.

Katherine caught sight of Mrs Welsh sobbing on one of the benches outside the court, and was relieved to be distracted by the prosecuting counsel who came across to congratulate her. Eventually, Katherine extricated herself and set off for the robing room. Half-way there, she felt a tug on her gown. Stopping, she found herself face to face with Mrs Welsh, her face contorted with rage and humiliation.

'How could you?' she screamed at Katherine. 'How could you? Another woman!'

Katherine could only mumble that she was sorry, pull her gown closer around herself, and walk away. Although Katherine never looked back, she knew Mrs Welsh was still watching her. The woman's cries seemed to keep echoing around the building.

The Ladies' Robing Room was deserted when Katherine walked in. She removed her wig and looked at herself in the mirror. No matter how she tidied the hair which had started to fall down at the back, she still wasn't satisfied. She pursed her lips to make sure that her lipstick was evenly applied. Finally, she looked into her own eyes, and she came to a decision.

Suddenly, she knew that if she remained at Grimshaw's she would no longer be able to live with herself. Frank had made her an offer. It was time for her to stop agonizing, and accept. She put her wig and bands in a small tupperware box which she used for storage, and collected her coat from her locker.

*

Katherine found Alex Grimshaw in his customary haunt, the Bar mess. She stood in the doorway as he came across from lunch with his usual cronies.

'I'm sorry, Alex,' she said.

Alex waved his hands elegantly, as if to say that it was nothing, and looked at her quizzically.

'Well.' Katherine paused, took a deep breath and came out with it. 'I've decided to go.'

Alex nodded. Katherine saw that he had been expecting

this news for some time. She guessed that he would be sad to see her go, even though he must know that the rest of the set would be delighted.

'Any point in trying to persuade you to stay?' he asked.

'No.' Katherine shook her head.

'Well, our loss is Cartwright's gain.'

Katherine smiled.

'Please, one thing,' she added. 'No "do" of any kind.'

Alex Grimshaw nodded and returned to his meal. With a sense of anti-climax, Katherine went off to pack up her things.

CHAPTER FIVE

Frank Cartwright waved to James Bingham as they parked their cars round the back of Southwark Coroner's Court. Frank got out of his rapidly rusting Volkswagen Beetle, and watched with bafflement as James set the alarm on his brand-new, top-of-the-range BMW.

Frank prided himself on being non-materialistic, but still occasionally experienced a secret twinge of jealousy when confronted with such evidence of James's extreme wealth. He presumed that James had a private income, or that James's wife Gloria did. Frank suspected that the cost of his whole wardrobe was about the same as that of one of James's suits. And James seemed to have about a dozen of them.

Even worse, they had been to each other's houses. Until Frank went to James's, Frank had thought he was doing quite well. True, the Laura Ashley wallpaper was peeling a bit, and stripped pine was no longer that fashionable, even in Islington; but both Frank and Annie had been amazed to walk inside James and Gloria's house in Cheyne Walk and find themselves in a series of immaculate rooms such as Frank had only previously encountered in glossy magazines.

Frank had wandered around in a daze at first, unused to a house where there weren't sticky fingermarks on the walls and dents in the skirting board where children had attempted to ram the wall with dumper trucks. The kitchen looked as if nothing had ever been cooked in it, and there were fresh flowers everywhere. Just wait till they have children, Annie had said; but Frank had a strong suspicion that if James and Gloria ever procreated, their progeny would emerge from the womb in designer nappies.

The two men walked together round to the front of the Coroner's Court building, where a large crowd of demonstrators was gathered. There were anti-racist groups, members and supporters of the Association of Black Families, and a considerable police presence standing to one side. A crowd of journalists was clustered around Alton Phillips and the Marshalls, who were standing in a group on the steps, posing solemnly for the press photographers. A news reporter from the BBC was doing a piece to camera for the lunchtime news. Frank and James pushed their way into the building, as Alton wound up his impromptu press conference.

'The whole black community,' Alton concluded, 'will be looking to this inquest for justice and for the truth finally to begin to be established about the death of Nola Marshall.'

Alton raised his hands as if to ward off any more questions, and shepherded the Marshalls inside. Frank and James paused, and then walked into the courtroom alongside them, past a long queue of people waiting to get into the public gallery. Frank noticed that the policemen on duty looked at his small party with obvious distaste.

The most noticeable aspect of the courtroom was that it was awash with black faces, except for twenty or so policemen ranged along one wall, at right-angles to the public but facing the jury. Ivan and Jo Marshall sat sadly in the front row of seats behind their lawyers, facing the coroner.

The buzz of conversation died away as the coroner's officer called for quiet. The coroner was a severe-looking man with aquiline features. Dressed in a sombre grey suit and dark blue tie, he looked round the courtroom and made his opening remarks.

'Many of you,' he said, 'will never have had cause to attend a coroner's inquest before. Let me begin by making one or two things clear so that there is no subsequent confusion.'

He spoke very slowly, as if the assembly were slightly simple.

'Firstly, a coroner is completely independent.'

A murmur of disbelief went through the public gallery.

'Secondly, despite similarities in the trappings, this is not a criminal court and I am not a judge. Look, no wig!'

The coroner looked around the court, visibly perturbed when nobody laughed. There were a few forced chuckles from the coroner's officer and the policemen in the court; but no one else seemed to find the situation at all funny.

'Nor is this a trial,' continued the coroner. 'No one is accused.'

There was angry murmuring from the public gallery at this.

'It is not a crime which is being investigated, but a death. No blame will be apportioned. I, along with the jury, am charged with the task of ascertaining as nearly as I can the cause of the death of Nola Marshall. There are many witnesses to be heard and I anticipate a lengthy hearing. We'll begin today by hearing Mr Coleman, the assistant medical officer, read the report of the autopsy.'

As soon as the coroner had stopped speaking, Frank sprang to his feet.

'Sir,' said Frank, 'will the jurors be given a sight of the photographs taken at the post-mortem?'

'They are unnecessarily distressing,' the coroner replied. 'The autopsy report is full and detailed.'

'Sir,' Frank continued, 'may I ask if the police officers we see here are to be called as witnesses?'

'Yes, they are.'

'May I ask if you intend to allow them to remain in court throughout each other's evidence?'

'That's for me to decide,' said the coroner, 'and I see no reason why not.'

'May I ask, sir,' continued Frank with a glance at the jury, 'why you think it appropriate for the police to have the benefit of hearing all the evidence but – ?'

Before Frank could finish, the coroner snapped back at him.

'No, I'd rather we got on with it, actually.'

'May I ask you, sir,' said Frank with elaborate politeness, 'to consider the idea that, for some interested parties, including the one I represent, it may seem baffling that seventeen policemen are apparently required to give evidence and that such a heavy and constant police presence throughout the hearing might seem intimidatory?'

The coroner surveyed the police witnesses ranged along the wall, many of whom Frank noticed scowling back at him.

'No,' said the coroner.

'Sir,' persisted Frank, 'is that "No, I won't consider the idea" or "No, I don't think it's true"?'

'It's a "No, I'm not listening to any more of this nonsense,"' snapped the coroner. 'Sit down, please.'

Frank sat down, unperturbed.

The coroner nodded to his officer to bring on the first witness. Mr Coleman walked to the witness box carrying his medical report. A small, serious-looking man, he read his report in a slow but precise manner. It outlined in graphic detail the injuries that Nola Marshall had sustained before her death.

'There were 17 small contusions on the chest and upper abdomen; there were 11 contusions on the back and shoulders; the upper arms had severe gripping contusions; the face and neck were very severely bruised. It was not possible to separate the number of contusions.'

Frank watched Nola's mother scan the policemen in the courtroom. Nola's father, Ivan, seemed to shrink deep inside himself as the list of injuries was read like an inventory of goods.

'In all,' concluded Coleman, 'I counted 63 separate external injuries, mainly abrasions and contusions to the face, body and legs of the deceased, in addition to the brain haemorrhage which was the actual cause of death.'

There was silence in the courtroom as Coleman concluded his report.

'Thank you, Mr Coleman. We will now adjourn for lunch.'

The coroner pushed back his chair and rose. He left the courtroom by his own private door behind his chair.

Frank continued to watch the reaction of Nola's parents. Ivan sat like a broken man, while Jo looked in astonishment at the policemen, as they filed out, cheerfully chatting and joking among themselves. Alton leant round and patted Jo comfortingly on the hand; but Frank didn't think it was comfort that she wanted: only justice.

*

At about the same time, Katherine walked into her old Pump Court Chambers for the last time. She found the whole place strangely deserted, until she walked into Alex

Grimshaw's office, where she found the barristers gathered en masse.

They all stood clutching a glass of sherry each, ready to toast her departure. Katherine's heart sank. She'd asked for no fuss to be made, and this was what Alex did. She looked round the room at the forced smiles, and realized for the first time with absolute certainty that not one of the men in the Chambers actually liked her. An embarrassed silence pervaded the room, broken by the sound of Grimshaw at his most pompous.

'Well, I won't keep you all too long,' he said. 'It's a sad day indeed for our set to be losing such a distinguished and valued colleague as Katherine.'

Somewhat belatedly, Edward crossed the room and offered Katherine a sherry, which she sniffed and then gave back to him.

'And at such short notice,' added Grimshaw.

Katherine pretended not to notice Tom's muttered comment of 'About bloody time', nor the chuckles of some of the barristers nearest him.

'But we hope,' continued Alex Grimshaw, 'she may be happier in her new home. *Bon voyage!*'

They all raised their glasses and drank. A few voices muttered, '*Bon voyage.*' Tom, who evidently had had a glass or two already, murmured 'Good riddance'. Again, Katherine heard laughter behind her back.

'Speech!' called out a couple of the rowdier elements.

Katherine looked around the room, and wondered what she had ever thought she had in common with them all. She knew that every one of them was more interested in a booze-up than in her.

'I see you've given them your cheap South African muck, Alex,' said Katherine.

There was an awkward silence. Grimshaw chuckled.

'Completely apposite, of course, that Katherine should choose to leave us with a taste of her sharp tongue.'

Katherine looked at him steadily.

'It won't taste as sharp as that rubbish,' she said, indicating the glass which she had given back to Edward. 'You might at least have opened a bottle of decent amontillado.'

The smile faded on Grimshaw's face.

'Well,' concluded Katherine, 'goodbye.'

Katherine smiled sweetly, turned on her heel and left. As she closed the door behind her and walked to her room, she knew that she had wanted to behave as badly as that for years. She performed a most uncharacteristic, impromptu dance. Entering her room for the last time, she felt a wonderful sense of release; and she threw the last of her books and files into large cardboard boxes, labelled 'To be collected and taken to Fetter Court.'

She charged downstairs, swinging her briefcase, and went home to change. Let Grimshaw's celebrate her departure in a cheapskate way, she was going to have a much more enjoyable evening. Annie had rung up to say how delighted she was that Katherine had finally taken the plunge, and suggested a girls' night out.

As she soaped herself under the shower, Katherine couldn't remember the last time that the old threesome, Annie and Claudia and she, had had one of their long, boozy evenings.

Claudia seemed to spend half her life abroad, but was grounded for the moment in Shepherd's Bush. Her TV series had gone so far over budget that the final episode (about world poverty) was having to be shot not in Ethiopia and Bangladesh but in Birmingham and Bradford.

It would be Annie's first free evening for several months. Ever since Mrs Thatcher came to power, she had taken a doom-laden view of the future of social work, and had wanted to change career. Now, at last, she was taking a correspondence course with a view to becoming a psychotherapist.

Katherine met Annie outside the Curzon cinema, where they had arranged to see the latest film by Eric Rohmer. As usual, Claudia was late and arrived breathless and brimming over with apologies – the traffic was dreadful, she had had the most terrible day in the editing room, ending up in the most appalling row, etc, etc. . . .

Katherine and Annie, both tall, thin women, grinned at each other over their voluble, petite friend. They had never known Claudia to be on time for anything. How she ever got on a plane to all these exotic overseas locations – or even a train to Birmingham or Bradford – was a mystery to them both.

Katherine took great pride in not keeping people waiting. Her father had brought her up to believe that unpunctuality was a form of selfishness, but Claudia's privileged background had certainly given her a thorough grounding in that particular sin. She was the daughter of minor aristocracy and had rebelled against doing the usual cooking course. She had demanded to go to university, where she had espoused radical politics with a passion which surprised her friends and appalled her family.

All three women were rebels in their way. Katherine was the working-class girl who had torn up her roots; Annie was the Anglican vicar's daughter who had flouted convention and lived in sin; while Claudia had pursued a career rather than a husband.

The Eric Rohmer film turned out to be another of his meticulously crafted essays in adolescent yearning, grown-up philosophizing and sexual hypocrisy. All of them said they enjoyed it but none of them thought it memorable.

Annie said how much Frank would have fancied the leading actress.

After the film, Claudia announced that she had booked a table for them all at Orso's. When Annie asked where it was, the other two looked at her pityingly.

'I'm a married woman with children and a correspondence course to support,' said Annie defiantly. 'I don't get out much.'

Claudia saw a cab and hailed it.

'Orso's,' said Claudia.

'Right you are, ladies,' said the cabbie, as they all piled in. 'You been to the pictures?'

'Yes,' said Katherine. 'Do you go to the cinema?'

'I'm more into videos, me,' said the cabbie. 'Have you seen that *Death Race 2000*?'

Katherine felt slightly sick as the taxi rounded a corner at fifty miles per hour.

'I've been feeling very depressed recently,' said the cabbie, conversationally. 'Where do you think you are, mate? The dodgems?'

This last remark was aimed at a car which had edged out of a side street and nearly collided with them.

'Coon driver,' explained the cabbie. 'If I had my way, I'd have 'em off the roads. Them and those Yids in funny hats.'

'Great,' muttered Katherine.

For some reason, the cabbie had decided that the quickest route to Covent Garden lay via Holborn.

'Is this the right way?' enquired Claudia.

'Don't you worry your pretty little head,' said the cabbie, swinging round a corner on screeching tyres.

Katherine felt sick, and wondered if the cause was the sudden movements of the cab, or the conversation of its driver.

'You heard about that bloke on the train?' asked the

cabbie. 'Stabbed a couple of darkies in self-defence. If you ask me – '

'We'll walk from here,' said Katherine, firmly. She had had enough.

The cab-driver drove off, with a few obscenities about passengers too mean to give tips; and Katherine took some deep breaths, to make herself feel better.

'What a frightful man,' said Claudia, who took such encounters in her stride. 'Are you all right, Katherine?'

Inside the restaurant, the three sat round a corner table and regained their composure. Katherine loved the subterranean restaurant with its white-washed brick walls and pretty waiters. One of these immediately produced a bottle of Italian bubbly, ordered by Claudia.

She raised her glass.

'New jobs,' she said. 'For the three of us.'

The three of them drank.

'The three of us?' asked Katherine.

'Yes,' said Claudia. 'An uncle of mine has just popped his clogs, left me some money. So I thought I'd leave the Beeb and set up as an independent producer.'

The women were so busy catching up on their gossip that they had to send the waiter away three times before they could concentrate on reading the menu. When they had finally given their order, Katherine looked round the restaurant to see which celebrities were in that night. A large, noisy table at the back of the restaurant caught her attention. It was the young cast of alternative comedians from a cult television series. To her surprise, there was a familiar figure sitting among them. Robert was sitting with his back to her, his arm draped round the anorexic shoulders of a spiky-haired blonde.

'Ladies, you want another bottle?' asked the waiter, bringing them their first course.

'Why not?' said Katherine brightly.

'You're right,' said Annie, making short work of a stuffed courgette. 'The waiters here are very sweet. I suppose they're all gay.'

'He's very pretty, and he doesn't appear to be gay,' said Claudia, nodding in the direction of Robert, whose hand was straying down the spine of his dinner companion. 'Oh my God, isn't that Robert?'

'Cheers,' said Katherine.

'Well,' said Annie, in a valiant attempt to retrieve the situation, 'this is a far cry from my usual existence. The people here don't resemble my clients at all.'

'Oh, come on,' said Claudia, 'the only difference is that these are social inadequates with money.'

'Money,' said Annie, 'makes a considerable difference.'

'You OK, Katherine?' asked Claudia. 'You look a bit green.'

'Still recovering from the cab,' Katherine replied.

She concentrated on wiping up the olive oil from the plate with a chunk of bread. Her appetite for her favourite starter of tomato and mozzarella salad had suddenly disappeared. Robert looked at home with the young actors preening and showing off to each other. Annie, despite numerous ups and downs, was deeply committed to Frank, and Claudia, although perpetually complaining, was satisfied with her spasmodic affair with a married BBC executive. Katherine felt very alone.

Suddenly, Claudia let out a shriek, pushed her chair back and scampered across to another table.

'CHARLES!' she screamed.

'CLAUDIA!' bellowed a man in an unstructured jacket, his orange hair noticeable despite the dim lighting.

'Isn't that Charles Bulkhead?' asked Annie. 'I think I've seen him on the telly. On one of my rare evenings in.'

Katherine smiled at her friend's ironic tone.

'What's up?' asked Annie. 'Robert?'

Katherine nodded.

'Really?' exclaimed Annie, incredulously. 'You're not pining for *him*?'

'Of course not. I mean, no. Not really,' Katherine answered. 'He's back with his sort of people. But he did have his good points, you know.'

'If you say so,' said Annie.

'Sorry about that,' said Claudia, returning. 'That was Charles Bulkhead. Absolute sweetie, even if he has got the mentality of a tree-stump.'

Annie patted her friend's shoulder in sympathy.

'Don't brood,' said Annie.

'Absolutely,' said Claudia. 'This is meant to be a celebration.'

'By the way,' Annie added, 'this is on me. Well, Frank actually. I won my bet with him about you joining Fetter Court.'

'What?' It was Katherine's turn now to be incredulous.

'Yup,' laughed Annie. 'He was so despondent after that lunch he had with you, that he bet me you would never leave Grimshaw's. Naturally, I took him up on it.'

'Why?' asked Katherine.

'ROBIN!' yelled Claudia, careering off to another table.

Katherine and Annie looked round the room and then smiled at each other. Each realized she would never belong here in the way that Claudia so evidently did.

'It's human nature,' said Annie. 'Don't they call it networking, these days? I knew that in the end *you*'d want to be with *your* kind of people too.'

CHAPTER SIX

'You look cheerful,' said Michael Feingold, as he and Katherine sat together in an interview room in Brixton Prison.

'Do I?' asked Katherine. 'Sorry.'

She and Feingold were waiting to see Blinkho. Katherine wondered what he would look like. Charles Bronson? Clint Eastwood? A wimp? When he appeared, he looked like none of them. He looked fit, weary and fairly normal, except for something about his eyes.

'Hello, Gavin. How are you?' Feingold greeted the man.

Blinkho did not reply. He merely nodded and sat down.

'How are they treating you?' Katherine asked the usual opening question.

'Not bad,' said Blinkho.

Katherine looked sympathetic and glanced down at her papers.

'Michael has talked to me already about what went through your mind on the night, as you watched those boys doing what they did. And we've got a lot of good witnesses who also say you were all being subjected to a very frightening and intimidating ordeal. Now what I'm

125

rather glad about in a way – and you will understand this, I think – is that two of those lads, including the lad you stabbed, are backward. I don't know if you knew that.'

Katherine looked up at Blinkho, who shrugged his shoulders and looked back at her blankly. Katherine realized she would have to explain further.

'The reason I'm glad about it is, it means that the jury doesn't have to decide who's wicked, you or him. They can sympathize with the lad and understand why you did what you did. We don't have to do the beast on the 10.40 to Peckham Rye routine. OK?'

Blinkho stared straight ahead, and showed no reaction to what she had been saying. Katherine looked at him shrewdly.

'Are you always this quiet, Gavin?'

'Yeah,' he said almost inaudibly. 'I don't believe in a lot of talk.'

Katherine looked at him again. Alarm bells began to sound inside her brain. This young man was weirder than she had originally imagined.

'Well, I'm afraid I have to talk a bit more,' said Katherine. 'You're pleading not guilty to attempted murder, but we accept that the stabbing took place. I understand from Michael that you wish to say that it was self-defence. Now, they will in all likelihood reduce the charge to grievous bodily harm; so I take it you will still be saying you acted in self-defence.'

There was no reply.

'Is that right?' she prompted him. 'Self-defence?'

'Yeah, self-defence,' responded Blinkho finally. 'He came at me.'

'Only one of the witnesses says the lad touched you.'

'So?'

'So I wouldn't want to rely too heavily on that.'

Michael intervened.

'Luckily, Gavin, self-defence can be broadened to include defending others. The man they were assaulting, for instance.'

'Well, right,' said Blinkho unemotionally. 'I was defending other people.'

Katherine looked up from the papers she was studying.

'You say here that that's the point at which you drew the knife? Why then?'

'They could have killed him.'

Katherine was pleased by this reply.

'OK,' she said. 'Fair enough. Now as it turns out, the guy you were defending, the guy they were riding, didn't sustain any real injuries. It all seemed a bit worse at the time than it really was. But *at the time* you thought there was *real* violence happening, didn't you?'

'Thought?' Blinkho asked.

'I mean, you were presumably pretty terrified?'

Katherine looked at Blinkho, fascinated by his lack of emotion. He considered her question for a few moments without speaking.

'Or concerned, anyway?' she prompted him.

'Concerned, yeah,' he assented.

Katherine continued whipping her mule along this well-beaten legal track.

'I think this is what we have to concentrate on,' she told Blinkho, 'the whole *atmosphere* of violence that was there *at the time*. Now, this is where the witnesses really do the business for us. I'll get them all to relive the nightmare in front of the jury; and believe me, it'll be bingo, because if there's one thing we're all worried about – and juries are no different from anybody else – it's The Threat.'

By now, Katherine was seriously worried about Blinkho. He had sat throughout her exposition as if in a coma. He appeared not to have taken in one word of what she had said. Katherine saw out of the corner of her eye that Michael Feingold was studying Blinkho anxiously as well.

'I just need to talk through some legal technicalities with Michael for a second,' she said. 'OK. Do you smoke, Gavin?'

'No,' said Blinkho.

'Well, just bite your nails or something then, eh?' said Katherine. 'Won't be a tick.'

There was not a flicker of reaction on Blinkho's face, as he took out a book from his pocket and found his place. The cover read 'Hard-Core Survival', and depicted a man in combat gear not dissimiliar to the clothes which Katherine knew Blinkho had been wearing on the train.

Katherine left the room, followed by Michael. A prison officer came up to them thinking that they had finished their interview; but they signalled that they were only outside temporarily. They huddled close to each other and spoke in whispers, while people passed them in the corridor.

'Am I seriously briefed to stand on my hind legs in front of twelve intelligent people and say, "My client was so threatened by this youth and by media images of the violent breakdown of urban society, blah blah, that he panicked and over-reacted"?' Katherine asked.

Michael grimaced.

'I know. I must admit, I hoped he might open up a bit for you.'

'Michael, this bloke wouldn't even notice if a herd of elephants got on at Penge and stampeded through the buffet car. I mean: is he in a coma or what? You know what I'm beginning to think, don't you?'

Michael nodded. The same thought had occurred to him too.

'I'm sure he's just a *straightforward* psychopath,' he said unconvincingly.

'I certainly hope so,' Katherine muttered.

They returned to the interview cell and resumed their seats.

'Gavin,' said Michael. 'Remember how we talked about how, before the night of the attack, you'd been thinking for some time about the possibility of something like that happening sooner or later?'

Blinkho grunted his assent to Michael's question.

'You said you felt a growing sense of panic.'

'I think I said anger. I don't panic,' said Blinkho simply.

'I recall a particular, telling phrase,' continued Michael. 'You said there was a sea of crime and it would reach your door one day.'

'Well, I was right, wasn't I?'

Katherine decided this was getting nowhere.

'OK,' she interjected. 'Look, I have to look at this through the prosecution's eyes for a second. And I ask myself: how do I discredit this man Blinkho? How do I get rid of all his jury sympathy and transfer it to the victim?'

Blinkho looked alert for the first time.

'Victim?' he said, incredulously.

Katherine leant forward and stared hard at the man.

'Yes, victim. Gavin, you're on trial, not them. You knifed this lad. A black lad.' She stared at him. 'They were all black, in fact, weren't they?'

'Black? Yes,' said Blinkho. 'So? They're blacks. I didn't go looking for blacks, they came looking for me.'

'But you see I might say,' Katherine decided to take the plunge. 'Or the prosecution might say: OK, they're black, and you're telling me that's irrelevant. But all this business about a sea of crime and a fear of walking down the street at night, this is all code for saying what you really want to say: that this was racial.'

'They came looking for me.' Blinkho seemed to stare right through Katherine.

'Perhaps you don't understand. The prosecution is going to say "What we have here, whether he knows it or not, is a white racist. The victim of his own prejudices. There never was an attack on him. It was just his warped imagination."'

Silence.

'You see, we have another problem,' persisted Katherine. 'None of the witnesses is black. There were blacks on the train, but they didn't come forward.'

'Well, they wouldn't, would they?' said Blinkho.

Katherine took a deep breath and tried to control her worst fears about the man.

'Why were you carrying a knife?' she asked, trying another tack.

'I'd been living rough. In the hills in Brecon. Ten days. I could have done longer, but I'd proved my point,' he said proudly.

Katherine tried to understand.

'Which is what? Why bother? Why see how long you can survive in the hills in Brecon?'

Blinkho looked at Katherine as if she was a moron.

'Because one day we're all going to have to, aren't we?'

'So you're worried about nuclear war, are you?' asked Katherine.

Blinkho smiled, disparagingly.

'What then?' she asked.

Still, there was no response.

'What is this sea of crime that's going to drive us all into the hills?' Katherine persisted.

The three of them sat silently for a few moments as Blinkho thought. Then Blinkho pushed back his chair and half stood, in a crouching position. He pushed out his lips and began to scratch his armpits.

'Oo, oo, oo, oo, oo!' he said, dancing, crouching and leaping, as he made his monkey noises.

*

Katherine and Michael Feingold shared a taxi back into the centre of town. Feingold was the first to break the silence.

'I think,' he said slowly. 'I think . . . if we go through it with him very thoroughly, we can probably stop him from talking himself into a life sentence.'

'He's a head case,' said Katherine, leaning back in the seat, with her eyes shut. 'I can't believe this is happening. The Crown'll offer us "grievous bodily harm". Blinkho will plead guilty. And I'll be standing there making a mitigation speech. What are the mitigation circumstances? Defending himself against four attackers? There isn't a mark on him. No. His mitigation is that they were black.'

Katherine sighed, and opened her eyes.

'I'm sorry, Michael, I've made a mistake. I can't defend him. It would be better if I returned the brief to you.'

'OK, he's a prick,' Michael said, 'but somebody's got to defend him.'

Katherine closed her eyes again. She couldn't believe she was in this nightmare situation again, so soon.

'Not me,' she said firmly.

CHAPTER SEVEN

That afternoon at the coroner's court, the Police Constable who had arrested Nola Marshall gave his evidence. Referring continually to his notes, PC Turnell described how he had found her in a drunken state, sitting on the pavement.

'It was obvious to me that she was very drunk,' he said, 'that she was too drunk to stand. Her speech was very slurred, and she had had a recent fall.'

When asked by the coroner how he knew this, PC Turnell referred again to his notebook.

'She had a swelling on the side of her face, on the right cheek. Also I asked two members of the public who confirmed to me that the drunken woman had fallen heavily against the wall some minutes previous to our arrival.'

It was established that Nola was well known to PC Turnell, who had arrested her several times before for drunkenness. He described how, on this occasion, she had been taken to the police station and then to Willesden Magistrates' Court, where she was remanded in custody to Holloway Prison. Holloway would not take her due to industrial action about overcrowding. Nola had been taken back to Yew Tree Road police station and put in a cell at about 6.45 that evening.

'And what kind of state was she in by then?' asked the coroner.

'Her speech was still slurred, sir, but she could walk upright without assistance.'

'What sort of thing was she saying?'

'As far as I could make out, sir, just general abuse directed towards the police. I couldn't really make it out.'

'Was she complaining about her injury?'

'No, sir.'

'You're sure she didn't complain of a headache?' suggested the coroner.

The policeman looked grateful for the suggestion.

'She did complain of a headache, sir.'

The public benches muttered at this. Frank paused from scribbling for a moment and shook his head.

Turnell looked across the courtroom at the police doctor.

'I believe that's why Doctor Taylor was called, sir, but I'm not sure. At this point – my shift having ended at 6 o'clock – I went off duty.'

The coroner then asked when the policeman had next seen Nola, and what state she was then in.

Turnell looked up from his notebook and stared at the public benches.

'Well, frankly appalling, sir,' he replied. 'She had been sick in the night. She had also – how can I put it? – been ill in the night, so that her underwear was heavily soiled, and both her underwear and, well, practically everything was totally saturated with her urine.'

The coroner nodded sympathetically as Turnell continued.

'Well, sir, we carried her into another cell. The main

problem, as you can imagine, sir – and I don't want to give any offence to anybody – was the appalling smell.'

'But, once again, this was not the end of it for you?' enquired the coroner.

'No, sir. I had to clean out the cell.'

There was another murmur of outrage on the public benches, causing the coroner's officer to call for quiet.

'No, I mean you saw her again,' explained the coroner.

'Sorry, sir, I hope I haven't offended anybody,' said the constable. 'I misunderstood. I saw her again in her cell before going off duty. As I understand it, she unfortunately went into a coma shortly after that. But again it was the end of my shift, sir.'

The coroner turned to James, who began his questioning. James rose to his feet and addressed PC Turnell.

'Constable,' James said pleasantly, 'as you know we are not allowed a sight of police statements from witnesses, so we're a little bit in the dark over here. You say you spoke to two members of the public who said they witnessed Nola Marshall having a heavy fall a few minutes before you arrived to arrest her. Did you take statements from them?'

'No, sir.'

'Why not?'

'At that point, we had no reason to think it would be important.'

James nodded.

'I see. So we have no way of checking this? I mean, except with your colleague who was with you; and his memory will no doubt coincide with your own.'

Frank suppressed a smile, as James hammered home his point.

'So . . . we can't hear from those witnesses to this alleged fall.'

'No, sir,' admitted the policeman.

The coroner leant across his table and interrupted.

'But they were in no doubt about it?' asked the coroner.

'No, sir,' said the policeman, gratefully.

James continued.

'Constable, you say you recognized Nola Marshall because you'd arrested her before. Was she known to you apart from that?'

'In what way, sir?'

'As a doctor who had twice given evidence against police in criminal cases involving alleged police brutality, and as a person who was involved in black community work.'

Turnell denied any knowledge of Nola, apart from as a drunk.

'I see,' James continued. 'Constable, on the evening of her arrest you say: one, that her speech was too slurred for you to make out anything but general abusiveness; two, that she made no complaint about any injury; three, that she complained about a headache.'

The policeman nodded.

'Which of these is true?' enquired James, coolly. 'As I see it, you can have one, but not then two or three. Or you can have two, but not one or three. Or you can have three, but not one or two. Which are you plumping for?'

'I think we will proceed better without sarcasm, Mr Bingham,' interjected the coroner.

'Sir,' James responded, 'either she complained of a headache, in which case she was speaking intelligibly, or she didn't, because she had no headache.'

'The officer has made himself plain,' said the coroner firmly. 'Do you wish to ask anything else?'

'No, sir.'

As Turnell left the stand, Frank saw other policemen grin at him and give him the thumbs-up sign.

*

Turnell's colleague, PC Milnes, proved to be a more confident performer. James made little headway; and when Frank rose, he saw an insolent look on the young constable's face.

'Constable,' said Frank casually, 'you say that at noon, on Saturday 16th August, you and other officers carried Nola Marshall bodily into another cell. This is now nearly twenty-four hours after her arrest?'

The constable nodded.

'So, presumably,' said Frank, 'she had shaken off the effects of her drinking. Why did you need to carry her?'

'She wouldn't walk.'

'Wouldn't or couldn't? Why do you say she wouldn't?'

Milnes looked blank.

'Could she stand?' Frank asked.

'No, sir.'

'Was she conscious?'

'Yes, sir.'

'I see. Was she warm or cold?'

'Cold, sir.'

'I see. So, here was a woman who we've already heard had had a lot to drink and a heavy fall less than twenty-four hours before. She'd vomited and been ill during the night, and she was saturated with urine. She was incapable of standing and her body, as you say, was cold. And four of you picked her up bodily and put her in the cell? On the floor?'

'Yes, sir.'

'Handcuffs?' asked Frank.

'Yes. She was thrashing out at the police officers and had to be restrained. She was handcuffed to a seat.'

'So she was lying on the floor, handcuffed to a seat. Did you put her in the three-quarters prone position, as you are required to do by your own regulations?'

'Well . . .' For the first time during the interrogation, Milnes seemed unsure of himself.

'Why not?' Frank probed.

Again, there was no response.

'Your rules require, do they not, that this is the procedure when dealing with drunks?'

Milnes remained speechless.

'But she wasn't drunk, was she?' said Frank. 'She can't have been, not twenty-four hours after her last drink.'

Milnes finally responded.

'No,' he said. 'Obviously, it was the blow on the head. Beginning to take effect.'

'So you,' said Frank, 'were very conscious of the fact of an injury to her head?'

'Yes,' said Milnes.

'And that's why you dumped her on the floor of the cell, and handcuffed her to the seat,' said Frank.

There was a murmur of appreciation on the public benches.

'Mr Cartwright,' interposed the coroner, 'only you are using this unpleasant word "dumped". Please be more careful. Nothing that has been said so far suggests she was treated with anything but due care and attention by these officers.'

More murmurs, this time of disbelief, came from the public benches.

'Quiet!' shouted the coroner's officer.

The murmurs subsided.

'I do hope that you've finished, Mr Cartwright,' said the coroner, in a long-suffering voice.

'No, sir,' said Frank, with a searching look at him.

'Well, I must warn you,' said the coroner, 'my patience is wearing thin.'

Nevertheless, the coroner nodded for Frank to continue. Frank consulted his notes.

'Constable Wilson, yourself, Constables Pearson and Turnell were all present with Nola Marshall?'

'Yes, sir,' replied Milnes, whose confidence seemed to have returned.

'What happened?'

'I'm sorry?'

Frank decided he might as well try and pull a fast one.

'Did anything happen which accounts for the fact that when Nola Marshall was eventually examined at a hospital, at least one member of staff said she'd never seen such injuries on a drunk?'

The coroner was livid, as Frank had known he would be.

'Mr Cartwright, I hope you're not making speculative accusations! You know very well no such evidence has been heard by this court.'

'I will ask you to receive exactly that evidence, sir,' replied Frank. 'Will you, on my application, recall PC Milnes after you've heard from the witness from the hospital?'

'As you well know,' said the coroner, 'that is a matter for my own discretion.'

This time, there was uproar on the public benches. As soon as the noise subsided, the coroner spoke firmly, surveying the sea of black faces.

'I did not invent the rules of a coroner's inquest,' he said. 'All civilized societies have rules, and they must be obeyed. That's what civilization is.'

Amidst general consternation on the public benches, the coroner turned back to Frank.

'Mr Cartwright, have you finished?'

'No, sir,' replied Frank, evenly. 'Constable, what head injuries did Nola Marshall have already, when she was moved?'

By now, Milnes had had time to think out his response.

'She had some very bad bruising on her face from the fall.'

'So, bruising under her right eye on her cheek, where you say she'd fallen in the street? But no other bruises elsewhere on her face or body?'

'No. Not that I'm aware of.'

'And she sustained no further injuries during the move?'

The coroner was looking angry again; but Frank pressed on.

'I'm merely asking the officer whether or not Nola Marshall may have hurt herself, or accidentally hit herself. She may, for instance, have had a convulsion?'

For a moment Milnes looked tempted to respond positively to Frank's suggestion; but one look at the row of the constable's colleagues seemed to dissuade him.

'No,' he said, finally.

'Thank you,' Frank replied. 'So whatever her injuries were when she reached hospital eventually, she had sustained them in Yew Tree Road police station, with the exception of the bruising under her right eye, caused by a fall in the streets to which we have no witness?'

There was no response from the witness.

'What is your answer?' pressed Frank.

'I don't know,' said Milnes.

'Thank you,' said Frank, sitting down. Frank noticed that Milnes puffed out his cheeks in relief, as he stood down from the stand. He went over to his colleagues, some of whom slapped him on the back.

'I think we'll adjourn at this point,' said the coroner, 'until Thursday.'

'All stand!' called the coroner's officer.

Frank looked across at Alton Phillips, who winked back, and smiled.

CHAPTER EIGHT

It was after seven, and the bedlam of the Fetter Court Chambers had subsided. Katherine hadn't had time to get used to the place yet, and had installed herself in a far corner of the vast, open-plan office, by a window. The aspect was not as attractive as the one she had at Pump Court; but at least there was an interesting view of rooftops.

'Got used to the open plan?' asked Frank.

Katherine smiled.

'I still find it a bit noisy. But in principle I approve of lawyers and clerks working together in the same room. And Lorraine is a lot easier to get on with than Tom.'

Frank looked across to where Lorraine was doing a bit of general filing and tidying up before going back home to her communal squat in Hackney.

'She's good,' said Frank. 'I did mean to bollock her about showing photos of Nola Marshall's injuries to Tessa, but I think I missed the right psychological moment.'

'Good night!' called Lorraine.

Frank looked at his watch.

'Are you sure Feingold is coming?' he asked.

'He said he needed to see me urgently.'

'I thought you'd got yourself off the Blinkho case.'

'I have,' said Katherine, firmly.

She saw Frank look at his watch again.

'You don't have to wait,' she said.

'It's all right,' smiled Frank, who had hung on to take her home that evening to have dinner with the family.

'Ah, here he is,' said Katherine.

Michael Feingold looked all of his sixty-four years, having puffed his way up the stairs. He also looked anxious. Nevertheless, he beamed at Frank.

'Hello, Frank. Are you going to win that inquest?'

'How do you win an inquest?' Frank asked wryly.

'By not letting the coroner screw you. You'll do it, you have to. You have to,' Feingold repeated, putting his briefcase on the floor and sitting opposite Frank and Katherine.

Katherine looked at Feingold.

'Well?' she asked.

Feingold looked miserable.

'If only life could be simple,' he said. 'Your friend Mr Blinkho has confided in me – oh, what a lucky man I am! – that he's a member of the National Front.'

Katherine and Frank exchanged looks of dismay.

'Which particular version of the one and only true National Front,' continued Michael, 'he doesn't specify. I understand a press release along these lines has been prepared just in time for tomorrow's committal. We now have a full-blown legal nightmare on our hands.'

'We?' Katherine shook her head. 'No, no, no, Michael.'

'Hear this,' said Michael. 'Blinkho insists you are still his brief.'

'Oh no, I'm not.' Katherine was adamant.

'And if you refuse,' continued Michael, 'he'll drag you in front of the Bar Council.'

'What?' said Katherine.

'I keep on underestimating this man,' said the solicitor. 'He's not stupid, believe me. Whatever else he is, he's not stupid.'

'I've returned the brief and that's all there is to say.'

'I've told him you'd say that. I've told him I can get him a better barrister than you. He's not interested. You've got a monkey on your back.'

'Why don't you tell him to find a new solicitor as well?'

Feingold looked sadly at Katherine.

'This is the acid test of whether my job is a sham. You must defend the rights of your opponents. Besides, that's what he's hoping I'll do. Why else did he come to me?' He pushed back his chair and stood up to go. 'Cheerio for now.'

Katherine could not stop herself.

'You lost your family to these Nazi pigs,' she said.

She saw Frank blink at her audacity. Michael stopped walking, turned, looked at her thoughtfully for a moment and nodded.

'Precisely. But they weren't able to build the camps until they'd destroyed the rule of law.'

'Before they destroyed it, they hijacked it,' said Katherine. 'I'm sorry, Michael. I won't lift a finger to help Blinkho or his kind – or do anything that'll help get him a platform for his filthy ideas.'

'I think,' said Feingold softly, 'you'll find that you've already done that. I wish you well, Katherine. This could be the one they've been waiting for.'

Feingold walked slowly towards the main entrance, waving a hand to them both in farewell.

Frank pushed his chair back and groaned. Katherine felt even more upset.

'The one who's been waiting for?' said Katherine. 'They're nobodies. They don't exist. Michael's crazy to let them use him. Complete stupidity. For a man like him to help them attack black people in court!'

'We could cobble together a story about a clash of dates,' suggested Frank. 'Lorraine could do a bit of creative diary entering.'

'Frank, I could have stayed at Grimshaw's and done that.'

Frank still looked troubled. She leant across, squeezed his shoulder, but could find nothing to say.

'Come on,' said Frank, finally. 'You can come and help me choose the wine we're having with our meal tonight.'

*

The minute he read Gavin Blinkho's press release, Clive Curran smelt a story. Curran prided himself on knowing what the tabloid-buying public wanted to read, and what his editor wanted him to write. So Curran spoke to Blinkho's family on the phone, met Blinkho's brother Kenneth for a drink or three, after which Curran alerted the editor to the fact that he was definitely on to something.

Curran was at the magistrates' court bright and early, to watch Blinkho being committed for trial at the Old Bailey. He was keen to drink in the atmosphere, get a look at the man himself, and make sure he had the right angle. He barged in past the loony-left demonstrators outside, sat on the crowded press benches and looked around the courtroom.

Blinkho's press release had certainly done its work. The public gallery was packed with National Front supporters including Blinkho's brother, who sat next to Findlay, the current leader of the party. Curran nodded at Kenneth, who nodded back. Curran also caught the eye of Findlay, who had helped Curran with stories on a number of occasions. Findlay nodded back. Curran also noticed that the court had been infiltrated by blacks and whites whom he recognized as coming from various rent-a-mob organizations on the left.

Sure enough, the court proceedings rapidly degenerated into farce. As Blinkho was committed for trial, his supporters chanted the name of Blinkho's absent barrister. Counter-chants calling Blinkho a racist came from the blacks in the public gallery. Before Blinkho was taken down to the cells, he looked up at the gallery, shouted the name of Katherine Hughes, and complained that he was a victim of a conspiracy.

Curran ran outside and watched the police escort the National Front members out of the court and down the steps. Suddenly, both police and Front supporters were charged by the large crowd of anti-racists demonstrating outside. Curran slipped away from the fracas, and caught up with Findlay.

CHAPTER NINE

'You can wave that newspaper in my face as much as you want, Michael,' said Frank. 'Katherine's her own woman, and – for what it's worth – I support her.'

It was a sunny spring day. Frank and Michael Feingold were having a sandwich and a polystyrene cup of coffee in the Temple Gardens. As they sat together on a wooden bench by the lily-pond, the pleasantness of the surroundings seemed to have done nothing to improve Feingold's temper.

'So you won't take Blinkho's brief either?' demanded Feingold.

Frank took a sip of coffee, and thought.

'No,' he said.

'In that case,' said Feingold, 'I have been instructed to offer the brief to each of the Fetter Court barristers in turn.'

'You must do as you see fit,' remarked Frank.

'You think I like doing this?' Feingold wagged his finger in Frank's face. 'Take my advice: persuade Katherine. Somebody has to defend this maniac before we turn him into a celebrity! You people aren't taking your responsibilities seriously. It isn't enough to be right. Who does she think she is?'

Frank noticed passers-by beginning to stare, and he did his best to calm Feingold down.

'All that this newspaper coverage does is confirm that she made a brave decision. Did you know she's already had threats on her life?'

'Threats? Threats?' said Feingold, thrusting the newspaper into his raincoat pocket, and standing. 'I walked out of Buchenwald! I ate my own shit to stay alive! How dare this woman talk to me in your office about losing my family? How dare she say that? Or lecture me about people hijacking the law?'

He calmed down as quickly as he had blown up.

'My client wants an answer,' he said.

Frank sighed. He liked Feingold, and appreciated the difficulty of his situation.

'Can't it wait till after the Nola Marshall inquest?' asked Frank. 'Blinkho's case isn't even listed yet. Can't you baffle him with science, tell him he has to wait?'

Feingold looked at Frank pityingly.

'Be clever, Frank. *I* can wait. *I* can wait for ever, but what is this all about, do you think? Who is running this man Blinkho? Not me. It's that child molester, Findlay. And who runs him? Who has what Findlay needs to spread the good word?'

Feingold brought the newspaper out from his pocket and waved it again at Frank.

'Ask *them* to wait! You think they're going to be nice about this? You think these animals are going to wait, now that Katherine has offered them her throat? Does she even know what she has done?'

*

146

After Curran's first article appeared, and Katherine received the first batch of phone calls threatening her with injury and death, she didn't bother to leave her answering machine on. Even when hate mail started to arrive, she refused Frank and Annie's offer that she should move in with them for a time. But she did make a point of always double-locking her front door.

Fortunately, too, Katherine had another case to occupy her; and Tessa, the young black barrister with whom Katherine found herself working, strongly supported her decision not to defend Blinkho. So the first time Katherine became aware of any feeling against her in her new Chambers came when Tessa and she returned from court, the evening before the Nola Marshall inquest reconvened.

Katherine slid back the massive door to the Chambers; and she and Tessa staggered in laughing, weighed down with papers and briefcases.

'How did your man in the jockstrap do?' asked Lorraine as the two women dumped their belongings and picked up their mail from the pigeonholes.

'He got three months. Can you imagine it for him?' Katherine shook her head. 'He's so pathetic. Little weedy fella. They were all laughing at him. All this stuff about him poking his little winkle through a hole in the cubicle wall and . . . ugh, it was humiliating for him, wasn't it, Tessa?'

'Revolting,' replied Tessa, wrinkling up her nose.

'A pointless, spiteful waste of time catching, trying and imprisoning a man like that,' Katherine said, shaking her head again.

Michael Khan looked up at Katherine as she went past his desk to fetch herself a cup of coffee.

'Still it's a job, isn't it?' he said.

Katherine smiled. She knew that Michael hadn't had much work recently, and was still smarting from the fact that two white barristers, Frank and James, had been briefed on the Nola Marshall case.

'Oh, Katherine,' said Lorraine, remembering, 'the *Guardian* rang.'

'Saying?' asked Katherine.

'Asking for a comment on the Blinkho case.'

'I have nothing to say that won't get me into more trouble,' said Katherine.

'That's what I thought,' Lorraine replied.

Katherine finished pouring herself a coffee and looked up, to find James staring at her thoughtfully. He was leaning against one of the pillars, and had crossed the room to speak to her.

'You could say you were double-booked on Blinkho,' he said.

'I could,' she said, continuing to sort through her letters.

'Why should she?' Katherine found herself supported by Hugh, the black junior clerk. 'The guy's a racist.'

'What about the man in the jockstrap? Might he not have been a racist?' said Michael Khan.

'I didn't ask,' snapped Katherine, going to sit at her desk.

Another of the barristers, Ken Gordon, joined in the interrogation of Katherine. Katherine felt that Ken – certainly the most successful barrister in the Chambers, after Frank and James – resented Katherine's arrival more than most of the others.

'What about rape?' Ken asked. 'I mean, nobody likes rapists either.'

Katherine put her letters down on the desk and looked from Ken to Michael, and then to James.

'I don't do consent rape cases,' she said. 'If I can avoid it.'

'Why not?' Ken asked. 'Don't women sometimes consent to sex? I mean, they don't with me; but some men occasionally get lucky, I hear.'

Katherine took a long sip of her coffee, her irritation rising slowly within her. Really, she thought, I might as well be back at Pump Court.

'Yes, we do consent occasionally to sex,' she said. 'We sometimes even initiate it.'

Ken and Michael grinned at each other.

'But we don't ever consent to rape,' said Katherine. 'And we never initiate that, despite what some judges think.'

Katherine was pleased to see Lorraine and Tessa nodding their agreement.

'But that's the point at issue,' interjected James. 'It isn't rape, if it's consented to.'

'You can't consent to rape. It's self-evident,' said Katherine, patiently.

'No,' said James, 'but you can consent to sex and then change your mind.'

'Then you're not consenting. Do you do consent rape cases, then? Willingly?' Katherine asked James.

'I have done, yes. Willingly.' James nodded.

Katherine turned to Michael.

'Do you?' she asked.

'I've never been sent that kind of brief,' said Michael. 'But I would do it.'

'Do you?' Katherine asked Ken.

'Of course,' Ken replied.

Katherine sighed.

'You know, I have to say this, Mr Bingham, Mr Khan and Mr Gordon, but you've got your heads up your arses about this.'

She rose and walked across to put some post in the out-tray on Lorraine's desk.

'But,' she said, 'I accept it. I accept your heads wherever

you want them. Fetter Court is in the grip of libertarian democracy.'

Young Hugh snorted with delight at Katherine's diatribe. James looked at the junior clerk with some annoyance.

'Hugh,' Lorraine said, warningly.

Katherine was on her way through the door of the Chambers, when James called out to her.

'Why do you accept my right to be wrong, but not Blinkho's?'

Katherine stopped and turned round.

'Because, James, you're not asking me to mouth your opinions in a serious criminal trial.'

'But that's your job,' James replied, taunting her.

The atmosphere in the room worsened noticeably as Katherine walked back across the floor. Tessa frowned at James, to show her support for Katherine.

'Hey, get your hand off it, James!'

'Well, isn't it?' James ignored Tessa, and repeated his question to Katherine.

'Criticize me, but don't tell me what my job is,' said Katherine coldly.

Hugh ignored Lorraine's warning, and wandered across to James.

'Can you see anything up there, James? Want a torch?' he joked.

'Thank you, Hugh, that'll do!' snapped James.

'Hugh,' ordered Lorraine, 'go over to the list office *now*!'

Hugh turned to go, then looked back at James and bowed ironically.

'Yes, boss,' he said, rolling his eyes in the manner of a southern slave.

'What does that mean?' asked James, angrily. 'I don't want that rubbish from you!'

'OK, bwana!' Hugh tugged an imaginary forelock and cringed in front of James.

By now, Lorraine had had more than enough of her junior.

'Hugh! Go!' she shouted.

Katherine suddenly noticed that Frank had entered the Chambers and was standing by the door, watching the argument with mounting dismay. Before she could intervene to defuse the situation, Michael Khan had joined in again.

'You're out of order, Hugh!' Michael wagged his finger at the lad.

'He isn't out of order. Let's have a straight answer,' Tessa said, poking her finger at James. 'Would you defend Blinkho if they asked you to? Knowing that he's National Front?'

'Yes,' said James, 'and I'd try my hardest to get him off. Of course. There is no other answer to that question.'

Tessa looked at him with utter disgust.

'Well, there's a word for that, isn't there?' she said.

'Whoa, whoa, hold it!' said Katherine, looking over her shoulder at Frank. 'Everybody. Please.'

They all went quiet, as they noticed Frank standing mournfully by the door.

'Katherine,' James spoke quietly and reasonably. 'All I'm really trying to say is that we as a Chambers are heading for trouble on this. If it hadn't become public, OK, fair enough. But it has. Politically, it would be clever to bite the bullet and help Blinkho to his day in court.'

'For the sake of the Chambers?' Katherine asked ironically, recalling Alex Grimshaw's similar argument after Alan Ackroyd's attempted suicide.

'If for no other reason,' said James, in his best public school manner.

'We must all "muck in"?' Katherine savagely mimicked his superior tone.

James was now white with anger.

'We – are – a – team!' He spat the words out, one by one, as if she could not be expected to know what they meant.

'I – will – not – defend – Blinkho!' she stated with equal vehemence.

Katherine walked out of the room, without looking at any of her colleagues. Not even Frank.

Frank wandered into his Chambers, and sat down.

'One thing you may as well all know,' announced Frank, 'is that Katherine is under enormous pressure. Among other things, she's had a warning from the Bar Council. Blinkho's lodged an official complaint.'

*

Frank's day proceeded effortlessly from bad to worse. He was just settling down to go through his papers for the inquest in the morning, when Alton Phillips rang up to demand his and James's presence in the Law Centre that evening, at an emergency meeting of the Association of Black Families. Alton wouldn't tell Frank why they had to attend, but was emphatic that the matter was of great urgency.

Frank and James both felt tired and disgruntled as they sat in reception at the Law Centre. Frank and Annie had had a row, when he rang up to say he was going to be home late yet again. James was annoyed at having to pull out of a drinks party that Gloria had arranged for some of her colleagues from Christie's.

Neither Frank nor James were prepared for the bomb-shell which proceeded to explode. James's statement that he would defend a racist had been reported back to the Association of Black Families; and a committee from the

Association now asked James to explain himself. There was no great mystery how the Association had heard of James's views, since one of the most prominent members of the committee in question was Tessa.

The night before the resumption of the Nola Marshall inquest, James found himself in the dock, one white face stared at by a room full of black ones. Frank increasingly wished that the floor would open up and swallow James, whose speech of self-justification was full of neat metaphors and clever argument, but rather more appropriate to the Bar mess than to a radical Law Centre.

At first, members of the committee merely stared at James impassively. After a time, they began to heckle. By the end of the meeting, a motion was passed unanimously that James no longer be involved in the Nola Marshall inquest.

'Sorry about that,' muttered James.

'Don't worry about it,' said Frank.

Tessa looked apologetic but elated, as she wished them both goodnight.

'Well, Frank,' said Alton Phillips, showing him and James out of the Law Centre, 'it looks like you're on your own.'

'Yeah,' said Frank. 'Thanks a lot, Alton.'

CHAPTER TEN

Frank stayed up all night, to familiarize himself with James's papers. He tried to push the troubles within his Chambers to the back of his mind, and concentrate on the job in hand: namely, to demonstrate that Nola Marshall had received her fatal injuries whilst in police custody. The next morning, after a shower and a change of clothing, Frank was back in court.

The police surgeon, Dr Taylor, was a grey-looking, middle-aged man in a grey-looking, middle-aged suit. He had the world-weary air of a man well used to giving unpleasant evidence about violent death.

Frank began his questioning of Dr Taylor by asking about his first visit to Yew Tree Road police station. Frank established that this visit had been at four o'clock in the morning.

'Sixteen hours after Nola Marshall's arrest,' Frank emphasized. 'This was because she had apparently been found to be unable to stand. We therefore assume somebody had been asking her to stand, although it was the middle of the night.'

'Police regulations covering drunks require them to be

observed every thirty minutes,' explained the doctor, 'and in this case the officer in charge had obviously taken the wise precaution of requiring her to move around.'

'I see,' said Frank. 'That's an assumption on your part?'

'No, that's what I've been told by the senior officer.'

'Right.' Frank prodded the air with his pen. 'And you say you found Nola Marshall unable to stand or speak. Was she injured?'

'She'd had a fall.'

'Yes, we've heard about this fall.'

'No, she had apparently fallen in the cell during the night.'

Frank could hardly believe his ears, and reiterated Dr Taylor's statement.

'She had another fall?'

Dr Taylor nodded. One or two people on the public benches hooted and whistled.

'She had *another* fall,' repeated Frank. 'Well, this is news to some of us, you see. PC Turnell was apparently unaware of this when he gave evidence last Tuesday.'

'Well . . .'

Before the doctor could continue, Frank pressed on.

'Am I to understand, Dr Taylor, that where your statement referred to "conditions caused by the recent fall" you mean this later fall, not the original fall?'

'Yes, sir.'

'Very well. When did this later fall happen?'

'I'm told at about 2.30 a.m., after she'd been roused to check on her condition. She'd fallen against the wall and struck her face on the concrete floor of the cell.'

Frank consulted his notes on the policemen's evidence.

'So she was now heavily bruised,' said Frank, 'and couldn't stand or speak? Was she conscious?'

'Yes.'

'This must have been of great concern to you?'

'Well, of course, she was in a rather pitiful state; but I felt, from what the police had told me, that she was still getting over her drinking bout.'

'Had she been sick at this point?' enquired Frank.

'No.'

'What did you do?'

'I advised that observation be kept on her, and that – should her condition change – she should be taken to hospital. I also said if accommodation was obtained at Holloway, they should be fully informed of her history and condition.'

'What did you do then?'

'I went home to my bed from whence I'd come.'

'You next saw Nola Marshall another fourteen hours later at 6 p.m. that evening, twenty-eight hours after her arrest. Why were you called to the station?'

'She was in a coma.'

'A coma,' repeated Frank. 'What did you do?'

'I immediately arranged for her to be an emergency admission to the Royal Free Hospital.'

'Where a surgeon operated to remove a brain haemorrhage. But in vain. Is that correct?'

'Yes.'

Frank looked across at the coroner, who was gazing at the doctor intently.

'Let's go back,' said Frank, 'to the night you first saw her. You advised the police officers in whose care Nola Marshall was, that she should be taken to hospital if necessary. In what circumstances did you advise them to do that?'

'If she was repeatedly sick.'

'You know she was never taken to a hospital?'

'So I understand.'

'You know she was sick repeatedly?'

'So I understand,' Dr Taylor said again.

'Would you expect that sickness, uncontrolled urinating and inability to speak might have alerted the police that something was wrong?'

'Well, I suppose it could be confused with drunkenness,' suggested Dr Taylor.

'Twenty-four hours after the event?' Frank asked with incredulity in his voice.

'I can't speak for the police,' replied Taylor, hurriedly.

'But they had certainly not followed your instructions.'

'It would seem not,' admitted Taylor.

His reply prompted cheers from the public benches.

'Thank you,' said Frank, pleased to have pushed the point home.

As the coroner dismissed Taylor, a row erupted between the police and members of the public who were shouting abuse at the officers. The coroner's officer tried to restore order as the coroner bustled out of the courtroom, through his private door.

Frank packed away his papers and gave a tired smile as Alton congratulated him on denting the police evidence. Nola Marshall's parents, Ivan and Jo, seemed shocked by the whole experience. Frank helped Alton shepherd them out of the courtroom and into the open air.

Outside, a large crowd of demonstrators and people from the media had gathered. As Frank and Alton emerged, one on either side of the Marshalls, a couple of TV news crews filmed the group as they walked down the steps and through the mass of demonstrators supporting them.

Suddenly, a little, bent old man with lank hair pushed his way through the crowd towards the old couple. He was wearing what was obviously his best suit, shiny and well worn but brushed for the occasion; and his left pocket was emblazoned with World War II medals. He leant forward to grasp Ivan Marshall's hand.

'Mr Marshall, I'm Gavin Blinkho's father,' said the old man.

Frank was tired, but not too tired to sense that this was an occasion which had been engineered. He looked round quickly, and saw press photographers going mad to capture this meeting. One TV news cameraman was elbowed aside. The other swore as one of his cables became disconnected.

'How come they can spare the time for your daughter, but Gavin still hasn't got a barrister?' the old man said bitterly. 'Can anybody say this is a fair country? My son's the forgotten man in Brixton Prison!'

Alton pushed his way to Ivan Marshall's side and pulled him away from Mr Blinkho. In the commotion, both old men were knocked and shoved, and Blinkho fell to the ground.

'Now,' yelled Clive Curran.

Curran's photographer moved in and started shooting close-ups of the old man on the ground. Blinkho looked into their camera, and then at the TV cameras, beseechingly.

'Is this why we gave our lives in the war? For England? This isn't the England we fought for,' the old man wailed, with tears coming into his eyes.

CHAPTER ELEVEN

The next day, in Fetter Court, Frank snorted as he studied
the front page of Curran's paper. It consisted of a huge
picture of Mr Blinkho falling to the ground, apparently
drowned in a sea of angry black faces. The headline read
'IS THIS ENGLAND?'

'See page 14,' said James, gloomily.

Frank turned to the centre pages, where a banner
headline straddled the centre spread. 'LOONY LEFT AT THE
BAR' read the headline.

'Shit a brick!' exclaimed Frank, as he saw the photographs of Katherine and himself.

He threw the newspaper across the office; but James
picked it up.

'No,' said James. 'You might as well hear the worst.
"The head of this set of Bar misfits is Frank Cartwright,
one-time member of the Communist Party of Great Britain,
who has never publicly renounced his Soviet-style
beliefs ..."'

Frank had heard more than enough. He stuffed his gown
and wig into his bag.

'I'm late and I'm off to court,' he said, and stormed out
of the Chambers.

'What else does it say?' asked Lorraine.

James continued.

' "Cartwright's speciality is attacking the police in court and in print. He has never been known to pass up an opportunity to accuse the police of racism, sexism, brutality and all the other smears of the loony left." '

James smiled as various members of the Chambers cheered ironically.

' "But the undoubted star of this Chambers is Katherine Hughes, who mixes her similar brand of far-left politics with a raunchy lifestyle of blokes and booze. Attractive Katherine is the lady who breaks all the rules of her profession. She won't defend men on rape charges: won't defend white people accused of offences against black people; speaks out publicly about senile judges and the immorality of prison. We ask 'Who does she think she is?' This holier-than-thou attitude rings as phoney as a crocodile's tears, coming from a woman who has had a succession of live-in lovers since her marriage to teacher Eric Dewar ended in divorce, when he could no longer tolerate her lengthy and public affair with black American civil rights lawyer Bobby Russell during his two-year stint as visiting lecturer at the London School of Economics. Unfortunately for Ms Hughes, no sooner had her divorce come through than 6 ft. 4 in. Russell promptly returned to his wife and children in Detroit, leaving the raunchy Radical older but apparently not wiser." '

James threw the paper down in disgust, just as Katherine entered the Chambers.

'Have you seen this?' James asked, indicating the paper. 'If not you'd better have a look.'

Katherine nodded grimly and went across to Lorraine's desk to pick up her letters.

'You're probably all wishing I'd stayed at Grimshaw's,' said Katherine.

Tessa came across from her desk and smiled at Katherine.

'I'm very glad you came here,' she said.

Katherine smiled her appreciation, but wondered whether Tessa might not currently be in a minority of one.

*

Frank arrived at the court with only seconds to spare. He noticed a buzz of excitement and support from the public benches as he took his seat in court, and arranged his papers. His entrance seemed to be the cue for the police to file in, each ostentatiously carrying a copy of Curran's newspaper. One by one, they sat down, opened the paper, and paid studious attention to the centre pages.

Frank turned round, to see how Jo and Ivan Marshall were coping. They smiled but looked drained and much older than they had been at the start of the inquest. Alton gave Frank a friendly pat on the arm for encouragement.

Soon the day's business was underway. Now it was Frank's turn to call witnesses. The first witness he called was Mr Barnes, who had called the police when Nola Marshall caused a scene outside his newsagent's shop. An elderly man with a moustache and dignified bearing, Barnes entered the stand and looked around the courtroom with interest.

Frank quickly established that Mr Barnes had witnessed the whole incident, and then asked the crucial question.

'Did she have a fall?'

Ted Barnes's answer rang out confidently.

'No.'

'You're sure about that?' Frank wanted there to be no doubt.

'Yes.'

'Did you see her face before she was taken away?'

'Oh yes,' Barnes nodded.

'And did you see any injuries on it?'

'No. None at all.'

'Thank you.'

The coroner leant towards the witness.

'Can you explain how it can possibly be,' asked the coroner, 'that no fewer than eleven policemen have stated that they saw clearly the evidence of this fall, whether at the time of arrest or very soon afterwards.'

'No, sir.'

Frank looked meaningfully at Alton. At long last, the tide seemed to be turning in their favour. However, the next witness was the crucial one. After a whole evening spent waiting at the police station, Alton had finally been told who the other inmates of the cells at Yew Tree Road police station had been on the night that Nola Marshall died. A little more detective-work had yielded a most interesting result.

The coroner turned to address the jury.

'Before I call this final witness,' he said, 'I feel bound to point out that the man you're about to hear evidence from is himself an habitual drunkard and this is indeed why he occupied a nearby cell on the night in question. I'm not suggesting he would deliberately mislead you, but his credibility must be weighed against his record as an offender.'

Then a portly figure in his forties entered the stand. He had a florid complexion and was perspiring heavily, as he placed his hands on the balustrade at the front of the stand. The coroner addressed the man with some distaste.

'Mr Collins, you've seen enough courtrooms in your time to know that perjury is a crime.'

Mr Collins nodded.

'Yes, sir.'

'When did you last have an alcoholic drink?' the coroner enquired.

'Two days ago, sir.'

'Very well.'

Frank stood up and started his questioning.

'Mr Collins, you were in a cell next door to Nola Marshall.'

'Yes, sir.'

'Because you were drunk yourself.'

'Yes, sir.'

'How long had you been in the cell when Nola Marshall was brought in?'

'Five hours, sir.'

'So you were sobering up. What time was this?'

'About seven o'clock, sir.'

'How did you know it was Nola Marshall?'

'She talked to me, sir, through the walls. If you raise your voice, you can talk. It's a regular thing. She said, "I'm Nola Marshall. Who's that?" I said, "I'm David Collins." She was very merry. We sang two or three songs together. She was calling out to the police, telling them to come and sing and dance.'

There was a murmur of amusement in the court.

'She was inviting policemen to sing and dance?' asked Frank.

'Yes, sir. She sang "Put down all your cares and woe, here we go, singing low, bye, bye blackbird."'

'What else did she sing?'

'Well now, sir, I . . .' Collins looked uneasy, glancing at the Marshalls.

'You can speak freely,' said Frank. 'We realize Nola was very drunk and that she was in high spirits.'

Collins paused for a moment before replying. He produced a scruffy handkerchief and mopped his forehead.

'Well, sir, she shouted out that she was feeling randy. And could anybody oblige her?'

Ivan and Jo stared into their laps. Several of the policemen sniggered.

'What happened then?' Frank pressed on.

'Well, sir . . .' Collins looked diffident. 'This went on for a while. She was telling these fellas they weren't real men and what have you. Then all of a sudden a group of, I should say, four or five of them came into the cell block from the stairs, and they went into her cell.'

Collins paused for a moment before continuing.

'And there was a lot of shocking abuse and she was screaming.'

'Why was she screaming?' asked Frank.

'Well, they was giving her a terrible battering, sir. Kicking and punching her. And calling out "black slut" and "black slag" and "black whore". I would say they lost control of themselves.'

*

There was a hush in the coroner's court as the jury filed back in. The jury foreman stood to give their verdict.

Frank closed his eyes.

'We find that Nola Marshall was unlawfully killed.'

Frank opened his eyes. Pandemonium had already broken out in the courtroom. The policemen were filing out, trying to ignore the scene of celebration around them, and pretending not to hear the abuse which was being hurled at them. Alton pumped Frank's arm up and down, with a great beam on his face; but Frank couldn't help but look down at Ivan and Jo Marshall, who sat motionless while everyone around them jumped, danced, laughed and embraced.

*

That night, Fetter Court was festooned with balloons and streamers. The Chambers had won its first big case, and everyone there was celebrating. Only Frank and Katherine were still missing. A sound system pounded out loud music, chosen by Hugh.

All the barristers and both clerks were there, plus an

extraordinary number of friends, colleagues and miscella-
neous hangers-on. All the desks had been pushed back
against the walls, so that there was a large area for
dancing. Everyone seemed to be dancing, drinking or
shouting to each other over the hubbub.

Tessa smiled at James, and pulled him on to the dance
floor.

'Am I forgiven?' she asked.

'What for?' asked James.

'You know. Getting you off the Nola Marshall inquest.'

James concentrated on his dancing for a few moments,
and then delivered his verdict.

'Well, we won,' he said. 'And as we're a team, I suppose
that's the important thing.'

*

'Nice place you have here,' said Frank, admiring Alex
Grimshaw's office in Pump Court.

'I'd have thought you'd be out celebrating,' remarked
Alex Grimshaw, drily.

'I shall be, later,' said Frank. 'I just wanted to get this
Blinkho business sorted out.'

'You think a lot of Katherine, don't you?' said Alex,
turning down the Mozart on his CD player.

Frank sipped his sherry.

'Good sherry, this,' said Frank.

'Yes,' said Alex, waving his cigar. 'Amontillado.'

'Ah,' said Frank.

'So what do you want?' asked Alex.

'You owe her something, Alex. Help her. Take the
Blinkho brief. Get this monkey off her back.'

Grimshaw twirled the stem of his glass. He paused and
then looked up.

'If Feingold offers it, I'll take it. But Blinkho will get ten
years, whoever defends him.'

A look of relief crossed Frank's face.

'Thank you.'

Alex topped up Frank's glass and smiled at him. Frank raised his glass.

'Cheers,' said Frank.

'Cheers,' responded Alex. 'And well done at that inquest. Very pleasing to see that coroner with both tits in the mangle.'

*

Frank's arrival back at Fetter Court was greeted with cheers and congratulations. He hung his coat by the door, and looked round the throng. James came across and thrust a drink in his hands.

'Where's Katherine?' asked Frank.

'Licking her wounds, I should imagine. Or getting some slim-hipped youth to lick them for her.' James saw the look of disfavour on Frank's face, and stopped. 'Only joking, Frank.'

'You believe what you read in the papers, do you?' asked Frank.

'Look,' said James, 'they weren't exactly flattering about me either, but there was a grain of truth in it.'

'The attack on her was different,' said Frank.

'Quite,' agreed James. 'Well, that's all I'm saying: no doubt if I was Katherine, I wouldn't feel like a party either.'

'Katherine!' said Lorraine.

Frank and James turned, to see Katherine — smiling and confident — stride through the doorway. Tessa and Lorraine ran towards her, each offering her a glass of wine.

Frank gave his male colleague an appraising stare.

'I think there's something you still haven't grasped about Katherine, James. She's fearless.'

PART III

CHAPTER ONE

Katherine was in bed when the phone rang.

'Katherine, I think you had better come home.'

It was the Yorkshire accent of Aunt Susan, her father's sister. Usually, she sounded cosy: now, she sounded anxious, tentative.

'It's Dad,' Katherine said.

She had been expecting the news, even though her father was only sixty-two. Bob Hughes had spent his life fighting, first as a shop steward, then as a Labour councillor, and finally as an invalid; but not even Bob could conquer pneumoconiosis, the disease he had contracted as a result of a lifetime spent working in textile mills. Katherine knew how much Bob had resented having to take early retirement, even though his job had literally been killing him.

Katherine had often argued with her father and been infuriated by his obstinacy; but she knew she would miss him. She recognized that it was from him that she had inherited her own terrier-like tenacity. It was he who had pushed her to win an 11-plus scholarship to the local grammar school and then encouraged her to go on to university. It was he who had taught her the basics of Marxism and the class struggle.

As a widower, Bob had seen education as the only way for his child to escape poverty and have the opportunities which he had never had. Katherine smiled, though, as she remembered his determination that she should never forget where she had come from.

She rang Lorraine to cancel her appointments for a few days, packed an overnight bag, and set off for Yorkshire.

*

The cemetery overlooked a narrow valley, along the whole length of which lay a straggling ribbon of once-prosperous industrial towns. A large crowd of mourners stood around the graveside, hunched against the wind and rain driving straight off the Pennines.

Katherine had expected mainly relatives, and was pleased to see how many colleagues from work, the union and the council had turned out to remember her father. She felt guilty that she either didn't know, or had forgotten, the names of most of the people there. They all seemed to know who she was: Bob's daughter, the clever one, the one who there'd been all that fuss about in the papers.

The rain turned to sleet as earth was shovelled on top of Bob's coffin. The mourners started to walk back along the gravelled path to the car park. Katherine remained at the graveside, watching raindrops form puddles on the newly dug earth. She was trying to work out why a progressive, no-nonsense man like her father had insisted on a full-blown funeral, rather than a quick, quiet cremation. She supposed he saw it as doing things 'properly'.

When she looked up she was relieved to see someone whom she recognized, hanging on to a small collapsible umbrella.

'Katherine,' said Ellen.

'Oh, Ellen.'

The two women hugged each other. Their respective umbrellas became entangled, and they both got soaked.

'Thank you for coming!' said Katherine.

They walked slowly away from the grave.

'Look,' said Ellen, 'when are you going back to London?'

'A couple of days. I have to clear his things out of the house. I don't know what I'm going to do with it all. I suppose I'll give it all to Oxfam. My dad was such a hoarder.'

'How are you?' Ellen asked.

'Oh, you know.' Katherine shrugged her shoulders. 'What about you? How's the practice?'

'Same as ever. Maintenance claims, divorce, petty theft. Look, why don't you come over? It's been ages.'

*

The following evening, Katherine took Ellen up on her offer and went round to have dinner. From the outside, Ellen's two-up-two-down terraced house was identical to the ones in which both Ellen and Katherine had been brought up. Inside, however, the two downstairs rooms had been converted into one large living area, decorated with indoor plants of every conceivable shape and size.

Ellen had painted the walls white and covered them with posters from Cuba and Nicaragua. There was a small but expensively fitted kitchen at one end of the room, over-looking the back yard. After a meal of lasagne and salad, Katherine helped pile the washing up in the sink. She offered to wash up, but Ellen told her not to be silly.

They returned to the front part of the living area. Katherine examined the shelves on either side of the fireplace, and was not surprised to discover that she and Ellen had many of the same books. The two of them subsided on to a sagging sofa; and Ellen opened a second bottle of wine, the one which Katherine had brought with her.

'This is nice,' said Ellen, looking at the label. 'You're getting very sophisticated!'

Katherine laughed. Ellen Thompson was a small, slim woman with shoulder-length, tousled chestnut curls and large dark brown eyes. Her appearance of physical fragility was deceptive. For as long as Katherine had known her, Ellen had been ambitious. She and Katherine had been the two girls from their junior school to make it to university and a job in the professions. Whilst Katherine had gone to London to make her career at the Bar, Ellen had returned to Yorkshire and eventually had set up her own solicitor's practice on a large council estate.

Although they had occasionally lost touch with each other for months and even years at a time, Katherine knew that their friendship survived. The geographical distance between them had not diminished their mutual respect for what each was doing in the law. At a more fundamental level, each felt she understood the other. No explanations were needed to account for their actions. Both had emerged from the same sort of background; and even now, their personal lives retained many similarities.

Both women had suffered broken marriages in pursuit of a career; and both thought, on balance, that they'd made the correct decision. Katherine revealed that she was 'between men'. Ellen laughed and said that she'd given up men altogether or at least they'd given her up. She wasn't sure which.

Ellen got up and turned on the television.

'Do you mind?' she asked. 'There's something on the news I want to watch.'

They continued chatting; but Ellen hushed Katherine in

mid-sentence and turned up the sound, when an item about a twelve-year-old missing girl began.

There was the inevitable press conference, with mother and father looking strained and nervous, and the father reading out an appeal for information. The police looked solemn, as though they thought they would soon be investigating a murder case.

'The family lives on the Brightpool Park Estate, round where I work,' said Ellen. 'Terrible place.'

'Tracey, if you're watching,' said the father, hesitantly into a battery of microphones, 'we know you're out there somewhere. Come home, love. Or get in touch. Your mam and me know things has been bad. Things have been bad for all of us. We've hit rock bottom. But we want you back.'

He paused for a moment and lit a cigarette. Katherine noticed that his hand was shaking. The mother was asked if she wanted to say anything.

'Just . . .' said the mother, who looked sallow and unhealthy, 'if somebody's got Tracey, please don't harm her.'

'How old do you think she is?' asked Ellen.

'I dunno,' said Katherine. 'Forty-nine?'

'More like twenty-nine,' said Ellen.

The camera cut to a shot of the journalists at the press conference. Katherine noticed with distaste that Clive Curran was among them.

'Mr Charnley, do you think your stepdaughter might've been abducted?' asked one of the journalists.

There was a long silence as Mr Charnley thought.

'There are some people capable of it. I've asked the police that they should be rounded up, all the known ones, and looked at,' he said. 'But I don't know where she is. All I know is, animals shouldn't have to live like we've had to.'

There followed a background report on the Charnleys' estate, which had won awards when it was built, but was now considered one of Europe's worst. The open spaces between the flats were littered with rubbish and burnt-out cars. The camera went inside the communal lobby of one of the blocks, and found the floor and walls daubed with graffiti and excrement. The lift had, of course, been vandalized.

Inside the Charnleys' grubby, sparsely furnished flat, the camera panned across damp walls and cracked, dirty windows.

'Talk about two nations,' said Ellen, bitterly.

The reporter, Dan Schumacher, stood in front of the Charnleys' block of flats to do his final piece to camera.

'Tracey Wilson may well have run away from a life too bleak to contemplate,' he said in his usual tone of concerned urgency. 'Whatever the truth of this particular tragedy, the harshness of life on Brightpool Park poses a challenge to this country's apparently slumbering social conscience.'

Ellen snorted as she turned off the television.

'More like terminal coma,' said Katherine.

'Are consciences slumbering in Kensington?' asked Ellen.

'Notting Hill, if you don't mind,' Katherine retorted.

Ellen smiled.

'Was it a problem for you and your dad?'

'The fact that I've lost my accent and live in a big flat in London?' Katherine considered the question. 'Yes. He thought I should've stayed up here and done ... well the sort of work you do. Basic, nitty-gritty work helping ordinary people in trouble with the law.'

'But surely,' said Ellen, 'isn't that what Fetter Court is all about?'

Katherine laughed. Perhaps, during the meal, she had been coming on a bit too strong about her new Chambers.

'Ellen,' she said, 'don't ask me what Fetter Court's all about.'

CHAPTER TWO

When Frank arrived at Fetter Court, he was in a filthy mood. Annie had complained of a headache so he had had to drive the children to school and he was late for his appointment with a client and his solicitor. On top of all that, Frank arrived to discover Lorraine bickering with Joanna Davis, youngest of the four black barristers in the Chambers.

'I can't do more than keep asking, Joanna,' said Lorraine.

'Yes, I know, but . . .' sulked Joanna.

'Is he upstairs?' asked Frank.

'In the conference room,' said Lorraine.

'Who?' asked Joanna.

'Tim Hudson, megastar,' said Lorraine, in a tone which chided Frank for keeping the teenagers' heart-throb waiting.

'Thanks, Lorraine,' Frank muttered.

'You aren't the only one.' Lorraine returned to her argument with Joanna. 'Frank's got unpaid fees going back twelve months.'

'Yes, but Frank's a big earner,' said Joanna. 'I haven't worked for four weeks.'

Frank swore, as he searched his desk for the correct brief.

'Yes, I know. Hugh, take that, will you?'

Lorraine turned to her junior, as the telephone started ringing. Joanna refused to be fobbed off.

'I find it hard to believe, Lorraine, that there's nothing for me. I mean, there's got to be a reason . . .'

Frank found the brief and bounded up the stairs, still listening to the altercation.

'Ignoring me won't solve the problem!' Joanna shouted.

By now, Lorraine was equally angry.

'So what you're actually accusing me of is pushing work towards the whites in the set!'

Frank turned and saw Lorraine glaring at Joanna.

'Let's start speaking plainly, shall we, Joanna,' continued Lorraine, 'or we'll be here all week!'

Frank swore again, under his breath, and burst into the conference room.

*

Frank found his client even more irritating. Tim Hudson's story sounded to Frank like a pack of lies, even when delivered with the famous doe-eyed expression which had won the actor thousands of teenage fans.

'You don't believe me,' Tim whined.

'I don't have to believe you,' Frank explained. 'I have to construct an account based strictly on this.'

He pointed at the brief.

'An account which a jury will believe in the face of some rather persuasive police evidence.'

'Oh come on,' said Hudson. 'Juries are getting pretty wise to the way the filth get their arrests.'

Frank couldn't believe Hudson's naïvety.

'You think so?' said Frank. 'OK, this is my story then.'

He started to retell Hudson's story.

'Ladies and gentlemen of the jury. I'm sitting at home one night in Hampstead minding my own business when a group of detectives from the drug squad arrest me for dealing in a quantity of cocaine which they've brought specially for the occasion. I see you asking yourselves why. Why should they do this to me? Well, what other motive could it be than the time-honoured obsession which repeatedly drives detectives to nick actors with uncles in the Tory government?'

Frank looked him in the eye.

'I should think you'd get five years,' said Frank.

Tim Hudson looked shocked and turned to his solicitor, Nigel Conway, a prematurely balding young man with a floppy bow tie and a large showbiz practice.

'Well,' said Hudson, 'I have to say, your reputation and your fees had led me to expect you might come up with something rather more irresistible than that.'

Frank looked over the top of his glasses at this unbearably vain and shallow young man.

'Really?' he asked quizzically. 'Please don't feel obliged to me. There are many, many barristers in the Temple who would be delighted to charge you even higher fees to run this engaging story past twelve intelligent people!'

Frank wandered over to the glass window dividing the conference room from the gallery, and looked down at the main work area. His mood was further soured by the full-scale row he saw going on beneath him. Lorraine was standing by the clerk's desk, shouting her head off. Michael Khan spotted Frank at the window, and made frantic signs for him to come out.

Tim Hudson stirred from his sulk and stood up.

'I think Nigel and I should have another talk before we go any further.'

'Yes, so do I,' said Frank shortly.

He opened the door for Hudson and Conway, who

walked down the metal staircase with Hudson grumbling so loudly to Conway about Frank's attitude that the two visitors hardly seemed to notice the argument raging around them. When they had gone, Frank tried to work out what the fracas was about. Hugh, for once, was not joining in. Neither was James, or the new pupil, Brendan Hollingsworth. Joanna, Lorraine and Ken Gordon, however, were having a heated disagreement.

'Nor, frankly, do I see why I should be responsible for having to chivvy you lot into paying your rent!' Lorraine shouted. 'If you want the bills left unpaid for months on end, that's fine by me!'

Ken Gordon stabbed his finger in Lorraine's face.

'Money! This is it,' he said. 'This is what really annoys you. Money!'

Lorraine glared at him.

'Nothing annoys me. I'm not annoyed!' she said, unconvincingly.

'You're complaining about being a hired hand, aren't you?' Ken obviously felt he had got to the nub of Lorraine's grievance. 'If you want a rise, why not come out and say so?'

'I'm not asking for a rise and *I* didn't start with the complaints,' said Lorraine, now glaring at Joanna. 'Only don't blame me if the phones get cut off!'

'We're not talking about phone bills, and this is not a personal attack on anybody!' retorted Ken.

Michael Khan picked up a brief from his desk and moved towards the door.

'I have to go to court,' he said. 'This whole matter has to be aired by the entire set, Lorraine.'

'Well, air it then!' snapped Lorraine. 'But I'm not prepared to be the whipping boy for everything that goes wrong. I can't help it if solicitors won't pay fees promptly!'

At this point, Joanna stamped out of the Chambers, slamming the door as hard as she could behind her.

'And I'm not the person to complain to if you don't happen to like the tea bags,' Lorraine continued, looking at Ken.

'We're not talking about tea bags, darling,' said Ken, with a sigh.

'Don't call me darling, you great sexist slob!' said Lorraine.

'Oh, that's great!' Ken sneered. 'A post-feminist critique!'

'Frank, we have to get this sorted out,' muttered Michael as he passed.

Frank nodded at Michael.

'I know,' said Frank, only to find Lorraine staring at him belligerently.

'The trouble is, Frank,' said Lorraine, 'you are running around like headless chickens because you never sorted yourselves out about who you are and what you are.'

'Oh, bollocks to this!' said Ken, going back to his desk in disgust.

Lorraine started gathering up various documents and papers from her desk.

'I'm going to the Clerks' Office now to try and help some of you get your cases into court, because I'm not a lawyer. I'm not paid to stand around arguing. Frankly,' she added, 'that's a luxury I can't afford on these wages.'

Frank watched her departure with dismay.

'God!' said Ken. 'She'll not be happy till she's on a percentage and pulling in fifty grand a year like all the other clerks. And that's not on in this Chambers.'

Frank sighed.

'Is Katherine in?' he asked.

Hugh spoke for the first time. 'In court as usual.'

Brendan, too, had been quietly following the argument with some interest.

'It seems to me what Lorraine's saying is,' said Brendan, in his laconic Liverpudlian accent, 'what really is the difference between Fetter Court and, you know, Pump Court or Grimshaw's or anywhere else? I can't say it's immediately visible to the untrained eye, apart from in Fetter Court, we all sit around in one big draughty room.'

Everyone looked at Frank for a reply, but right now, Frank couldn't be bothered to think of one.

CHAPTER THREE

The Cartwrights' evening meal was a bad-tempered affair. Frank was tired and disagreeable, and spent the time going over every aspect of the morning's arguments, until Annie told him to shut up about the bloody Chambers. Frank suddenly realized that Brendan's youthful, but all too pertinent, cynicism had hurt him more than he would have considered possible.

Sensing the atmosphere, the boys had disappeared upstairs as soon as possible to watch television in the ground-floor drawing-room. The only person who seemed unaffected by Frank's mood was Alethea, who spent the entire meal staring at her pretty thirteen-year-old face in her mother's hand mirror. Now and again, Alethea moaned about how ugly she was; but she still failed to attract the attention of her father.

Annie merely toyed with her food, pushing the bits of osso bucco round and round her plate. Frank leant across the table to empty the wine bottle into her glass, which was still half-full; but Annie placed her hand across the rim of the glass to stop him.

'Are you OK?' he asked, uttering the first comment he had made that evening which did not concern Fetter Court.

'Headache,' muttered Annie.

'Oh I'm sorry, I've droned on. Here, have some wine.'

'I've got a headache,' Annie repeated more loudly.

Annie got up and stacked the dishes.

'Homework, Alethea,' she said to her daughter, who was still gazing at her reflection.

Alethea sloped out of the room, a picture of disaffected adolescence.

'Thank God,' said Frank. 'I thought they no longer gave them homework.'

Annie carried the dishes through from the dining-room into the kitchen and started running the water. Frank filled his glass and reached for the telephone. He dialled a number, then called across to his wife.

'Oh, Annie, I'm sorry. I forgot to say I was going out again.'

'That's all right,' Annie replied grimly, her hands deep in the soap suds.

'Come on, Katherine. Be in for a change,' Frank muttered into the telephone.

'Frank,' Annie warned. 'You'll get ulcers!'

Frank put down the telephone and desperately searched for something else to talk about. But all he could come out with was:

'Bingham wants me to apply for silk.'

'He wants you to be a careerist like he is.'

'Advise me,' asked Frank as he got up and stood beside her.

'You've always said you wouldn't allow them to absorb you or buy you off. Unless you've changed your mind, you're not going to apply for silk.'

Frank watched Annie doing the dishes, then kissed her.

'I was thinking about us today,' he said. 'We're not the greatest marriage in the world, but we've survived. Nineteen years. I feel rather proud of us.'

Something about this speech seemed to irritate Annie.

'You're never going to let me live it down, are you?' she snapped. 'I have one brief affair, which God knows wasn't worth the effort and . . .'

Her voice trailed away. Frank looked at her forlornly.

'I'm talking about us,' he said, 'not you.'

He knocked on the wooden plate-rack over the sink for luck, and started for the door.

'Look, I've got to go,' he said. 'I'll try not to be late.'

'What does it matter?' said Annie, dully. 'I've got a book to read. You've got a key.'

CHAPTER FOUR

Katherine was driving back to London when she heard on the radio that Mr Charnley had disappeared.

A day later, the body of Tracey Charnley was found, hidden deep in a beech wood. She had been the victim of what police described as a vicious sexual attack.

A few days later, the tabloids were full of the fact that Charnley had been found and was assisting police with their enquiries. Curran's newspaper called Charnley the Beast of Brightpool Park. I'd like to see *him* get a fair trial, thought Katherine grimly.

The next day, Ellen Thompson rang Katherine up to say that the Charnleys needed her help.

*

Superintendent Keith Gee was relieved when they found Charnley. For a start, it got the gutter press off his back. In addition, he didn't like the idea of a man like that roaming free. When Charnley was found, he'd been living rough for several days. A couple of policemen spotted him sleeping in a shelter on the sea front. Charnley tried to escape by running into the sea; but it had only reached his waist when the two policemen caught him.

Now, in New Road police station, Charnley sat slumped over a table, watched by Gee and his assistant, Grucock.

'When did she die?' Charnley whispered.

'Why do you ask?' asked Gee.

'How long was she kept alive?'

'You tell me,' said Gee.

'How can I tell you?' Charnley asked pathetically.

There was a pause as Gee walked round the room and leant over Charnley's left shoulder.

'I can understand how one thing leads to another,' said Gee. 'I've got two daughters. I have always enjoyed a cuddle with them, there's nothing more natural. And I can understand it getting out of hand. You wouldn't be the first or the last. Maybe you can tell me when she died if I remind you how she died.'

'Why should I kill her?' Charnley whimpered.

'Because she was threatening to expose you,' suggested Gee.

Charnley dismissed this idea with something between a groan and a laugh. He shook his head, hopelessly. Gee looked at Charnley, and was barely able to keep his revulsion under control.

'Because,' Gee continued, 'of the damage you did her in the last sexual attack.'

'Damage?' asked Charnley.

Gee was starting to get impatient.

'Where did it happen? Not at home? Somewhere on Brightpool Park or elsewhere? You lost control of yourself. There must have been a lot of blood. You were drunk maybe? You couldn't stop the blood. The child was hysterical. You couldn't take her to hospital, could you? But you had to stop her crying somehow.'

'How bad was the damage?' said Charnley.

'If she'd survived,' Gee said, 'she'd have needed a colostomy bag.'

Charnley gasped and gagged.

'You couldn't stop the blood but you could stop her crying, couldn't you?' Gee continued inexorably, taking a roll of sellotape out of his pocket. 'With sellotape, round and round her face.'

Gee wound the tape round and round his clenched fist, and thrust it into Charnley's face.

'Is that when it began to get out of control?' asked Gee. 'It wasn't really Tracey, just a rag doll. Was it? It wasn't real pain. And she was going to bleed to death anyway, so why not find out how it feels when you really let go of everything inside you?'

Charnley groaned and slumped forward on the table, but Gee pulled him upright and produced a large photograph.

'Do you want to see what you did?'

Charnley refused to look.

'You're making a mistake,' muttered Charnley.

'*You* made a mistake,' spat out Gee. 'Why did you wait four days before you reported her missing? Did you think you could wipe this little chicken off the face of the earth and nobody would notice?'

'I thought she'd run away,' said Charnley. 'She'd done it before.'

'Because of your filthy abuse, but why this?'

Charnley still refused to look at the photograph. Gee grabbed him by the hair and held the photograph in front of his face.

'Why this?'

Charnley opened his eyes, saw the photo, and screamed.

CHAPTER FIVE

Frank sat at the head of the conference table in Fetter Court, and tried to restore some order. All the barristers were present, and the meeting was turning out to be both long and acrimonious. Coffee cups and ashtrays littered the table. A large bottle of whisky, full at the start of the evening, was now nearly empty.

Frank was disturbed to notice that the four black barristers in the Chambers – Michael, Tessa, David, Joanna – had started to sit together, and had clearly worked out a united position on several of the issues beforehand.

'If people will stop shouting for a minute,' yelled Frank, banging the table, 'I might be able to hear you!'

Everybody went quiet; and then David Milner repeated the question which had been lost among all the shouting.

'Why are you defending Tim Hudson?'

Frank blinked.

'I'm not sure that I am any more, but why not?'

'Because he's a rich man who wants a left-wing lawyer to do his dirty work for him,' said Joanna.

'This is the point,' said Michael Khan. 'Deep down, what are we? Who are we serving?'

Katherine leapt to Frank's defence.

'Maybe he briefed Frank because he needed a good barrister, you know?'

Frank smiled at her, gratefully.

'Nobody's having a go at Frank,' said David defensively.

'I know when somebody's having a go at somebody,' snapped Katherine, 'and I don't like it. And shame on anyone here who says they're not interested in earning a living!'

David refused to back down.

'The point is: we can't afford to be seen to be operating as just another set of mercenaries.'

Michael Khan nodded, and elaborated the argument.

'We need a very clear policy,' he agreed. 'We can't have a kind of de facto First Eleven that gets political, criminal and trade union work, while the Second Eleven slogs away at the bread and butter: immigration, gay rights, petty crime. Nobody has to take any notice of us.'

Frank put his hands together, and placed his thumbs under his chin as if he were praying.

'You want a co-operative?' he asked.

The black members of the set nodded enthusiastically.

Ken groaned and rolled his eyes.

'Why don't we just go for total anarchy?' he asked.

'Nobody's talking about committees or anarchy – just a commitment to an agreed policy,' explained Michael Khan.

'Which would include all members taking on a share of the less sexy work,' added Tessa.

Murmurs of 'Hear hear' came from around the table.

'Where would the "sexy" work I would thereby be passing up go to?' asked Katherine. 'Would a solicitor whom I've turned down therefore offer his murder case to you, Tessa, or you, Joanna?'

'Eventually, yes,' said Michael.

Katherine lost her temper.

'Oh that's garbage, Michael. "Eventually" they will be offered those cases anyway or not, but it won't have anything to do with anybody else moving aside. It'll be to do with you lot gaining experience and getting your communities to instruct its solicitors to brief black barristers!'

Frank tried to re-establish order.

'OK,' said Frank. 'Say we've got our co-operative. Do we pool our fees and each draw a salary? Purse-sharing?'

'Based on years of service. Graded. Solicitors all do it. It's a perfectly easy thing to organize,' suggested Michael.

Katherine shook her head.

'Nobody's saying it's a perfect solution,' Joanna told her. 'There's a price to pay for progress.'

'Who's being asked to pay it?' asked Ken, angrily. 'That's what I want to know!'

'We are, at the moment,' said David Milner.

The room was silent as everybody considered their various positions. James now spoke up.

'Going back to something Michael said, I think the entire Chambers lacks a bit of credibility.'

Frank looked hard at James, and knew what was going to come next.

'I think,' said James, 'we'd all benefit if Frank took silk.'

The room went silent.

'It isn't being absorbed or bought off,' James continued. 'It's saying the left should have its share of senior counsel.'

Katherine butted in.

'James, I understand what you're saying,' she said. 'But I've listened to this for fifteen years. Taking silk is joining the establishment. Full stop.'

All eyes turned to Frank.

'I'm not in principle against any of us applying for silk,'

he said, 'but for me it's a personal decision I made years ago, which I see no reason to change.'

There seemed to be general approval for Frank's statement; but James found an unlikely ally in Tessa.

'I think you should,' she said. 'If I thought I'd get it, I'd apply.'

Joanna, David and Michael all looked at her, totally taken aback.

'Ridiculous,' said Brendan.

'No, it's not ridiculous,' said Tessa. 'You don't know the difference it would mean to me and what I could do with my practice.'

'No, *Frank's* ridiculous,' Brendan replied.

Frank looked at Brendan, amazed.

'You're going on as if this was 1968, Frank,' said Brendan, with evident lack of respect for Frank's seniority. 'It isn't radical politics any more, it's more important than that. The politics of gesture are buried. The class war is now being waged increasingly in the courts. That's what we've been talking about all night, I thought. If that's where the war is, let's get serious about it. There's nothing sell-out about strapping on the best armour if you're in a fight. That presupposes it's some kind of self-indulgent personal crusade. It isn't. The basic rights of a whole class are being stripped off us by the most reactionary government for fifty years and there's no time for pussy-footing about. If Frank Cartwright QC can speak louder in the fight than Frank Cartwright can, then get your form and fill it in. The world's moved on.'

They all sat, stunned by the passion of Brendan's speech.

'Well, that's what I think,' he added, as an apologetic coda.

The silence was broken by a knock on the door. Lorraine poked her head round, asking whether they were ready for her.

'Yes,' said Frank. 'Sorry about this, Lorraine.'

'That's all right,' she said.

Lorraine shut the door and stood facing the assembled barristers.

'I asked to be allowed to talk to you. I won't mince words. I joined Fetter Court for the same reasons as everybody else: because I believed in it and I was led to believe I would be treated as somebody who had a share in what we were trying to do. But I find that there are basically two workers here – me and Hugh – and eleven bosses. And there have been times when, I have to say it, you have simply exploited us. So I'm going to make your choice very simple for you. You must either devise a means of paying me which reflects the relationship I thought you wanted, or find someone else to employ. I'll leave you to it.'

She left the room to stunned silence. Ken finally broke the hush.

'Why don't we break a habit of a lifetime, and actually make a decision?' he suggested.

'OK. A vote. Do we offer her more money?' Frank put Lorraine's ultimatum to the gathering. 'In favour?'

He raised his hand and looked round the room. He counted votes for: Katherine's, Ken's, James's.

'Against?'

Michael, David, Joanna, Tessa and Alison all raised their hands. Those opposed to giving Lorraine any more money had won the day.

'Well, that's a crying shame,' said Katherine, as the meeting broke up, leaving Frank and Katherine on their own.

Frank poured himself the final drop of whisky and looked at Katherine.

'Would you leave if we became a co-operative?' he asked.

'Yes,' said Katherine, 'because it wouldn't be a co-operative. It would be me, you, Bingham and Ken Gordon subsidizing the others. That's a recipe for disaster.'

Frank groaned. 'I'm going home.'

Another thought struck him, as he turned off the lights in the conference room.

'Actually, I'm not. I have to go and tell Lorraine. Shit, shit, shit.'

Katherine did go home to read through the brief that she had been sent by Ellen; the Charnley case. She forgot her worries about Fetter Court as she read through the evidence against Charnley with mounting revulsion. The details set down in black and white were so disgusting that she felt contaminated herself. She was having a hot bath when the phone rang. It was Ellen, wanting to know if Katherine would take the case.

Standing by the phone, dripping wet with a towel wrapped round her, Katherine expressed her reservations.

'Just come up and have a look round,' urged Ellen.

'Give me time to think about it,' said Katherine, after a long pause.

CHAPTER SIX

So, for the second time in as many months, Katherine returned to her roots. Ellen took Katherine on a less than scenic walking tour of the Brightpool Estate. The Charnleys' flat had been boarded up; but Ellen had it specially opened, so that Katherine could have a look at the living conditions inside. Katherine emerged from the flat, holding a handkerchief to her face, and feeling extremely ill. Ellen immediately had the door boarded up again.

Katherine and Ellen walked away across the wasteland. Katherine found that she needed Ellen to support her by the arm.

'Ellen, you know me,' said Katherine, slowly. 'You know the sort of work I do. I don't spend my time doing dry-boned civil law cases, or traditional female work like custody cases or whatever. I'm in there doing heavy crime and politics. Murders, rapes, robberies, bombings, blackmail, treachery, violence. And that's before you get out of the robing room. You also know that I live alone.'

Katherine closed her eyes, trying to marshal her thoughts. She opened her eyes again.

'What I'm saying is: there's only so much of this sort of

thing you can do. Only so much of yourself you can use up when you . . . when there's not much in your life to renew you.'

There was a long pause.

'Yeah, well,' said Ellen, disappointed. 'Thanks for coming up.'

'Where's the wife?' asked Katherine.

'Annette? In a safe house with a journalist called Curran,' answered Ellen. 'She's given Curran's rag the exclusive story of My Life with The Beast of Brightpool Park.'

'Oh, Christ!' exclaimed Katherine. She was beginning to feel haunted by Clive Curran.

'Know him?' asked Ellen.

'Yeah. And how.' Katherine nodded grimly. 'Do you have access to her?'

'If we must, but he's not keen on the process of justice screwing up his exclusive. The two boys are in care. She'll have a hard job getting them back.'

'Does she know that?'

Ellen sighed and looked at Katherine.

'God, Katherine, it's hard to figure out what she knows. She's a mess really.'

The women continued walking. Katherine looked around at the dismal squalor of the council estate.

'I don't know. I don't think I can help you,' she said slowly.

'I don't think he killed her.'

Katherine was surprised at the conviction in Ellen's voice.

'Why?'

'How did he get the girl to the place where she finally died? He has no transport. They say he must have taken her there by public transport and carried out the final sexual attack there in anger because she was threatening to expose him, but there's not a hint of a witness to the journey. And I don't think he's the sort of man who would do . . . what was done.'

Katherine thought for a moment.

'You think briefing a woman will help Charnley's case?'

'I think it'll help *me*,' said Ellen.

'I expect there are people round here who don't think you should touch this case,' said Katherine, sympathetically.

'There aren't that many people round here who'll even talk to me.'

'Ever done a case like this before?' enquired Katherine.

'No.'

'You'll be OK, don't worry. Just don't spend too much time looking at the post-mortem stuff. OK?'

Katherine put her arm round Ellen's shoulders.

'How is he, mentally?' asked Katherine, as they walked on.

'Falling apart at the seams. He's in Risley. He's also been attacked by other prisoners twice. One lot beat his head in and another lot tried to sit him on a hotplate.'

'And he's tried to kill himself?'

'Yes and I think he'll try again.'

'And despite that and despite the fact that he's confessed, you think he's innocent?'

'He's not a monster. I think he's an ordinary man in trouble with the law.'

Katherine thought about what Ellen had told her, stopped walking and looked her in the eye.

'What made him confess?'

'I don't know,' Ellen said.

'Has he ever tried to claim the cops beat it out of him?'

'No.'

'Is the other stuff true, Ellen? Was he raping her?'

'I don't know.'

Katherine looked once more at the misery of her friend, and made a decision.

'Let's go and ask him, shall we?' suggested Katherine.

*

Charnley was sitting at a table in the middle of the interview room. He made no acknowledgement of Katherine and Ellen's arrival. An unlit hand-rolled cigarette hung from the corner of his mouth. He wore a grubby grey shirt which had once been white, and baggy navy trousers.

'David,' said Ellen, 'this is Katherine Hughes. She's going to defend you.'

Katherine smiled tentatively at Charnley.

'Hello,' she said softly. Charnley nodded slowly in acknowledgement but did not lift his eyes from the table. The two women sat down opposite him.

'We're told you've taken no food today, David,' said Katherine.

He did not reply, but turned to Ellen.

'Ask them for a match, please.'

Katherine produced a lighter from her coat pocket and leant forward to light his cigarette. He held it with an unsteady hand.

'Have there been any more attacks on you?' Katherine asked.

Charnley shook his head, and took a deep drag on the cigarette.

'What about the screws? Are they OK with you?'

Charnley nodded.

'David,' said Katherine, 'whatever else you may have done to Tracey and we are going to have to talk about all of it, you didn't kill her. Despite what you confessed to.'

David nodded his head, once.

'Hang on to that, then. You're not guilty of what you're charged with. That's all that really matters.'

Charnley made no further acknowledgement. He stubbed out his part-smoked cigarette and put it back in his shirt pocket.

Katherine continued.

'David, what they say was your motive, that you'd been sexually abusing her, what about that?'

Still there was no response.

'David, I have to ask you. How is it that there's clear forensic evidence of long-term sexual activity?'

Charnley seemed to crumple up in front of them. Cries of animal pain came from his sobbing body as he slumped to the floor. He crawled into a corner, and cowered there, hiding his face in his hands.

*

Afterwards, they got into Ellen's car and sat there. It was Katherine who finally broke the silence.

'Ellen, this fellow's never going to get to court. I've seen this before. He wants to die. Jesus Christ, he should die. She was only a little girl. He deserves to die, the shit. I'd like to kill him myself.'

Ellen did not reply.

'Listen, if he won't eat he'll very quickly go beyond the point at which we can help him. Get the shrinks back to him. I think he should have something drastic. Come on, get us out of here. I want to go home.'

CHAPTER SEVEN

'Oh, please! I'll sit quietly!' whined Alethea.

'He's horrible, anyway. He's a fat bore,' Frank said, trying to ignore his daughter as he gathered up his bits and pieces before setting off to the Chambers.

'Actually, he's fantastic,' said Alethea, pouting. She had been pestering Frank for days, wanting to go with him to Fetter Court and catch a glimpse of Tim Hudson.

Frank grunted in such a way as to imply that she should get some other fantasies.

'He's a true star! And he isn't fat!' argued Alethea. 'I wouldn't be in the way. I could stay in Lorraine's bit of the office.'

'Lorraine's left,' replied Frank.

'Because you're so horrible to her, I expect,' she said, putting her arms round her father's neck and kissing him.

'I can come then, can't I?' she crooned into his ear.

Impressed by such transparent wiliness on the part of his first-born, Frank knew there was only one thing he could do. He poked his head into the dining-room, where Annie was lying down on the sofa.

'Alethea is coming with me to ogle Tim Hudson,' Frank said. 'Is that all right?'

Annie sighed and pulled the quilt up under her arms.

'I need her to look after the boys,' she said.

'No! Why should I?' Alethea said, stamping her foot.

Suddenly, the phone rang. Frank looked at Annie with concern, as the noise made her pull the quilt up over her head and bury her face in the cushions as the phone rang. He'd never seen her looking so dreadful. She obviously needed stronger painkillers.

'Alethea, listen,' said Frank. 'Behave. I'll make it up to you. I'll get a signed photo.'

'I'm sick of her,' Alethea moaned.

Annie's voice emerged from the cushions.

'Oh, for God's sake go,' said Annie.

'No, listen,' said Frank, trying to assert his authority. 'Let me handle this . . .'

But Alethea had already run out of the room, to get ready. Frank picked up the telephone in the dining-room.

'Yes? Yes, Hugh, I'm on my way. We said 5.30. You *told* me 5.30. Oh, shit!'

He slammed the phone down.

'Why do you always have to make so much noise!' groaned Annie.

*

Frank and Alethea dashed up the stairs to Fetter Court, two at a time. The room was busy with people quietly working. Frank parked Alethea at the clerks' tables and introduced her to the new junior clerk.

'Alethea, this is Moira. Moira, Alethea. Where are they?'

Hugh pointed upstairs to the gallery.

'Have they had some coffee?' Frank asked Moira.

He saw Moira flush with guilt, and swore impatiently.

Ken Gordon waddled up to Frank.

'Frank, I want a word with you,' he said.

'I'm afraid it'll have to wait,' said Frank.

'Frank,' said Ken, carrying on regardless, in a voice loud enough for Hugh to hear. 'Tell me, have you ever tried finishing a case in Snaresbrook at 12.30 and starting another one in Aylesbury Crown Court at two?'

Frank shook his head and looked across at Hugh, who was studiously ignoring Ken's outburst.

'Does our clerk,' continued Ken with heavy irony, 'know something I don't about British Rail, or does he think we all possess bloody helicopters?'

Ken turned on his heel; but before Frank could escape, James also joined them, a brief in his hand.

'Moira, what's this?' he asked.

'It's your brief for tomorrow. It's just arrived.'

'But I'm not in court tomorrow,' he said.

'OK,' said Hugh. 'It's a cock-up, James. I'm ready to admit it.'

'It's my fault,' piped up Moira.

'No, it's my fault,' explained Hugh. 'Well, it's her fault in a sense. It came over the phone and I scribbled it on a piece of paper and . . .'

The phone started ringing. As no one bothered to answer it, Alethea leant across the desk and picked it up.

'I didn't realize Moira hadn't put it in the diary,' continued Hugh, 'and it just got forgotten about.'

'Who?' said Alethea into the phone. 'You want Mr Cartwright?'

Frank looked across at his daughter, and shook his head.

'Sorry,' said Alethea. 'He's tied up.'

'I see,' sighed James, resigning himself to the inevitable. 'And what is it?'

'Well it's incompetence,' said Hugh, shamefaced. 'I know that.'

James lost his temper and shouted at Hugh.

'I mean the case! I'm talking about the case I'm apparently doing tomorrow! What is it?'

Moira burst into tears.

'Look, sorry,' said Frank. 'We'll talk about this later.'

As he ran up to the gallery, Frank looked down at his daughter, who seemed to be making a good job of answering the phone. God, these Chambers miss Lorraine, he thought.

'I'm afraid he's unavailable at the moment,' said Alethea, waving to her father. 'He's in a meeting.'

*

Frank had not been in the meeting for long, when he heard the screaming. At first, he tried to ignore it. In any case, he was trying to take in what Tim Hudson had just told him.

'You're now telling me the entire cast used illegal substances?'

Frank stood looking at his client with mounting disbelief, as Alethea burst in. To Frank's amazement, she ignored Tim Hudson and ran sobbing to him. Hugh and James were close behind her.

'Frank, you'd better come,' said James, who looked white-faced.

'Is it a wrap?' asked Tim, with a grin.

'Oh, er . . . yes,' said Frank. 'Excuse me.'

Outside, Frank looked down from the gallery and saw everyone looking up at him. He turned on Hugh angrily.

'What's wrong now?' asked Frank, trying to comfort his sobbing daughter. 'What on earth is happening to these Chambers?'

Hugh looked at James, who took a step towards Frank.

'Frank,' said James, putting an arm on his. 'It's not the Chambers.'

*

Frank remembered only fragments of the next few hours. He remembered being too numb to say or think anything, as James drove him and Alethea through the rush hour to the Whittington Hospital. He remembered cradling Alethea in his arms, as she sobbed great gulps of tears. He remembered his two boys, John and Peter, holding hands with a neighbour outside the intensive care unit. They too had been crying.

'Look after your brothers,' Frank told Alethea.

A sister took him into the glass booth where Annie was lying inert, linked up to a machine. A woman doctor spoke to Frank. Most of all, he remembered feeling completely helpless, just sitting on the edge of Annie's bed and stroking her hand.

*

Katherine arrived at the hospital within minutes of Lorraine. There was no sign of Frank.

'He's still in intensive care with Annie,' said James.

James and a neighbour of Frank and Annie's were doing their best to comfort the children; but all three of the Cartwrights went to Katherine, as soon as she arrived and were sobbing their hearts out.

'Look,' said Katherine to James, 'why don't you run Mrs Morris home? Lorraine and I can look after the kids.'

James did as he was told. Katherine was surprised by how shocked he seemed to be; she'd always thought of him as being cold. She was even more surprised when James returned to the hospital, later in the night.

'I couldn't sleep,' he said, rocking backwards and forwards as he sat with them, waiting for news.

John and Peter slept fitfully on either side of Lorraine. Alethea cried herself to sleep, draped over Katherine. Eventually, a nurse came into the day-room and sat down next to Lorraine.

'Should we take them home?' Lorraine asked quietly.

The nurse nodded agreement. Katherine and Lorraine gathered up the children, and left James to maintain the vigil.

*

Much later that night, there were still no signs of life in Annie. A woman doctor suggested that Frank come outside. Frank found James in the day-room. James told him something about Katherine and Lorraine and the kids, but Frank couldn't take it in. The doctor came and sat with them.

'With this kind of massive brain haemorrhage there's really not much doubt,' she said. 'Only the ventilator is keeping her going. I'm really terribly sorry. Perhaps you should go and attempt some sleep. Come back later.'

She looked to James to take Frank home. Frank nodded.

'I see. Thank you,' said Frank, allowing James to pull him to his feet.

For the last few hours, one thought had been going through and through Frank's head. He knew he had to voice it now.

'Would it have made any difference,' he said, 'if I'd been there when she collapsed?'

The doctor looked at him reassuringly.

'None whatever,' she said. 'Your boys were very sensible. They alerted your neighbour straight away.'

'I see,' said Frank. 'Thank you.'

Dawn was breaking. Birds were starting to sing. The streets were eerily empty of traffic as James drove Frank home. James pulled up outside the house.

'Want me to come in?' asked James.

Frank shook his head.

'Got a key?' asked James.

Frank nodded and got out of the car. He suddenly remembered to thank James, who rolled down the window and asked him if he was in court. Frank had no idea.

'Don't worry,' said James. 'I'll sort everything out. Just get some sleep.'

CHAPTER EIGHT

It was almost a relief for Katherine to return north to the Charnley case. Frank's grief was so overwhelming that Katherine could hardly bear to speak to him. He never came out of his study, and he looked as if he'd hardly slept since the night of Annie's collapse. Katherine had to put such a bold face on everything, organizing the children and so on, that she hadn't had time to grieve herself. It was only now, as she drove north, that she allowed herself the luxury of weeping for her dear, dead friend.

At first, Katherine did not think that the ECT treatment had had any effect on Mr Charnley. He was as reticent as before, slumped opposite Ellen and Katherine, with a cigarette between his lips. Katherine leant over to light it for him. After a few sucks on the cigarette, though, he began to speak.

'All I've had was physical strength,' he said, slowly and deliberately. 'I've worked my arse off on farms, in factories, wherever there was labour wanted. I worked on the roads, on the M62, M63, M56. When they didn't want any more roads, I moved on. Pickin' spuds. Smashin' up batteries for the lead in them. Three years carrying carcasses in an abattoir. Then finish, knackered. Forty-nine years old, finished.'

'What's this got to do with Tracey?' asked Katherine.

Charnley stared hard at Katherine and spoke in a matter-of-fact-voice.

'You have to sell what people want to buy. That is a law of life, Katherine, a law of life.'

*

Ellen's car pulled up outside a small, detached house.

'This is it,' said Ellen.

'Do you really think she'll testify on his behalf?' asked Katherine.

'It's worth a try,' said Ellen.

'Who would think,' said Katherine, watching some schoolgirls walk past, 'that a man would put his own daughter on the streets?'

'Stepdaughter,' said Ellen.

'Whatever,' said Katherine, shaking her head. 'The man's an animal.'

'Talking of animals . . .' said Ellen.

'Good day, ladies,' said Clive Curran, who had evidently been watching from the window and had come out to greet them.

'Where's Mrs Charnley?' asked Ellen.

'Upstairs,' said Curran, 'with a couple of our best minders. A right waste of space, she is. Sits all day in front of the telly, like Nelly the Elephant. What do you want?'

A horrible thought seemed to strike him.

'Charnley hasn't topped himself, has he?' he asked.

'Ruin your investment, would it?' asked Katherine. 'No, he hasn't topped himself.'

'See you in a moment,' said Ellen to Katherine, and walked inside the house.

'You don't want to talk to her?' Curran asked Katherine.

'Barristers aren't allowed to talk to potential witnesses,' said Katherine.

'Witness?' said Curran, turning to face the house. 'Listen, I've got a right to be in on this if it affects the case.'

'You have nothing of the sort,' said Katherine.

Curran turned to Katherine. 'I've been good to you . . .'

'How do you mean?' said Katherine, amazed at his audacity.

'I mean, letting your friend see Mrs Charnley.'

'You only did it because otherwise she'd have got a court order.'

'Well . . .' said Curran, evasively. 'What I'm saying is . . . if there was any chance of a copy of the post-mortem photos, you know, pics of Tracey after . . . you'd be astonished at how grateful I could be.'

'Like what?' asked Katherine.

'I don't know,' said Curran. 'What are you in it for? What is it you really want, Katherine? Tell me what you'd like.'

'Well, Clive, what I'd really like,' said Katherine slowly, 'is to hang your balls around your neck.'

Curran looked at her with an expression of deep shock.

'Here,' he said. 'Are you a dyke?'

Any further conversation was halted by the return of Ellen.

'That woman needs help,' Ellen accused Curran.

Curran smiled back at her.

'I've got certificates saying there's nothing wrong with her mentally,' he retorted. 'She needs a roof over her head and food in her mouth. She needs thirty grand, darling. Are you going to give it to her, or am I?'

'Provided her husband is found guilty of murdering her daughter,' said Ellen. 'If not she gets nothing, right?'

Curran looked at Ellen in injured amazement.

'You mean she should get paid either way – like you two?'

Katherine suppressed a smile, as she watched Ellen make a final appeal to Curran's humanity. 'Why don't you arrange for her to visit the kids?'

Curran shrugged his shoulders.

'I've offered,' he said, 'but they won't allow a photographer.'

As they drove away, Ellen told Katherine about Annette's pitiful state.

'She's not all there,' said Ellen. 'Just sits. Can't even talk, or doesn't want to.'

'Do you think she knew what was going on?'

'If she did, she's not admitting it now,' said Ellen. 'Even to herself. I dunno. I don't think we should put her in the box.'

Katherine nodded grimly.

'OK,' said Katherine. 'In that case, Charnley is going to have to do it all alone.'

*

James decided the time had come to try and shake Frank out of his depression. Thank goodness, Frank's absence had meant that the arguments over democracy, co-operatives and the like had rather gone into abeyance; but, with Katherine out of town so much, the whole job of leading the Chambers fell on James's shoulders. Following Lorraine's departure, the clerks of the Chambers were in disarray; and James spent hours, well into the night, trying to make sense of the Chambers' accounts.

The following evening, James went round to Frank's house. The door was opened by Alethea, who seemed to have grown up a lot over the past few weeks. She brightened at the sight of James and took his hand in hers as they walked up the hall. She nodded upstairs in the direction of Frank's study.

'He never seems to come out of there these days,' she remarked, before returning to her homework.

Frank was sitting at his desk, gazing into space, and hardly noticed James's arrival. James brought a brief out of his raincoat pocket, waved it in front of Frank's face and chucked it down on his desk.

Frank stared at the brief as if he had never seen one before.

'Oh yes,' he murmured vaguely.

'Hudson's solicitor is getting rather desperate. Word around the Bailey is that Cartwright's retired,' said James, deciding that the time was past for mincing words. 'Burnt-out case.'

Frank tossed the brief aside and sank back into his misery. James put a hand into his other pocket and brought out an extremely good bottle of Beaune. For the first time since Annie's death, Frank's face cheered up for a moment.

'Ah!' he said in appreciation, and went downstairs to fetch a couple of glasses and a corkscrew.

When Frank returned, James opened the bottle while Frank put some Mozart on the record player. The two men sat down and listened to a sublime rendering of the clarinet concerto. The record came to an end and it was time for James to leave. He patted Frank sympathetically on the shoulder.

'I know we can never be close friends, personally, politically, in the way for instance that you and Katherine are,' said James, apologetically.

Frank ran his hand through his greying hair and smiled wanly at James.

'You and Gloria have my undying gratitude and friendship,' said Frank. 'The things you've done for the kids and . . .'

As Frank broke off, James tried to cover his own embarrassment.

'Yes I know, I know. I know all that,' said James.

Frank sat in silence.

'I realize that I'm about to be presumptuous,' said James hesitantly, 'but I simply wanted to talk to you as a colleague and admirer. When you come back to Fetter Court, and I hope it will be soon, don't allow yourself to be sidetracked by esoteric disputes about democracy. You should go for the big issues and fix your mind on the important questions. And you should take silk.'

There was a pause.

'Thank you, James,' said Frank.

James waited for more but Frank remained silent. James took his cue and was turning to go when Frank handed him the brief.

'You know Hudson, don't you?'

'Yes, vaguely but . . .'

'Could you possibly manage it?' Frank pleaded.

'Yes, of course, Frank.' James took the brief and stuffed it back into his pocket.

As he reached the door, James turned and saw Frank still brooding motionless at his desk.

'I won't forget this, James,' said Frank.

James walked down the stairs and let himself out of the quiet house, filled with despair.

CHAPTER NINE

Tim Hudson smiled and waved cheerily to press, photographers and fans as he entered the Old Bailey. James Bingham smiled as well, although he couldn't help wishing that Hudson would treat it more seriously.

Inside, however, James noticed that Hudson was sweating and shaking.

'Are you all right?' asked James.

'Sure,' said Hudson, unsteadily. 'First-night nerves, I expect.'

'Look,' said James, 'I'm going upstairs to have a word with prosecuting counsel and I'll see you again before we go in.'

'I'm sure that justice will be done,' Tim muttered nervously.

'Well, if so, we can always appeal,' laughed James.

Hudson winced.

'Only a joke, Tim,' James added quickly.

James walked through the busy corridors and up to the men's Robing Room on the fourth floor. He looked round and saw Roger Arbish, a large and usually amiable man, arranging his gown.

'Roger, I'm glad I've bumped into you,' he said.

'James!' said Arbish jovially, as if their meeting was the greatest coincidence. 'What can I do for you?'

'We're against each other this morning.'

'Ah, yes,' mused Arbish, taking his wig out of its tin box. 'Mister Tim Hudson. He's a naughty man.'

'Not at all,' said James. 'It's all a ghastly mistake.'

'You astound me,' said Arbish ironically, staring at himself in the mirror, and patting his wig into place.

James smiled at his adversary and rehearsed his argument.

'Let me tell you the facts. I was given the coke by a dressing-room visitor, an American film star.'

Arbish looked remarkably unimpressed.

'Good heavens!' he said.

'It was a gift for the cast of the play to share at a party,' continued James. 'No question of me dealing in the stuff at all. A very common practice in the business. In fact, I have a theatrical knight to tell the jury all about this side of backstage life.'

'Will the jury have to wear costume?' asked Arbish, hitching up his gown and enjoying the game.

'I don't need to make money this way. I'm a very successful actor. I'm of good character, so good that I've got as a character witness a member of the privy council.'

'Well,' said Arbish with a twinkle, 'I know at least four members of the privy council who should be in prison themselves. What are you suggesting, James?'

'I'll plead possession with very heavy mitigation. The public gallery will be looking at a *Who's Who?* of the theatre and politics.'

'Ah. The full Monty, eh?'

'Frankly, I don't think the jury's going to believe I'm a dealer. I think you should think again about that charge. The police, God bless them, have made an honest mistake.'

Arbish did not wait long to make his response.

'I'm afraid not, James. Let's stand it up in front of a jury, shall we?'

*

Much to James's surprise and horror, Tim Hudson proved to be a terrible witness. He stood in the witness box with sweat pouring off him, stammering like an amateur player.

'He put it on the table, yes. No, no. Actually a tobacco tin.'

'We've understood that,' James said patiently. 'What I'm trying to . . .'

'Get me to say,' interjected Hudson. 'Right, OK.'

James could not believe this performance.

'No, not get you to say. I'm not trying to get you to say anything.'

James glanced at Arbish smiling quietly to himself. He was loving every moment of this.

'I'm trying,' said James, 'to get you to convey to the court what exactly became of the tobacco tin.'

Hudson looked beseechingly at the jury.

'The tobacco tin had nothing to do with me,' he said.

The judge intervened.

'Your counsel is doing his best to assist you, Mr Hudson. If you could listen to his questions a little more carefully . . .'

'I'm frightfully sorry,' apologized Tim.

'That's all right,' continued James. 'I'm grateful to your honour. It's my fault. I'm not making myself clear. Was the cocaine in the tobacco tin when you first saw it produced?'

There was a very long pause. James watched Hudson in disbelief. Another very, very long pause. The whole court looked on in amazement as the heart-throb actor leant forward in the witness box, and finally spoke.

'I'm sorry,' he said. 'I've completely gone. No, sorry, it's gone.'

James shot another anxious glance at Arbish, who by this time was shaking with suppressed hilarity.

*

James sat with Tim Hudson in the Old Bailey canteen, waiting for the jury to come back with their verdict. Both were feeling despondent, although Hudson had brightened up momentarily when one of the canteen ladies had asked for his autograph.

'The bloody ironic thing is,' said Hudson, 'I really was telling the truth.'

James shot him a quick look. For the first time he actually believed Hudson's story.

'Well,' said James, unconvincingly, 'let's wait and see. Juries are strange creatures.'

'If you've kept me out of prison, James, I'll do anything for you.'

'Well, actually,' said James with a laugh, 'there might be something.'

The tannoy sounded.

'Defendant and counsel in the case of Timothy Hudson, please.'

Tim groaned as they stood up.

'Oh, God, I'm on,' he said.

*

Frank couldn't help smiling as he saw Alethea dressed up for her birthday lunch date with James. James's wife, Gloria, had bought her the outfit, an outfit which made Frank uncomfortably aware that his child was now an attractive teenager. Alethea was wearing a very short, trendy skirt over a pair of leggings, and had tied her hair up on top of her head with a giant bow. Frank thought she looked terrific, but nervous.

'You look great,' he complimented her.

'You think so?' she asked, uncertainly.

The doorbell rang. Alethea turned from the mirror and went to open the front door.

'Alethea Cartwright?' said a vaguely familiar voice, from behind the largest bouquet of flowers she had ever seen.

Alethea just gawped.

'Yes,' she stammered.

'I hope you don't mind,' said Tim Hudson, handing Alethea the bouquet. 'James said I could join you for lunch. Is that all right?'

Frank grinned, as his daughter tried to regain her composure.

'Yes, that'll be all right,' she said, as if she went out every day with a star of stage and screen.

The pair walked down the steps to James's car. Frank looked anxiously out of the doorway until James approached him.

'Well, cheer up, Frank,' he called out.

'Cheer up?' Frank said gruffly. 'You're taking my daughter to lunch with a drug abuser.'

'He got off, didn't he?'

'The jury must have been fully paid-up members of his fan club is all I can say.'

'No,' said James amiably, 'they just thought anybody who would go to the trouble of inventing a story as bad as that would have learnt his lines better.'

'I don't want him touching her,' Frank reminded his friend. 'You sit in the middle, right?'

James grinned.

'OK.'

Frank smiled back.

'Thanks,' he said, and shut the door.

Frank walked along the corridor and downstairs to the basement. He felt the place was filling with silence again, and he didn't like it. He picked up the kettle to make a cup of coffee, then thought better of it. He went over to the telephone and dialled.

*

Frank perched on the end of Katherine's bed, watching her pack her suitcase for the north of England.

'How's your man?' he asked.

'Half crackers,' said Katherine, tossing a couple of packets of black, lacy tights on top of her neatly folded clothes. They helped to relieve the monotony of courtroom wear.

'And how are you?' Frank looked at her anxiously.

'Panicking,' Katherine admitted.

'You can never tell with juries,' said Frank, thinking of the astounding Hudson verdict.

Katherine looked at Frank. He seemed much less miserable all of a sudden, much more able to talk.

'How are you?' she asked. 'I can't imagine it.'

'Grief is like chronic pain,' said Frank, trying to think of the right words. 'It's very isolating. Still about ten per cent of the time I'm hallucinating. But what's really knocked me sideways is the guilt.'

Katherine looked at Frank.

'About what?'

'About everything, everything. Being alive. My marriage. My job. It's a revelation, I can tell you. You go through life thinking you're rational. You're not. You think you're emotionally placid. You're not. In fact I don't know what I am. I'm not convinced I know who this "I" is who takes over every sentence, every thought, every feeling. Here I am, this must be me. I've got my clothes on.'

He broke off.

217

'Sorry,' he said. 'It's very embarrassing.'

Katherine closed her case and sat next to Frank on the bed.

'The other thing about grief,' he said, 'is that it keeps delivering you into situations where you find your friends standing there looking sympathetic because you're talking incomprehensible crap.'

They both laughed.

'Actually I don't really want lunch,' said Frank. 'I want to say something to you. Katherine, the grief that has had me by the throat, and still has, is rooted not in a love that was cut down but in that guilt I've nursed for ten years about sacrificing my marriage and my family to my job, to my career.'

Katherine shook her head.

'So I'm saying to you: don't do it,' said Frank. 'Don't let yourself be crucified by Brightpool Park or anything else. It isn't worth it.'

'You're ready for work again.' Katherine squeezed her friend affectionately.

'Yes. Soon,' Frank agreed.

'And ready for silk too?' said Katherine.

'What would you say?' asked Frank.

'I'd say if that's what you want you should do it.'

'That's what I think.'

'Then you should do it,' Katherine said, decisively. 'I have to go. Give me a lift, I have a train to catch. The circus is moving town.'

CHAPTER TEN

Partly thanks to Clive Curran, the Charnley trial had become a national sensation; so Katherine was not at all surprised that she could sit in the cell below the court and still hear the lynch-mob outside the court-house. To her shame, she shared some of their feelings.

She had not thought that she could ever pity Charnley, but now she did. He looked old and broken, with his head in his hands, so riddled with shame that he could not bear to look at the two women. Katherine wondered whether he would survive the strain of the trial. Nevertheless, she had to get him to speak.

'Say it,' Katherine ordered.

There was a long pause and eventually Charnley looked up and whispered hoarsely.

'Not guilty.'

Katherine shook her head. He sounded as if he was admitting the crime, not denying it.

'I want you to say it as if you meant it,' she lectured him sternly. 'Say sorry to spoil the party, but cop this: Not guilty!'

*

When Charnley did plead not guilty, he did so in a strange strangled shout which confirmed to everyone present that he was either crazy, or soon would be. He stood in the dock, seemingly unaware of the proceedings going on around him.

The Victorian, panelled courtroom was packed. There was no elbow-room for anyone in the public and press galleries; and the ushers had turned scores of people away.

Katherine had made sure that the jury was predominantly working-class men by challenging the few elderly women and obviously affluent people that there had been. She needed a jury that would understand Charnley's plight, as far as such a thing was possible.

Katherine watched with dismay as Charnley closed his eyes during the testimony of Saville, the elderly forest ranger who had found Tracey's mutilated body. The usher had to bring the old man a glass of water to steady his nerves and Katherine leant round to speak to Ellen, who was sitting in the row behind her with her junior counsel.

'I'm going to cross-examine him,' she whispered.

'Why?' asked Ellen.

'I just want the jury to see me being nice to somebody.'

The judge called on Katherine.

'Miss Hughes?'

Katherine stood and started her cross-examination.

'Mr Saville, we've all been distressed by your description. It's easy for those of us who are here in a professional capacity to forget what being a witness can really mean,' she said gently.

Saville acknowledged her tribute.

'I want to clarify one small point,' she continued. 'Did you stumble across this croft or did you know its location already in what is, by your evidence, a very dense part of the forest?'

'No, I knew it well. I'd used it many times for shelter.'

'It can't be seen by chance, from any road or footpath, can it?'

'Oh no.'

'Thank you again, Mr Saville. No further questions, your honour.'

*

That night when she came down to dinner in her hotel, Katherine was nauseated by the behaviour of the journalists in the dining-room. They really are no better than reptiles, or – more appropriately on this occasion – vultures, thought Katherine, as she sat down at a corner table.

It was not until she had ordered her food that she noticed another solitary eater. It was Dan Schumacher, the TV journalist who had done the item she'd seen about conditions on the Brightpool Park estate. Katherine noticed with surprise that he had a large book on US intervention in Latin American politics propped up on the table. She watched him shut the book in irritation, unable to concentrate because of all the noise.

As Schumacher passed the journalists' table, on his way out, one of them shouted out to him.

'You'll have to excuse us, Daniel! It's the conditions we're forced to live in!'

As they all screamed with laughter, Katherine gave Dan a sympathetic look and gestured to him to join her. She poured him out a glass of wine as he drew up a chair opposite.

'You hear the news?' asked Schumacher.

Katherine shook her head.

'No.'

'Another girl went missing. She's been killed.'

'More lurid headlines for you lot,' Katherine observed.

'No, she ruined the story by being a prostitute. Who

cares about whores? Still we'll make something out of it. She dressed young for guys who are into schoolgirls. There's our story.'

Katherine stared at him in disgust.

'Hey, I'm joking!' said Dan.

Katherine thought about what he said and looked at him shrewdly.

'Are the police making any connection between the two?' she asked.

Dan held up his glass of wine.

'No. Should they?'

Katherine raised her glass and clinked it against his.

'Cheers,' she said.

Ideas were forming in Katherine's brain that were more interesting, and potentially useful, than going over her work upstairs. And, besides, she had a feeling that Dan Schumacher might prove stimulating company.

Over another bottle of wine, she found out that he was originally Canadian but was now based in Manchester. He had followed the Charnley case from the beginning when Tracey went missing.

'What was the feeling around the time of Tracey's disappearance?' she asked.

'Sick,' said Dan, pulling a face and nibbling at the remains of Katherine's cheese.

'Why?'

'We were waiting for a body to be found.'

'No, I mean right at the beginning. That she was a runaway?'

'Sure. Gee made it clear right away he didn't expect the girl to turn up alive.' Dan looked at Katherine. 'Is this helping your case?'

'What's Gee like?' Katherine ignored his question. 'Is he a villain?'

'He drinks a lot.'

'That's not unheard of in a cop.'

'Or a lawyer,' Dan remarked.

Katherine stopped herself from bristling, and laughed.

'Why do you want to know about Gee?' Dan was curious.

'What's your problem?' asked Katherine. 'You like this man?'

'He gets respect. He's honest. That's what I feel.'

'Well, he'll be all right then, won't he? Bedtime . . .'

For a moment, she saw Dan wonder if she was making him an offer. Then Katherine got to her feet and held out her hand.

'Good night, Mr Schumacher.'

He grinned back.

'Good night, Miss Hughes.'

*

The following day, Gee gave his evidence. He stood erect, smartly dressed in a suit and police tie. Katherine looked at him with interest. For the first time, she had a feeling that she was really on to something.

'Inspector Gee,' she said, starting her cross-examination, 'you've had the responsibility for this case from the outset?'

'Yes.'

'Its conduct has been your personal responsibility?'

'My professional responsibility, but mine solely.'

'My client was taken in for questioning on May 7th, on the day after the discovery of the body and eleven days after Tracey went missing. Is that correct?'

Gee assented.

'You must have been very relieved that my client had been apprehended. Is that correct?'

'I don't think that's what I felt.'

'But hadn't you by then already formed a very strong

conviction that my client was the murderer?' Katherine leant forward on her lectern.

Gee shook his head.

'No, not at all.'

'Are you saying you still had an open mind?'

'Of course,' he asserted.

'Because in fact there was no evidence to link him with the crime, was there?' Katherine looked at him intently.

'Forensic evidence showed matching traces of fibres of his pullover under the girl's fingernails.'

'Yes, forensic tests made after his arrest linked him with the girl, but not the crime,' pointed out Katherine, for the benefit of the jury. 'And it is hardly surprising, is it, that he should be linked with his daughter, since they lived in the same house? So it can't have been that that persuaded you that a nationwide manhunt was necessary.'

'It was clear from a preliminary examination that the girl had suffered sexual abuse over a long period of time. A number of years, not days.'

A murmur of revulsion swept through the public gallery.

'So you suspected him of having sexually abused his daughter, once you received this preliminary report?'

'Yes.'

'But not before then? You didn't suspect that before?'

There was a pause while Gee thought for a moment.

'Yes I did,' he said hesitantly.

'You did? That's interesting. Why was that?'

'Because I asked myself, "If you believe your daughter's run away, why wait four days before telling anybody?"'

'And what answer did you come up with?'

'I had an open mind.'

'Did it seem to you that my client was behaving like a guilty man?'

'He struck me as a man who had something he needed to hide.'

'I see.' Katherine paused for a moment. 'Did my client offer any other explanation of his stepdaughter's disappearance?'

'Yes.'

'He insisted that Tracey might've been abducted, didn't he?'

'He came up with this once or twice.'

'Did you question all the known sex offenders on your books?'

'Yes.'

'And drew a blank in each case?'

'Yes.'

'When was this?'

'My colleague, Sergeant Grucock, handled this within forty-eight hours of us knowing she was missing.'

'So you were in fact waiting for a body to be discovered,' Katherine stated rather than asked.

'Absolutely not!' Gee looked affronted.

'But you weren't looking for her with anything like the same commitment of time and resources.'

'No.'

'Why not? Was it because you were convinced she was already dead?'

'She was already dead. Charnley's confession makes it clear she died on the 26th and he waited four days.'

'But you did not know that at the time.'

'No,' conceded Gee.

Katherine looked around the court and back at Gee.

'So why weren't you looking for her? I put it to you again: you had already decided my client was guilty of a murder you couldn't even be sure had taken place.'

'Absolutely not.'

'But you've just said he looked like a man who was hiding something. What was it he was hiding?'

'Well, his confession makes that clear.'

225

'Inspector, I'm talking about then, not now.' Katherine's voice became razor sharp. 'At the time before my client made the confession which he retracted as soon as he had access to legal advice; at a time when – and the forensic report makes this perfectly clear – Tracey may well still have been alive; at a time when you were nevertheless winding down the enquiry which was your sole responsibility: what was it you thought my client David Charnley was hiding?'

There was a pause before Gee replied.

'Well, what else could it have been?'

Katherine had made her point.

'No further questions, your honour,' she said.

*

As the trial proceeded, so Charnley's condition deteriorated daily. On the morning when he was to give evidence, he cowered before Katherine and Ellen, as they spoke to him in the cell beneath the courtroom.

'I don't deserve to live. I'm just shit. I'm an animal. I should be put on telly and given rat poison.'

Katherine went and sat next to him.

'David, where would any of us be if we got what we deserved?' she said soothingly.

'I want to plead guilty. I'm guilty. I don't want to show my face,' Charnley said, weeping.

A look of panic crossed Ellen's face; but Katherine kept her head. She had to get Charnley to give evidence somehow. Swallowing back her revulsion, Katherine put one hand round Charnley's shoulders and the other on his clenched fists. The man flinched. He could have had no warmth or bodily contact for months. He shook his head in despair.

'Oh, Jesus Christ,' he moaned. 'Christ's blood . . .'

Katherine understood what he was trying to say.

'You have to say it all,' she said softly. 'Shall I help you?'

Charnley shook his head.

'Shall I say it for you?' Katherine continued. 'You told Gee the truth about how you felt about Tracey, didn't you?'

A cry of pain came from Charnley. Katherine herself tried not to flinch as he sobbed, his head on her shoulder.

'You say it now,' Katherine prompted him. 'Go on, you couldn't resist her, could you, this little girl? But you didn't kill her.'

Charnley shook his head and snuffled, burying his face in Katherine's lap. She forced herself to continue stroking his shoulder as if he were a wounded animal.

'No, of course not, she was your little girl. You can say it. You can say it out loud, all you did to her.'

Charnley howled.

'You're not guilty, David. When we get up there today, I want you to forget about everybody else in the court but me. Just talk to me, OK?'

Katherine visited the ladies' toilets to compose herself before going into court. She felt contaminated by Charnley. She scrubbed at her hands and dried them thoroughly on paper towels. Then she squirted cologne on her wrists and on her sleeves where they had held the man close. She tried to erase the smell of him.

CHAPTER ELEVEN

'Mr Charnley,' Katherine began. 'You know, don't you, that nothing that's been said here so far in this trial and nothing that will be said will do anything to bring Tracey back? You know that.'

'Yes,' Charnley replied in a quiet, forlorn voice.

'And nothing that we say can cause her any more suffering. You know that.'

'Yes.'

'And you know that what this court is concerned with is whether or not you murdered her, nothing else? You know that?'

'Yes.'

'Mr Charnley, did you murder Tracey?'

'No,' he said.

'On the night of the 8th May and during the following day, you made statements to Chief Superintendent Gee which culminated in you signing the confession which was read earlier in the trial. Is that correct?'

'Yes.'

'Was it in any part accurate?'

'Yes.'

'Which part do you say was accurate?'

'The bit about having sex with Tracey.'

'Mr Charnley, are you prepared to be completely frank with the court?'

'Yes.'

'When did you start having sex with Tracey?'

'After the boys were born.'

'What were your sexual relations with Annette like at this time.'

'She didn't want any.'

'How old was Tracey?'

'Eight.'

'What did you get Tracey to do with you?'

The pressmen's pens hovered in mid-air, waiting for Charnley's reply. He looked down at his feet and then swallowed hard and looked back at Katherine.

'At first . . . at first, it was just touching. I asked her to touch my private parts. And I touched her. Then I got her to masturbate me. Then in the end I was going all the way with her.'

Katherine tried to pin Charnley's attention on her, as if only she and he existed.

'Can you tell the court exactly what that means?'

'Intercourse.'

'You had full sexual intercourse with her?'

'Yes.'

'As well as normal sexual intercourse, was there abnormal sexual intercourse?'

'Yes. Um . . . anal intercourse.'

'How old was Tracey when you first had actual sexual intercourse with her?'

'Eight.'

'For how long did these sexual acts continue?'

'Till she went missing. Five years.'

'Mr Charnley, was Tracey in any sense a willing partner in this?'

Charnley hung his head and shook it.

'I'm afraid you'll have to tell the court. Was she a willing partner?'

'Oh, help me, God. No, she wasn't!'

'In your statement,' continued Katherine, 'you said that in the spring of this year it became clear to you that Tracey was becoming so desperately unhappy that she might expose you to the authorities in order to escape your sexual advances. Is this part of your statement accurate?'

'No.'

'What is inaccurate about it? Was she not miserably unhappy?'

Charnley did not reply.

'Was she?' Katherine repeated the question.

'Yes, she was.' He was almost whispering.

'Was she threatening to expose you?'

'No. She knew we needed her.'

'You needed her? You're not now talking about your sexual needs, are you?'

'No.'

Katherine sensed that the courtroom was tense with anticipation. Gee was watching Charnley intently. The press gallery couldn't believe the field day it was having.

'In what way did you need her?' asked Katherine.

'We needed the money.'

'What money?' probed Katherine, even though she realized Charnley was very nearly on the point of collapse.

'Mr Charnley, it's very important that you now tell the court the whole truth.'

'We needed the money she started earning.'

'How did she earn this money?' asked Katherine firmly.

Again, Charnley had to pull himself together. He gazed

at Katherine.

'At first pornographic videos. After that, prostitution.'

*

Katherine had to push her way through the pressmen hovering outside the court-house. She ignored their questions and set off at a smart pace towards the hotel. All she wanted now was a long soak in the huge tub in her antiquated bathroom. She felt contaminated not only by Charnley, but also by the animal hatred that she had felt in the courtroom.

Her tension eased slightly as she found herself suddenly in a modern shopping arcade. She must have missed her turning to the hotel. Carols were blaring out over the mall loudspeakers. All the shops were decorated with bright and gaudy Christmas decorations. She came to a halt outside a large department store and stood transfixed. A giant, nodding snowman was waving at her to come in and buy. She had become so wrapped up in the Charnley case that she had forgotten that Christmas was only a week away.

What possible chance have the Charnleys of this world, surrounded by such affluence, she thought sadly. Then, seduced herself by the music and the atmosphere, she forgot everything else but the Cartwright children. Those kids, she told herself, should have the best Christmas that money can buy.

*

It was Katherine's call that evening, to ask how he was, which triggered Frank into action. He had been intending to go back to Fetter Court for the New Year; but Katherine's treatment of him as if he were still dangerously ill made him think. The next day, Frank rang up James and brought himself up to date on the chaos in Fetter Court.

Then he had a long conversation with Lorraine at his house, and a shorter one with Hugh. Finally, in the late afternoon, Frank set off for the Chambers.

He walked through the sliding door for the first time in months, and stood looking at the room. It was the first Christmas at Fetter Court. Tinsel had been wound round the pillars and up the staircase. Christmas cards from solicitors and grateful clients were stuck all over the walls. The desk lamps were on, and there was a feeling of jollity in the air as people sat chatting and unwinding at the end of the day. At first, no one noticed him. Then Michael Khan looked up from his desk.

'Frank!' he cried, and dashed across the room to greet him.

All the others got up and gathered round. Frank felt touched; they looked so pleased to see him. He looked from one smiling face to another.

'Merry Christmas,' he beamed.

'Merry Christmas!' they chorused.

*

A couple of hours later, as Frank looked around him at the Chambers meeting which he had called, he wondered if the seasonal goodwill would continue. Frank sat forward in his chair and laid out his plans.

'I've just come from a meeting with Hugh, at which I made it plain that he cannot continue as our senior clerk. I also made it plain that it was our mistake, not his, to have asked him to do it in the first place. I asked him to consider staying on as junior clerk.'

'I think that's appalling,' muttered Joanna Davis.

'Just a second, Joanna, please.' Frank was eager to tell the whole story. 'I've also had a meeting with Lorraine, at which I asked her on behalf of Fetter Court to come back.

She has accepted and I have offered her the customary terms to clerks in the Temple.'

'A percentage?' asked Ken, spelling out the point.

'Correct. I have also made an application for silk.' Frank looked round the gathering to register the various reactions and continued, 'I apologize for my prolonged absence. I am coming back in the New Year to lead this Chambers into what I believe will be a crucial period. This is a time for those of us who value truth, justice and democracy to discipline ourselves and be ready to fight. This is what Fetter Court was set up to do. I hope I have your support.'

There was silence which was broken by David Milner.

'Is the implication,' he asked acidly, 'that anybody who doesn't share your approach is *not* committed to truth, justice and democracy?'

'Not at all, David.'

'Well, I'd like a democratic vote about Fetter Court becoming a co-operative.'

Frank had expected this.

'By all means,' he said. 'Will those in favour please show?'

Joanna, Alison, David, Martin and Michael raised their hands.

'Those against?'

Frank, James, Ken, Tessa and Brendan raised their hands. Five each. However, Frank had an extra vote to add to the nays.

'Katherine cannot be here tonight,' said Frank, 'but she wished to record her vote against this motion, should it come up. I hope that you would all accept that?'

'Yes, I do,' muttered David.

Michael and Alison also nodded in agreement; but Martin and Joanna shook their heads and left the room.

CHAPTER TWELVE

Katherine stood to make her closing speech. Every available place in the courtroom had been taken, and there was a large crowd gathered outside. Katherine had made sure she looked her most attractive, taking care with her appearance and make-up, and she smiled as she addressed the jury.

'Members of the jury, this is the part of the trial when I'm allowed to speak directly to you.'

Katherine saw the jury react in different ways. Some looked back at her with unrelenting hostility. Others pretended to study the floor. One or two appeared more interested in the ceiling.

'You have had the harrowing task of listening to the evidence of a quite repugnant crime committed against a child.'

A couple of the jurors turned to stare at Charnley.

'You have also heard a sickening account from the mouth of the defendant, filled with self-disgust and shame, about the way in which he exploited his young stepdaughter. How he slowly began the process of taking advantage of her sexually, subjecting her to indignity and misery for his own satisfaction, and eventually pressing her to provide similar sexual services for other men.'

Some of the jurors looked embarrassed. Katherine took a deep breath.

'But, members of the jury, to allow these deep and powerful emotions to cloud your judgement in this case would be adding another monstrous act to the ones we have heard about. It would be a clear miscarriage of justice. You've heard forensic evidence that Tracey was killed in the remote spot where her remains were found. You've also heard that David Charnley possesses no means of transport. You've heard Inspector Gee agree that no forensic evidence exists to link David Charnley with the crime or the location.'

She paused, to let these facts sink in.

'Then why, you may ask, was my client ever charged with this crime? It was because he confessed. Why did he confess? Imagine.'

Katherine had always known this would be the trickiest part: the point at which she had to ask the jury to put themselves in Charnley's place.

'Your stepdaughter has been missing for eleven days and you have reason to fear the worst for her. You and your family have become the focus of national concern and speculation, and you have two appalling secrets to live with, both of which cause you deep feelings of guilt. So much so that you can't stand it any more. You run away. Your stepdaughter's body is found in a shallow grave. You are apprehended and then interrogated by the force's most experienced detective.'

She looked across at Gee, and saw that he was flattered by the description.

'You are shown a photograph of her remains. What might that do to a mind struggling for eleven days to block out its own imaginings of the torments and indignities the child may have suffered in her last days and hours, at the hands perhaps of one of the men who for four years have picked her up on the street corners in order that she might serve them sexually?'

Katherine put on her most reasonable voice.

'Ladies and gentlemen, the fact is we don't know exactly how Tracey died. But we do know exactly how and where she lived. She lived in a corner of late twentieth-century England called Brightpool Park. She lived in the kind of grinding poverty that few of us in this room can imagine having to endure. If we pity her death, we should pity too her life, and ask ourselves, who is responsible for putting her on to the streets?'

Again, a couple of jurors looked towards Charnley.

'Well, surely this man here, David Charnley,' said Katherine. 'Yes, he's responsible. He let it happen. Yes, he put his daughter on the streets. The head of a family clinging to the ledge of existence, he took the only option that seemed open to him. He had no skill to sell and no one wanted to hire his strength any longer. But here *was* a market for his daughter. What is it to be reduced to the ultimate service industry, where your own flesh and blood is for sale? By his own words, David Charnley denies killing Tracey but confesses to you that he did the unspeakable.'

Katherine glimpsed Clive Curran out of the corner of her eye. He was looking at his watch.

'This case is an indictment,' she said, 'but not just of David Charnley. Members of the jury, David Charnley confessed to murder precisely because he had *not* lost all moral sense. Precisely because he *was* overcome with guilt. He took personal responsibility for her death, and you now know why. But you are not trying him for sexual abuse. You are not trying him for pimping for a child. You are trying him for the most serious crime in the calendar.

Your task has been harrowing but your duty is clear. If you convict David Charnley, then let it be understood what his real crime has been: not murder, but poverty and powerlessness.'

*

The court was packed when the jury re-entered. As the judge came back in, Katherine smiled nervously at Dan Schumacher in the press box. He nodded back, as did Clive Curran, sitting next to him.

The clerk of the court called out.

'Will the defendant stand, please?' Charnley rose to his feet and clutched the rail in front of him to give himself support.

'Members of the jury, have you reached a decision?'

The foreman stood, a youngish man in a sports sweater.

'We have,' he said solemnly.

'Do you find the accused guilty or not guilty to the charge of murder?'

'Not guilty,' pronounced the foreman.

A cacophony of shouting broke out in the court. Katherine stole a look at Curran, who evidently couldn't believe what he had just heard. Dan Schumacher was slapping him on the back, with a broad grin on his face.

Charnley swayed, and prevented himself from falling only by gripping on to the rail.

Katherine turned round and hugged Ellen. As they embraced tears came to Katherine's eyes. At last, the nightmare was over.

*

Ellen accompanied Katherine back to the hotel, for a celebratory glass of champagne. They were both exhausted by the strain of the trial. Each flopped into one of the plush red-velvet chairs in the hotel cocktail bar.

The one good thing that had come out of the trial, Katherine reflected as she sipped her drink, was that she had renewed her friendship with Ellen. They talked for an hour, about nothing much. The important thing was that they were not talking about the Charnleys.

'Well, family calls,' said Ellen, downing the last of her champagne. 'You're quite sure you won't join us? I know Mum would love to see you again. She's always mentioning you.'

It was Ellen's mother's sixtieth birthday party, an occasion that Ellen could not miss.

Katherine shook her head.

'No, thanks. It's a nice thought, but I'd feel a bit of an intruder tonight.'

'You wouldn't be,' said Ellen, putting on her jacket.

'I feel like being on my own at the moment,' said Katherine. 'Tell her I'll be back and meet her some other time. Do give her my love.'

A small posse of journalists entered the bar. Like Katherine, some of the ratpack had decided to stay over and catch the first train back to London the following day. Even though Curran wasn't with them, Katherine felt a need to escape.

'I'll walk with you,' said Katherine to Ellen and quickly finished her champagne.

The two friends kissed each other farewell in the hotel lobby. Katherine collected her key from the reception desk and went upstairs.

As soon as she entered her room, she switched on the television – that comforting modern equivalent of the old electric fire – and kicked off her high-heeled shoes. She flung herself down on the bed and stared up at the ceiling, with her hands folded behind her head. The television news burbled in the background as she reflected on how much she looked forward to getting home to London.

Ironic really, she thought, considering how – when she was in London – she always referred to Yorkshire as home. Now, she couldn't wait to get away.

She was wondering whether she could face another mediocre dinner in the hotel, or to risk the even more doubtful delights of room service, when the phone rang. It was Dan Schumacher.

'Katherine? It's Dan. Congratulations! I'm so glad you're still here. I thought you might have caught the train back to London.'

Katherine roused herself up on to her side. As she looked at the TV, she did a double take.

'Where are you?' she asked. 'You seem to be speaking to me in stereo. You're standing outside the court-house on the telly and you're also talking into my ear.'

'I'm still here. What are your plans for tonight?' asked Dan, laughing. 'Will you join me for dinner or will you be out carousing with your colleagues?'

'Actually, I was debating the relative merits of room service or Ye Olde Oake Grill Room for the umpteenth time.'

Sod it, why not? she decided. It would be pleasant to have company.

'I'll see you in the bar at eight then,' said Dan, who rang off before she had time to reply.

A bit bloody presumptuous, thought Katherine as she ran her bath, though she was pleased that she had packed a rather smashing silk dress which she had not had the opportunity to wear yet.

Besides, Dan was attractive in an obvious sort of way. She stood in front of the bathroom mirror and applied her mascara with an unsteady hand, feeling annoyed at how nervous and flattered she felt, more like an adolescent going on a first date than an experienced woman of the world.

Katherine knew she looked good as she walked into the hotel bar. The dress's creases had fallen out as they were supposed to, thanks to her old trick of hanging it in the steamy bathroom. For once, she had managed to put on her extremely sheer stockings without laddering them. Her hair was worn in a chignon and she was wearing her favourite pair of diamond drop earrings.

Dan turned round from the bar and appraised Katherine slowly.

'Mmm,' he murmured, licking his lips like a more up-market Clive Curran. 'You sure look good.'

She returned his look coolly, feeling her hackles rise and wondering for a moment why she had made the extra effort. Dan was at least sensitive enough to see that she was not impressed.

'Oops, sorry,' he muttered. 'But you dyed-in-the-wool feminists shouldn't be so schizophrenic.'

'Right then, shall we go and eat?' she enquired sharply. 'It should be quite cosy. Just you and the two of me.'

'You'd better go and fetch your coat first,' Dan answered, unflappably. 'We're eating out. I've booked us a table at nine.'

'Where?' asked Katherine.

'I thought that we might try the Bay Leaf.'

Katherine looked at him quizzically. He was certainly pushing the boat out. It was regarded as probably one of the best restaurants in the north: certainly one of the most expensive.

'It's on expenses,' he quickly explained. Katherine wished he hadn't said that.

As Dan drove out of town and up into the dales, the couple sat in silence. She found Dan full of conflicting signals. She knew from the conversations she had had with him that he was intelligent and amusing, his chat-up lines proved he was no 'new man'; and he owned the sort of flashy but bottom-of-the-range Porsche most favoured by barrow boys made good. Maybe it was he who was the schizophrenic.

There was more than one flashy sports car outside the restaurant, which was in a remote village. It was little more than a modest terraced house of stone, with two rooms serving about thirty customers. Katherine liked the place immediately. The tables were sufficiently far apart that you didn't feel overheard; but there was an intimate atmosphere.

The service turned out to be attentive without being obsequious. The food looked and was superb, a slightly more substantial, anglicized version of 'nouvelle cuisine'. The meal reminded Katherine of the glossy book by Raymond Blanc which Frank had given her on her last birthday, and which she knew that she herself would never find time to cook from.

She was pleasantly surprised when Dan asked her advice on the selection of the wine. She was delighted when he accepted her half-hearted suggestion of a bottle of Montrachet. She had only drunk this white Burgundy once before, and that was at someone's house. Here, with the restaurant mark-up, the price was astronomical. Dan must have a large expense account or plenty of chutzpah.

Slowly, Katherine began to relax. Gradually too, she revised her opinion of Dan. He quickly got the hint that she did not want to go over the court case like some big-game hunter reliving her finest kill. Instead, he did most of the talking. He entertained her with stories of his orthodox Jewish upbringing in Canada. He had come to Britain in the early seventies on a Rhodes scholarship and stayed.

Katherine was surprised at how impressed she was when he told her that he had been behind a celebrated series which had exposed torture around the world. The episode about Northern Ireland had led to questions in the House, and vehement editorials in the right-wing press.

'Not that I was ever considered important enough to have Clive Curran investigate my private life,' smiled Dan.

Katherine wondered if she should feel offended. She also wondered what sort of a reputation Curran's article had left her with. For the first time, she felt she knew how some film stars must feel. What was it Rita Hayworth had said? Something about all her men wanting to make love to Gilda, but waking up with her.

The way Dan was looking at her made her feel a bit like the sexual dynamo which Clive Curran had created. Ridiculous, thought Katherine. And Dan wasn't her normal kind of man at all. But there was an appealing, puppyish enthusiasm about the way he revelled in his work. He had a nice smile too, even if it did seem a bit too calculated.

When the waiter asked if they wanted coffee, they were looking at each other so attentively that they did not hear him the first time. Dan looked questioningly at Katherine, then shook his head.

'No. Just the bill, please,' he said.

Dan leant across the table. He picked up Katherine's hand and kissed her fingertips.

'Mmm,' she said, feeling her body relax totally, for the first time since the trial.

She stretched out one long leg, wrapped it around his and rubbed it up and down. She smiled at his surprise that she had taken the initiative. Then, she took his hand and licked each of his fingers in turn. She steered it under the table, and watched his face as his fingers encountered her suspender and stocking.

Katherine saw Dan's eyes dart around the room, to make sure no one was noticing, when her hand delved under the napkin in his lap. She found herself enjoying her role-playing of the femme fatale. If the waiter didn't hurry back, he might find them making love under the table. Lust, however, was temporarily interrupted by the arrival of the bill.

Dan's straying hand abruptly disengaged itself; and he visibly flinched as he read the total. Katherine seized the bill from him. It really was a colossal amount.

'You can't possibly claim that!' exclaimed Katherine. 'Let's at least go dutch.'

She opened her bag and reached for her credit cards.

'Rubbish!' said Dan, looking hurt, as if his masculinity were at stake. 'This is on me. I've had the most enjoyable evening for months, and I don't want to spoil it now with arguments about who pays what.'

Well, at least he's not a wimp, she thought. Robert never had seemed to mind about her paying for anything and everything. Katherine momentarily relished this return to the old tribal rituals of courtship. She felt like a teenager again.

She barely noticed the return drive to the hotel. She lay back in the car and let Dan's left hand creep up between her legs. She thought it better not to reciprocate. Dan must be over the breathalyser limit, and she didn't want him crashing the car.

'Your place or mine?' asked Dan, after he had successfully steered his Porsche into a hotel parking space at the second attempt.

Katherine wondered again about the corniness of the whole situation. She wasn't even sure if she liked Dan Schumacher that much, and now he simply assumed he was going to sleep with her. All for the price of a slap-up meal, which he wasn't even going to have to pay for.

'That's only if you want to,' Dan added, after a short silence. 'I mean, I'd understand if . . .'

His voice trailed away, miserably. Katherine looked at

Dan's profile, and saw in him the anguished Jewish adolescent he once must have been. A flood of affection and desire came over her. Both of them were alone, unattached and reduced by lust to the clichés of seventeen-year-olds. So what. Why not enjoy it while it lasted?

'Well,' said Katherine, 'I think I'm getting a bit old to do it in the back of the car.'

'I don't think there'd be room,' said Dan, looking over his shoulder at the cramped space behind them.

At least, thought Katherine, he can joke about the size of his car.

'Dan,' said Katherine.

'What?' said Dan.

'Kiss me,' said Katherine, unfastening her safety belt.

*

The ratpack of pressmen were in full voice as Katherine led Dan into the hotel. The night porter smirked at Dan as Katherine took her room key, and Dan didn't bother to take his. She didn't even object when Dan squeezed her bottom as they walked upstairs.

Once inside her room, the ferocity of Dan's embrace disconcerted Katherine. There seemed to be as much violence as passion in the way that he pulled her towards him. His tongue thrust into her mouth and his hands worked their way roughly down her body.

She helped him as he fumbled with the buttons on her dress. He seemed to want her so much that he could scarcely wait. Katherine let her dress drop to the floor. She watched his eyes travel down, over her bare breasts as she stepped out of her knickers and kicked them away.

'Mm,' he said. 'Stockings, suspenders, long legs and high heels. It's a journalist's fantasy.'

'You're still fully dressed,' observed Katherine. 'I don't call that fair.'

She eased off his jacket and threw it across the room. His shirt was already half-unbuttoned, revealing chest hair but mercifully no gold chains. While he removed it, she concentrated on undoing his trousers for him. They fell to the floor, followed closely by his silk boxer shorts decorated with flying pigs.

'Don't go away,' she whispered.

She eased herself away from him and scurried into the bathroom. Her mind and body were looking forward to sex, but not if it meant the patter of tiny Schumachers.

When she returned, they made love with enthusiasm. It wasn't until the small hours of the morning that they both finally went to sleep. Every time Katherine thought that it was all over, Dan surprised her with his renewed energies. Technically at least, he was the most wonderful lover. After the second or third time, Katherine even stopped worrying about whether he was making love to her, or to a completely erroneous idea of her.

She was the first to wake in the morning. She looked at Dan, lying next to her with his head buried in the pillow. Could this be the start of something more than sex? She swung her legs out of bed and went off to have a shower.

Looking at her watch, she couldn't believe how late it was. She had already missed the train she had intended to catch back to London. Never mind. They would have a lazy breakfast in bed; and perhaps if Dan wanted . . . ?

Katherine whistled softly to herself as she rescued her clothes from where they had been thrown in such a hurry the previous night. She picked up Dan's jacket, and something fell out of his inside pocket. It was his wallet. She was about to replace it when she noticed a photograph in pride of place inside.

She was surprised at the depth of her disappointment when she studied the snapshot, which showed a happy family picnic. Dan was smiling out of the picture into the camera with his arms round a pretty, auburn-haired woman who had a small baby in her lap. A dungareed toddler was sitting astride Dan's shoulders. There was no mistaking the Schumacher family.

Katherine replaced the photograph and started to pack her things. Sod's law, she thought ruefully, as she folded up her court gear. The first fanciable man in ages, and he's married. Claudia might be into affairs with married men; but such liaisons had long since lost their attraction for Katherine.

She wondered if Frank had ever betrayed Annie in this way. Katherine hoped not, although she knew that Annie had 'cheated' on more than one occasion. Dan stirred and turned over. He smiled at Katherine who was leaning on the lid of her case, trying to shut it.

'I'm going to have to hurry if I'm going to catch my train,' said Katherine. 'Would you mind if I left you to have breakfast on your own?'

'Something wrong?' asked Dan.

'I have to get back to London,' said Katherine. 'I don't expect we'll see each other again.'

'Why not?'

'Why didn't you say you were married?' asked Katherine coldly.

'You didn't ask,' said Dan.

'You could have said.'

'I didn't think you'd want to know.'

'You told me everything else about yourself,' Katherine pointed out. 'Family background, career, your hundred best jokes . . .'

'Well, I'm sorry. OK?' said Dan.

'OK,' said Katherine.

'You're a great lay, Katherine.'

Dan lay back, clearly awaiting a similar compliment. He

knew he was a good lover but she was damned if she was going to give him the satisfaction of telling him so.

'I'm glad,' she said, picking up her case and making for the door.

'Why not give me your number, and the next time I'm in London . . .'

'Dan, it was a lovely evening. But let's leave it at that. Despite what Clive Curran wrote about me, I'm not in the market for one-night stands.'

'So why not make it two nights?' Dan blurted out.

'I am not mistress material. I am not just someone you can bed, each time you come down to London.'

'Wouldn't you enjoy it?'

'Dan, I don't even know if I like you. Besides, can you imagine the effect on your wife and family if the Currans of this world found out about you and me?'

Dan looked shocked. He glanced up at Katherine suspiciously.

'But don't worry,' said Katherine. 'I know the rules of the game. I'm not the woman in *Fatal Attraction*. I'm not going to slit my wrists, or murder your children's pets, or come at you with a knife.'

'Oh,' said Dan, holding out his hand as if to some remote business acquaintance. 'Well, it's been real good to know you, Katherine.'

'Likewise, I'm sure,' said Katherine, shaking his hand.

PART IV

CHAPTER ONE

Even for London traffic, thought Katherine, this is ridiculous. She wished she hadn't offered to pick Hugh up from his flat. Thanks to his being so long getting ready (and they say women are vain, she grumbled inwardly) they were already late, and going to be later still. The traffic hadn't moved for five minutes. Anyone would think that there's a conspiracy against us getting to Fetter Court.

'Oh, for God's sake! Let's walk the rest of the way,' she said, spotting a parking space.

The pair got out of Katherine's Golf GTI and walked towards the main road, where the hold-up seemed to be. Katherine knew she was looking her best in high heels and an expensive dress, cut low both front and back. She ignored wolf whistles from inside a passing four-year-old Ford Sierra.

Hugh was looking less ostentatious on this mild spring afternoon; but only just. She thought he looked rather splendid in full evening dress – as he should, considering the time it had taken him to get ready. He smiled as he offered her his arm; and together they stopped and glared at an indecent suggestion from a beaten-up Bedford van, whose number-plate was held on with string.

Katherine and Hugh walked briskly along the line of stationary traffic. At the intersection with the main road, a small crowd had gathered. A young Asian boy, half-covered by a blanket, lay in the road. Two police patrol cars had already arrived, and a police officer was starting to direct the traffic around the accident.

It was then that Katherine noticed something strange. There was a blue, unmarked van parked at an angle, half up on the pavement. Evidently, it was the vehicle which had knocked the boy over. Its back doors had burst open and several large crates had fallen out into the street. She nudged Hugh, wanting him to reassure her that she wasn't hallucinating. Protruding from one of the crates really *were* two Russian-made machine-guns.

A slob of a man wearing a red-checked lumber-jack shirt threw up in the gutter. Katherine felt her own gorge rise. Then the man saw her, wiped his mouth and spat out a large gob of phlegm which landed at her feet.

'Take a walk, lady,' the man growled at Katherine in an American accent, and started to reload the van. An ambulance arrived; and Katherine and Hugh watched the ambulancemen place the small boy on a stretcher. A dazed Asian woman was helped into the ambulance to accompany the boy to hospital. As Katherine turned away, she saw the blue van drive off at high speed.

'Hey, Hugh,' she said looking at the disappearing number plate, 'remember this, D500 FYF.'

Then the ambulance, too, drove off.

'All over,' a young policeman told the crowd, trying to disperse them. 'Hit and run, little boy dead.'

'Was it the van?' asked Hugh.

'What van?' the policeman said blankly.

'There was a blue van. There was a crate in the road,' Katherine explained.

'I dunno, love. I got here too late.' The policeman shrugged and walked off.

Hugh went up to some passers-by who were hanging about on the pavement; but none of them had seen the accident take place, or noticed the blue van.

'C'mon, Hugh.' Katherine tugged his sleeve. There was nothing that the two of them could do here. Besides, Katherine wanted to get to Frank's celebration.

*

The party was well under way by the time Katherine and Hugh arrived. Ah! Katherine sniffed appreciatively, Tessa's famous curried goat recipe was simmering away on a hot plate. A trestle table was laden with a mixture of Afro-Caribbean food, as well as more standard party nibbles. Bottles of bubbly sat in buckets of ice. People were dancing to the jazz band in which Frank sometimes played on Sunday mornings. The whole Chambers was enjoying its first full-scale knees-up since Frank had returned to lead it.

Katherine recognized Frank's parents, and smiled at them. Frank Cartwright senior was an ex-Civil Servant, an erudite liberal who was telling Lorraine that he was glad to have retired from the Department of Education and Science when he had: as he said, pre-Basher Baker. Katherine kissed Lorraine, who was dressed up like Marlene Dietrich in *The Blue Angel*.

'Frank's mother was asking where you were,' said Lorraine.

Mrs Cartwright greeted Katherine warmly. The two women had liked each other ever since they first met during Katherine's student days.

'Look at those children,' said Mrs Cartwright, fondly.

Alethea did indeed seem to have reverted to childhood,

and was trying to make sure she was the centre of attention by marching round with her father's full-bottomed wig on her head. Young John Cartwright was talking very seriously to James's wife, Gloria, about the relative merits of hamsters over gerbils. Frank's youngest, Peter, seemed more overawed by the party, and wouldn't let go of his grandmother's legs.

'It's lovely to see you,' said Katherine. 'Could you excuse me a moment? There's a phone call I have to make.'

'Not work, surely?' said Mrs Cartwright, shaking her head.

Katherine went over to her desk, where Hugh was telling Michael Khan about the accident and the mystery van. Katherine got on the telephone to an old journalist contact. She wanted to trace the van while the registration number was fresh in her mind. After a brief, muttered conversation, she looked up to see Frank performing a deep bow in front of her. The man was obviously completely rat-arsed.

'As someone said, shall we dance?' Frank thought he was being extremely witty. 'After all, this is a party.'

She held him up as they shuffled round the dance floor to slow smoochy music. She looked into his half-closed eyes and smiled.

'Congratulations,' she said.

'Thank you, good evening and welcome, and thank you for your support,' he murmured. 'I shall always wear it.'

Katherine groaned, the way she always did when he attempted his David Frost impersonation, usually very late at night, after several bottles of claret.

'I've been a silk for an hour,' confided Frank, pointing up to the heavens, 'and I haven't been asked even once to do their bidding.'

Katherine laughed.

'Just think of me,' she said, 'when you're sitting with the Attorney-General in the Sheridan Club.'

'Who were you phoning?' Frank asked. 'Don't you ever stop working?'

Frank might be drunk; but he wasn't totally unobservant. Katherine thought for a moment before answering.

'I'm sorry, I didn't want to spoil your day. Hugh and I were held up by an accident. A little boy was run over, killed.'

Suddenly the music went up-tempo, and Frank made a face, as if to say that such a frenetic beat was quite beyond a man of his age and professional dignity. The dancing space filled rapidly with the younger members of the party. Tessa and Alethea were attempting to out-Charleston each other; while Ken and Lorraine were trying to forget their perpetual squabbles and performing a complicated and quite inappropriate tango.

As usual, Katherine found herself amazed at the way certain barristers took on quite different characters when they were dancing. For the first time, she realized why Ken Gordon was so grossly overweight: he evidently spent far too much of his time in front of the telly, watching old Fred Astaire movies.

Hugh waved at Katherine to catch her attention, and pointed to her telephone. She left Frank and went over to answer the call. As she took notes, she noticed Michael Khan talking to Frank. Evidently, they were discussing the machine-guns; for she saw a look of worry pass over Frank's face. Katherine felt annoyed with Michael. Couldn't Frank be allowed at least one afternoon of relaxation?

People were starting to drift away. A loud, offensive drunk whom nobody recognized was evicted, before someone realized he was a judge. Frank's parents took Alethea off for tea at the Savoy. James's wife, Gloria, took Peter and John to the pictures. Soon there was only the nucleus of the Chambers left.

'Well?' said Hugh, sitting on Katherine's desk.

'That phonecall was a journalist friend,' explained Katherine. 'He got a mate in the police to ring vehicle licensing at Swansea. The van number belongs to the Metropolitan Police.'

Katherine noticed that Frank and James were still around, holding glasses of Perrier in a belated attempt to sober up. Clearly, left-wing paranoia was of more interest to them than tea at the Savoy, or *Basil the Great Mouse Detective*. Ken, too, wanted to know what was happening. Word seemed to have reached most of the Chambers.

'You sure it wasn't little green men?' Ken teased.

'I know what I saw,' protested Hugh, who was getting irritated by Ken's cynicism. 'I know what Kalashnikovs look like.'

Katherine stepped in.

'What were they doing in a van in the middle of a London street? Hit and run. A little boy died. But what happened? I mean, you know me. I think our police are wonderful.'

They all laughed hollowly.

'And there was this American guy being sick,' added Hugh.

'How do you know he was American?' asked James.

'He was being sick with an American accent,' said Katherine.

'An American, eh?' said Ken, drunkenly. 'CIA. You know what CIA stands for, don't you?'

'Just about anything these days,' said James.

'I was going to say Caught In the Act but yours is funnier, James,' chortled Ken.

Ken and James broke into inane giggles.

'Look, OK, why not do the obvious thing?' Frank asked Katherine.

She looked at him, puzzled.

'Call the press office at Scotland Yard and see what they say,' suggested Frank.

Hugh looked at Frank as if taking silk had made him go potty. Katherine thought much the same, and picked up her bag.

'Come on, Hugh. I'll drop you off, eh?'

'Listen, I know I'm a bit pissed, but . . .' said Ken, shaking his head and looking straight at Katherine. 'Hugh's one thing, but how can you get to your age and do what you've done, and achieve what you've achieved and still believe all this conspiracy stuff? It's juvenile. You'll get the loony left a bad name.'

Katherine ignored Ken, and kissed Frank warmly on the cheek.

'Frank, congratulations,' she said. 'I'm chuffed for you.'

*

Of all the journalists Katherine knew, John Woodham was the least like Clive Curran. Several years ago, Katherine had defended John on an official secrets charge; and ever since, they had remained friendly. He had been an investigative journalist on a left-wing weekly at the time. Now he worked on the one remaining up-market daily with liberal pretensions.

In his hand-knitted, chunky sweater, John looked totally out of place in the modern, open-plan office of his newspaper. Every other desk but his seemed to have a computer terminal on it. John's files remained in bulging manilla folders.

Katherine flicked through John's folder marked CIA, while John read Hugh's affidavit, which described what he and Katherine had seen.

Katherine looked up from her research.

'Can you do something with it?' she asked. 'Run a little story?'

John Woodham scratched his beard doubtfully.

'Kalashnikovs on the streets of London aren't exactly unheard of these days.'

'Not a crateful,' Katherine emphasized.

'If I get a quiet day next week,' said John, 'I'll do half a column, seeing as it's you.'

'Say we're asking for other eye-witnesses, will you?' Katherine asked. 'Listen, if you get a quiet day next week, come to my peace camp case. Five women and three Japanese Buddhist monks. No?'

Woodham shook his head.

'Peace camp stories are last week's news,' he said.

'Can I borrow this?' she asked, nodding at the file.

'Sure, but only twenty-four hours.'

Katherine picked up the heavy folder and put it in her briefcase. She smiled at John as she turned to go.

'Thanks. See you, John.'

'Yeah, take care, Katherine,' John replied. 'How's your sex life?'

Katherine pulled a face. She knew John fancied her, but he wasn't the most subtle of operators and, although she liked him, she did not really find him attractive.

'Celibacy, John. Get into it.'

'I was into it for twelve years. We called it marriage in those days.'

Katherine laughed and walked away.

'I don't believe you,' John called out.

It wasn't that far off the truth, thought Katherine ruefully, as she walked out of the newspaper building. The nearest thing had been Dan Schumacher back in December. Maybe it was because Dan had been Canadian but at the moment, anyone with a transatlantic accent seemed suspicious.

It was not until late that night that Katherine had another chance to look at John Woodham's file. She made a pot of tea, opened a packet of chocolate digestive biscuits, and settled herself comfortably in bed. It really was the best place to work. Katherine was turning over the pieces of paper almost automatically and beginning to nod off, when suddenly she saw the fat American's face staring up at her. She picked up the photograph and examined it intensely. There was no doubt about it. This was the same man who had spoken to her, and had loaded the crate back into the van.

She leant across the bed and pulled the telephone towards her. She dialled John Woodham's number, but there was no ringing tone. She replaced the receiver, then picked it up. No dialling tone. Slowly, Katherine replaced the receiver and lifted it again. Still nothing. A flicker of suspicion entered her mind. Then she noticed that her phone was out of its socket. She smiled at her own paranoia, as she bent down to plug it in. The dialling tone came back, loud and clear; and she dialled Woodham's number.

'John? Katherine,' she said.

'Urgh,' he said. Clearly, she had woken him up.

'Hi. Sorry about the time, but listen. I think you're going to want to run that story.' She read the caption at the bottom of the photograph. 'The guy we saw was Geoffrey Katz. CIA, formerly ex-Deputy Station Tehran, now believed to be a member of the Secret Team.'

'Yeah?' John now sounded considerably more alert.

Katherine wanted to know one thing.

'What's the Secret Team?' she asked.

CHAPTER TWO

James was completely baffled. There was nothing at all about Bill Turner which made him a suitable client for Fetter Court; and yet the man had insisted on seeing James. James expounded the problem to Frank, as they both sipped their mid-morning cup of tea.

'I'm a forty-four-year-old man,' said James, in the character of Bill Turner. 'For twenty years I had my own little business, an electrical subcontractor. I'm one of the sparrows who get the crumbs when they divide up big contracts, mainly defence contracts. Very small beer but it's a good living. I vote Tory. I'm perfectly clear that I live in the best country in the world. I'm a blood donor.'

Frank chuckled as James continued.

'I'm involved in the Boy Scout movement. Apparently I not only do not think that's remotely funny, but I don't even *know* anybody who *would* think it was funny.'

Frank looked at James over his spectacles.

'I don't like you very much,' said Frank.

'One day, I'm on some trivial defence job and I'm suddenly ordered off-site. My contract is torn up because my work isn't up to scratch.'

'Serves you right, you toad-eater,' laughed Frank.

'My business goes bust. The building society repossesses the house, the finance company tows away the Volvo. I finally discover the explanation for all my troubles. I'm the victim of a conspiracy.'

Ken Gordon, who had been listening in on James's exposition, groaned loudly.

'Ah, that one,' said Frank, nodding. 'Lot of it about.'

'Why another conspiracy?' asked Ken.

'Because there's no other explanation,' said James. 'I write to my MP. She's no use. I write long letters to anybody I can think of. Nobody's interested. Except the people watching me from their cars, tapping my telephone when I had one, and interfering with my mail.'

Ken clapped his hand to his forehead in mock horror.

'Finally,' said James, 'after a bit of striptease in Mayfair, I go berserk in a Chelmsford police station, in front of a small but attentive crowd of police.'

By this time, both Frank and Ken were howling with laughter.

'Witnesses,' added James. 'I am now up on charges of wasting police time, actual bodily harm on two police officers, causing fifteen hundred quid's worth of damage to a police vehicle and property. What do you think?'

James stood, arms akimbo, glaring at his two colleagues who were creased up with laughter. Finally, he relaxed and let out a chuckle himself.

'Why *me*?' James sighed, as Mr Bill Turner and his solicitor arrived in the Chambers.

'Best of British,' said Frank.

James escorted the two men upstairs to one of the conference rooms. After initial pleasantries, he got straight down to business.

'Mr Turner, do you mind if I ask you this? When you went to Curzon Street and stood outside that building . . .'

'MI5 Headquarters,' insisted Bill Turner.

Turner was a squat man with bulging eyes. He reminded James of a latter-day John Bull. Instead of wearing a union jack waistcoat, though, Turner was bursting out of a disgustingly tight suit of loud brown checks.

'Yes,' James nodded. 'Why did you take all your clothes off?'

'That was my low point, Mr Bingham,' Mr Turner explained, in his nasal Essex accent.

James just managed not to laugh, and tried not to imagine Bill Turner naked in a Mayfair street.

'I felt like I was at rock-bottom,' said Turner. 'I felt, here I am, I'm nothing. You've reduced me to nothing. What next? What else can you take away? And of course I got my answer within the hour, didn't I? All I've got left is my liberty.'

Turner's solicitor, John Shandly, looked as if he was about to speak. James knew little about him, except that he had represented Turner in his business dealings over the years.

'I don't really think there's much point in dwelling on that part of the story,' said Shandly. 'The police are not charging Bill with indecent exposure, or with anything else he says happened in that particular street. In fact, they say they know nothing about you being in that street at all. They're solely interested in events after you arrived . . .'

Bill bristled. Shandly quickly corrected himself.

'Were *brought* to Lansdowne Road police station.'

'Well, obviously they would deny it. They're part of the conspiracy against me,' asserted Turner.

'Yes, Bill.' Shandly tried to clarify things for his client. 'All I'm saying is, let's not complicate things. You're charged with actual bodily harm, with attacking police-men. The reason I thought Mr Bingham would be a suitable barrister is that this Chambers specializes in that sort of, er, difficulty. But I don't honestly see the helpfulness of the other business.'

'The reason I asked,' explained James, 'is that I feel that, until I understand this conspiracy business, I can't get hold of Mr Turner as a whole.'

Bill nodded his head vigorously in agreement.

'Quite right,' he said.

'Well, can we at least *begin* with the strictly relevant information?' pressed Shandly.

James decided that he disliked Shandly at least as much as he disliked Shandly's client.

'All right,' said James, ignoring Shandly's intervention. 'Let's go back to Curzon Street.'

Shandly sighed, realizing that his protestations would get nowhere.

'You'd been drinking?' James asked Turner.

'Yes, I was drunk as a monkey, in fact.'

'But you have a clear memory of what happened after you were arrested?'

'I was driven out of London back to Essex, to a police station, and I was assaulted by police officers.'

'Well, there must be more to it than that?' suggested James.

Bill Turner looked James up and down.

'Let me ask you a question, Mr Bingham.' Bill Turner stared hard at James. 'Do you vote Conservative? I mean, habitually?'

'No. Not at all, in fact,' James replied.

'No, I didn't think you did. Do you believe in the profit motive? Is that what makes the world go round as far as you can see?'

'No.'

'No,' repeated Turner. 'Were you glad when we beat the Argies?'

'No,' said James. 'I can't say I was "glad" about that episode.'

'No. Fair enough,' said Turner. 'Would you say you believed in this country?'

'Believed in it?' queried James.

'Love it? Do you love this country?'

Shandly shook his head in despair at his client.

'Bill,' said Shandly, 'I've explained about the radical Bar.'

James was beginning to enjoy the conversation.

'Yes. I do love this country,' James replied.

'What do you call love? Answer me straight!' Bill thrust his head forward.

'I love my friends. I love the countryside. English literature, cream teas, white Christmases.'

Bill Turner looked as if he wasn't sure if he was having the mickey taken out of him.

'No, balls to that, excuse my French,' he said. 'Do you love this country, not the promised land, but do you believe we've got it basically right here? That we do a lot of things better than a lot of other people?'

'Such as?'

'For example, fair play. Do you believe in good old British fair play?'

'I believe a lot of people believe in it.'

'You're a slippery customer. John said you would be.'

'Well . . .' stuttered Shandly, going red.

'Let me tell you what I think.' Bill Turner leant forward like a belligerent Staffordshire bull terrier. 'I think it's all a load of shit.'

James could not prevent himself from smiling.

'Answer me one more question,' said Turner. 'Do you believe the British legal system can be relied on to give me justice?'

James thought for a moment, very seriously, and then replied 'No.'

At first, Turner looked disappointed. Then he nodded to himself and seemed pleased with James's reply. He sat back in his seat and beamed at James.

'I place myself entirely in your hands, Mr Bingham. Tell me what to do and I'll do it, with one proviso. I want the whole story told in court.'

'The court can only hear evidence which bears directly on the charges,' said James. 'I think you'll have to accept that it would be wise to plead guilty to the charges and then let me bring out the rest of the story in mitigation.'

'As long as you believe me, Mr Bingham.'

'Well, as it happens, yes I do,' said James, honestly. 'It occurs to me, Mr Turner, that there must be a possibility that what we are dealing with here is not a conspiracy . . .'

Turner scowled at James.

'But,' said James, 'that somebody somewhere might have made a ghastly mistake.'

'Who?' Bill Turner glared questioningly at James.

James shrugged.

*

'The Strange Case of the Hit and Run', as John Woodham's piece was entitled, appeared in his paper the following day, next to a photograph of Geoffrey Katz captioned 'Katz Eyed'.

Katherine pinned a blow-up of the article on the wall by her desk. She looked hard at Ken Gordon, who pretended not to notice what she was doing.

Lorraine was having an argument with a British Telecom engineer who was in the process of dismantling every phone in the Chambers.

'Not much wrong there either,' said the telephone engineer, as he examined Hugh's phone.

'Well, I'm telling you there's a fault,' said Lorraine.

'I'm not doubting it, but intermittent faults are tricky. Can I . . . ?' He picked up the telephone on Katherine's desk.

'Help yourself,' replied Katherine.

As the man took the back off her phone, Frank bustled over to admire Katherine's newspaper cutting.

'Great stuff,' he complimented her.

'Ta,' Katherine grunted.

'Making any progress?'

She shook her head.

'Not yet.'

The telephone engineer screwed Katherine's telephone back together.

'Well?' demanded Lorraine from the centre of the room.

'Not yet,' replied the sardonic engineer, who moved on to Michael Khan's phone.

'I dunno,' stormed Lorraine, crossing the room. 'How come it takes three days to get you round here? Honestly, you make 2 billion quid a year out of us.'

The telephone engineer nodded. He was used to verbal abuse.

'I know,' he said, as if it were nothing to do with him.

'Lorraine,' said Michael, 'he doesn't own Telecom, he's a worker.'

'Michael, will you leave this to me?' snapped Lorraine as she headed back to her desk. 'I know what he is. He's bloody inconvenient.'

'Well, actually, I have got a few shares,' muttered the telephone man, surprised when this comment brought him glares from all around.

Katherine stuffed the remaining bits of paperwork she needed into her briefcase, and put on her coat. She stopped at Lorraine's desk to tell her she was off to Ipswich on her peace camp case, but that she would be back as soon as possible.

'Oh, by the way, a Mr Woodham phoned,' said Lorraine. 'He says he's found another witness to the hit-and-run accident.'

'I'll give him a ring,' said Katherine. 'Thanks.'

*

James was quietly mulling over the Turner case, and trying to ignore the engineer at work on his telephone, when he heard a familiar voice. He looked up and, to his horror, saw Bill Turner gesticulating wildly at Lorraine. She was trying to prevent him from going any further.

'It's all right, dear. I can see him,' Turner assured Lorraine.

He made his way across to James's desk with her hovering anxiously behind. Dressed in jeans and an old anorak, and with unkempt hair, Turner looked madder than ever.

'Mr Bingham!' Turner stood in front of James waving a large envelope, from which press cuttings fell on to James's desk. 'I've been doing some research about what you said: mistakes. Mistakes have been made.'

Turner stood looking at James, like a dog expecting to be rewarded for some elementary trick.

'James, I'm sorry,' apologized Lorraine.

'It's all right, I'll explain,' said James, noticing with relief that Frank had come across to see what the fuss was about.

'The fact is, Mr Turner,' began James.

'Call me Bill,' said Turner.

'Bill,' said James. 'The fact is, Bill, I'm not allowed to talk to you except in the presence of your solicitor. You have to talk to him first and he'll arrange a . . .'

Before James could go any further, Turner interrupted.

'I've sacked him. He was useless. I'll get another one, but you'll continue with the case. I'm hanging on to you. You've got the right attitude. Read this!'

Bill picked up some of his cuttings and waved them in James's face.

'All cases of mistakes being made,' said Turner. 'Mistaken identity! There was one woman sacked from her job and it turned out she had the same name and similar national insurance number to one of these, you know, one of these bitches in CND, excuse my French, won't you?'

James could see Frank gawping at this unbelievable caricature.

'Well, look, I'll read it. I promise,' James assured Turner.

'And I've finally had a reply from the Prime Minister.'

This time it was James's turn to gawp.

'Prime Minister?' James repeated.

Bill fumbled in his pocket and brought out a cream envelope.

'Well, shall I say the Prime Minister's office.'

He pulled a letter out of the envelope and unfolded it.

'"Dear Mr Turner,"' he read. '"Thank you for your letter. I regret to inform you that this is not a matter with which the Prime Minister can become personally involved. She suggests you take it up with your Member of Parliament." As if I haven't. "Yours sincerely". Thirty-six words.'

He folded up the letter, and put it back in its envelope.

'In my opinion,' said Turner, 'the Prime Minister hasn't even read my letter. But it doesn't end here. I refuse to lay down and die. I will make my presence felt directly in Downing Street. What I need is publicity.'

'Please don't,' pleaded James. 'You're on bail.'

Bill Turner banged James's desk. James was horrified to see that the man was on the verge of tears.

'I've always behaved myself, Mr Bingham. It's against my beliefs to act like a hooligan.'

Turner suddenly seemed to realize that everyone in the room, including the telephone engineer, was mesmerized by his performance. He tried to pull himself together.

'OK, I'll do it the proper way, due process of law. Recommend another solicitor.'

'That's not really the correct thing,' said James.

Frank was busy scribbling a name and telephone number on a piece of paper.

'Here,' said Frank, passing the note to Bill. 'She's good.'

Bill read the name in a suspicious voice.

'Helen Robinson. Is she . . . ?'

'She's a communist,' said Frank.

Bill Turner hesitated, then smiled madly.

'Good. I need hard-liners if I'm taking on the secret state.' He nodded at James. 'I shall go now.'

The whole Chambers watched with astonishment as Bill Turner walked past Lorraine and Hugh, and out through the main door.

'You're going to put this maniac into the witness box?' asked Frank with incredulity.

James sighed a deep, heartfelt sigh and slumped back in his desk, flicking through Bill Turner's cuttings.

'It *is* amazing how many people believe they're being watched by, you know, the powers that be,' said James. 'CIA interfering with the milk deliveries, MI5 tapping their phones.'

The telephone engineer finished putting the back on James's phone.

'There,' said the man cheerfully. 'That should do it.'

CHAPTER THREE

John Woodham was unsure whether his secret caller would show up at the rendezvous. All he could be sure of was that the witness to Katherine's hit-and-run accident was a woman and extremely frightened.

He absentmindedly picked at the flaking paintwork on the pub table, while he sat waiting in the bright spring sunlight. She had been insistent about the time and the place; but as yet there was no sign of her. He was just wondering whether to get himself a second pint or call it a day, when a young woman came out of the pub and joined him.

She was wearing a dark car-coat over a policewoman's uniform.

'Now you know why I have to be careful,' she said nervously. She sipped her orange juice as she told him what she knew.

'Look, your sources were right,' she said. 'There was a van, and it was a police van. It killed that little boy, I'm certain. I was on the scene within minutes. There was no sign of any other vehicle, no other skid marks, no other debris, nothing. This is all wrong.'

She remained silent whilst Woodham finished taking it all down.

'Were the drivers policemen?' he asked.

'Yes, I know they were. They showed us their warrant cards.' She paused for a moment. 'Anyway, I knew one of them by sight.'

'What about the guy who was being sick, the American?'

'No idea. He'd crapped himself, that's all I know.'

The two stared into their glasses.

'The weapons?' Woodham broke the silence. 'Who's keeping quiet?'

The policewoman looked around the pub garden to check that there was no one else there, before she continued.

'I don't know,' she said. 'Somebody very senior, because the pressure we're under to shut up is nobody's business. Official Secrets Act, old pals act, you name it. It's sickened me and I'm not the only one. But it's wrong.'

Her voice broke and she started getting emotional.

'I for one,' she said, 'would like to know why that little boy was run over, and I'm not a hero, and I'm not looking for trouble, but I'm not going to help protect the people responsible. I've got a five-year-old myself.'

'It would really help if I knew who those cops were.' Woodham decided to seize his opportunity.

'Anti-terrorist squad,' she said after a long pause.

'You said someone very senior. Bob Fine?'

The policewoman shook her head.

'I find it hard to believe. If he'd had officers under him who'd done something like this, he'd be the first to do something about it. Commander Fine . . . I mean he's a legend.'

CHAPTER FOUR

The Radio Four newsreader spoke in his usual neutral tone.

'The trial of peace camp women at Ipswich Crown Court today ended in acquittals for all five women defendants,' he read.

Katherine slapped her hands on the steering wheel with non-neutral glee.

'Wallop. Take that!' she exclaimed to herself as she drove along through the flat Suffolk countryside.

Rather than take the motorway straight back to London, she had felt like celebrating her victory with a drive through Constable country, especially beautiful in Spring, before hordes of tourists could descend on it. The fields looked ethereal in the pale, late afternoon light.

Suddenly, the road narrowed and became a rutted lane. Katherine realized she was lost. She pulled up and looked at her road map, but still couldn't work out where she was. Noticing a signpost lying on its side, she got out of the car. Her mood of elation vanished as she felt the coldness of the wind, and looked up to see a flock of birds swooping across the sky like fighter planes. Dark clouds were building up on the horizon. She hurried along the side of the ditch to inspect the signpost. It was no good. Both names on the signpost had been obliterated by vandals.

Walking back to the car, Katherine decided to go for the quickest possible route back to London. A slow drive through East Anglian farmland had lost its appeal. A long way off, she thought she could see a farm house. Maybe they could give her directions. Back in her car, Katherine set off, twiddling the knob on the radio to retune it to Radio Three. Wagner blared out at her and she snapped the radio off.

Looking in her rear-view mirror, she saw that there was a van driving dangerously close behind her. She put her foot gently on the brake pedal, so that the lights would signal a warning, and was relieved when the van suddenly pulled out and overtook her at speed. It roared off round a bend and out of sight.

Light was beginning to fail as the farm house came into view again. It was set back off the road. She drove up the farm track through large puddles, sending chickens flapping out of her path, and parked in the yard round the back of the house. Katherine got out of the car, and looked to see if there were any lights on in the house. She had just formed the opinion that the place was deserted, when the van which had bothered her earlier suddenly reappeared and drove right into her car.

Katherine stood and watched in horror as the van reversed and drove at the car for a second time. This time, it rammed the car about ten yards across the farmyard. The back doors of the van swung open. Three men in combat gear and balaclavas jumped out and ran towards her. Katherine's heart pounded with fear. She did her best to escape, running through the farm outbuildings, dodging between farm machinery and then she stumbled through an open door into a large barn.

Petrified, she realized that she was trapped. She turned and raised her hands to protect her face as the men came at her with truncheons. She was knocked to the ground and two of them picked her up and threw her on to a pile of horse manure. She cowered, whimpering, face down, as they beat her and kicked her. Finally, they undid their flies and urinated over her.

When she came to, her attackers had gone. She crawled on hands and knees across the barn floor to the door which swung in the wind on creaky hinges. She gulped back her tears and continued her slow and painful progress across the yard to the farm house. There were lights on now. Katherine slowly pulled herself upright and banged feebly on the door.

*

The next day, Katherine woke in her own bed to see Frank and Lorraine standing over her.

'What happened?' croaked Katherine. Her memories of the last few hours were confused. What was dream, and what reality?

'Don't try to talk,' said Lorraine. 'The doctor says you've no broken bones, just severe bruising.'

'You're telling me,' groaned Katherine. She ached from top to bottom. 'How did I get home?'

'You don't remember?' said Frank.

'Shock,' said Lorraine.

'You got the farmer's wife to ring me,' Frank told Katherine. 'I picked you up.'

'Oh, Frank, I'm sorry,' said Katherine.

'Don't be,' said Frank, sitting on her bed. 'When we got back, I rang Lorraine. She gave you a bath and put you to bed. She's been here all night.'

Katherine's eyes filled with tears of gratitude.

'You didn't call the police?' asked Katherine suddenly.

'You wouldn't let us,' said Lorraine, with a curious expression on her face. 'Do you know who did this to you? Is it something to do with the peace camp case?'

'Maybe,' whispered Katherine. 'But I think it's this hit-and-run thing.'

'Katherine, you should tell the police,' Frank insisted.

Katherine felt dreadful, and she knew she must look dreadful. Even so, she felt determined.

'Come off it, Frank. What's the point?' she asked.

She felt angry with herself when her body shook and she began to whimper like a small, frightened animal. It was as if she was out of control.

'Give me a kiss, Frank?' Katherine asked, raising her bruised face up to him.

Frank took Katherine in his arms and hugged her to him like a small child. He brushed back the hair which had fallen over her face, careful to avoid touching her bruises and cuts, and planted two kisses on her cracked, swollen lips. He smiled when, almost immediately, Katherine fell asleep.

*

Later on, Katherine felt well enough to see John Wood-ham. Lorraine let him into the flat, and poured him a whisky. Katherine could see that he was shocked by her appearance, but she told him only in the briefest terms what had happened to her. She had no desire to dwell on the nightmare, more and more of which she was now beginning to remember.

'So what have you found out?' she asked.

'Geoffrey Katz is supposed to have left the CIA in 1981 when he fell under suspicion, along with two others, of running weapons to terrorists in the Middle East. He's now widely thought to be an important member of the Secret Team.'

'Yeah, you mentioned that. What is it?' asked Katherine.

'The Secret Team is a state within a state. Past or present members of the CIA, depending on your point of view, operating huge drugs and arms smuggling businesses in order to finance, well, who knows what, arms to the Contras, but what else . . .'

'Is there an English branch of this Secret Team?' asked Katherine.

Woodham shrugged his shoulders. Katherine saw him looking at her, as if she were a child.

'Katherine,' he said slowly, 'I don't honestly feel that having got this far *I* can let this drop. But there's no longer any compelling reason why *you* shouldn't take a very remote back seat.'

'No,' insisted Katherine, with all the spirit that she could muster. 'No back seat. I want to get as much of this public as soon as possible.'

CHAPTER FIVE

Over the next couple of days, Katherine watched a lot more television than usual, mainly because she could do little else, but partly because she wanted to see what the official response to John Woodham's front-page article was. She was not surprised when the Home Secretary made only a brief, bland reference to it in the House of Commons.

Later that evening, she was dozing off in front of the TV, when she heard the Home Secretary's statement once again. She opened her eyes to see a familiar BBC face.

'That was the Home Secretary answering questions about suspected MI5 involvement in the Khadri case, following a report by journalist John Woodham. With me now is an acknowledged expert and author on security matters, Michael Crowe.'

The camera cut to an elderly, dapper man.

'Mr Crowe, do you give any credence to the theory that the CIA and the police could be involved in some shady arms smuggling operation?'

The expert thought for a moment before replying.

'I think it's possible. Until a year or two ago, I'd have

said it was utterly non-feasible; but recent developments inside the security community have changed my thinking. Frankly, almost anything is now believable.'

'What sort of developments?' probed the interviewer. 'Are you talking about MI5?'

'I am talking about MI5. Basically, what I suspect is going on is this. There is a group inside MI5, a small but influential group – extremely patriotic, let it be said – led by a charismatic senior officer I'm obviously not at liberty to name, who have allowed their ideology to lead them into some very murky operational areas.'

'Surely a senior officer shouldn't allow ideology to intervene?' asked the interviewer.

*

Valentine sat in his office in Curzon Street, and stared at the television.

'What people don't understand at all well is the stresses and strains that a man like this lives with, day in, day out,' Crowe was saying. 'Is it any wonder if occasionally an element of instability creeps in?'

Valentine banged his glass down on the sidetable. Bloody cheek.

'Bastards!' he exclaimed, recognizing all the signs of a set-up.

Valentine got up from his chair and crossed to his desk. He sat down at his computer terminal and typed away. The screen lit up, but only with the words 'Sorry the registry is closed.' He was too late, then. Returning to the TV, Valentine poured himself another whisky and sat down to wait.

Within the hour, as Valentine expected, four large security men – accompanied, of course, by that smug smoothie, Tyler – arrived in his room. Wrenched unceremoniously from his chair, Valentine was frogmarched out of his office, along the empty corridors and down in the lift to the ground floor, where he was politely escorted out of the front door and thrown on to the pavement.

*

James felt incongruous, being fully clothed, as the old man in the pool swam his regulation five lengths, just as he did every morning. This indoor pool was one of the best in London; not surprisingly, since it belonged to one of the best gentlemen's clubs. James was glad that today it was deserted. The old man swam over to him, with an expression of great satisfaction.

'Not coming in, James?'

'Not today, Dad. I'm due back in court in half an hour,' he replied.

'Not staying for lunch?'

'Thanks all the same, Dad. Well?'

'Ah yes,' said Sir Charles, looking round to make sure they were not being observed. 'They weren't terribly keen to be helpful, even for an old friend.'

James could not quite suppress a smile. His father had always prided himself on his contacts within British Intelligence.

'And you certainly picked your moment to ask a favour, what with Fleet Street worried about your friend the harpy banging on about Scotland Yard selling Chieftain tanks to the Ayatollahs.'

James was pretty sure now that his father had discovered something, and tried to get him to concentrate on the subject.

'There's no connection,' said James. 'It's a simple question. Are they sure they haven't made a mistake and got the wrong Bill Turner?'

'But say the answer was yes,' remarked Sir Charles. 'You see, from their point of view, yet another opportunity

279

for somebody to get up a story in the papers, poking MI5 in the eye with a burnt stick. More opposition MPs sinking their yellow teeth into the poor old Home Secretary's legs.'

James could not feel the same sympathy which his father evidently felt for the Home Secretary's legs, but decided to let that pass.

'The answer was no, then,' said James.

'I'm promised this is definitely kosher, James. There's no mistake. Your client failed a routine security vetting.'

'Did they say why, for God's sake?'

'Now, James,' his father rebuked him, 'you asked me to ask a simple question. The answer was no. You didn't ask me to ask, and I wouldn't have agreed to ask, any supplementaries. It's supposed to be a bloody secret service, you know, though you wouldn't believe it these days!'

James watched gloomily, as his father submerged.

*

Katherine recovered more slowly than she had expected. The physical bruises remained for days, but the mental scars were far more frightening. She had always thought of herself as a strong, fearless individual. Yet now she hardly had the confidence to answer the phone.

When she did answer it, she felt as if she was still dreaming. The man spoke as if he was in a John Le Carré thriller. He had information. He wanted to meet her. Alone. In her flat.

'Certainly not,' said Katherine.

After a brief pause, the man gave her the name of a Thames riverboat as a rendezvous.

'Is this a joke?' she asked.

But he had already rung off.

*

Katherine forced herself to keep the appointment. What harm can come to me in broad daylight in the middle of London, she asked herself. As the boat left its moorings, she had to clutch her hat to stop it blowing off. She walked the length of the deserted top deck and descended steep steps into the cabin area.

The hot, steamy atmosphere engulfed her as she stood at the bottom of the steps. She glanced round the three rows of formica-topped tables and cheap, plastic chairs. A fat, bald man waved at her from one of the far window tables. He was drinking strong-looking tea from a polystyrene cup.

'I'm Valentine,' he said.

He spoke in the tones of the military establishment, and wore a camel coat exactly like James's. Katherine sat opposite him.

'How did you know me?' she asked.

'From photographs. What can I get you?' he asked with old-world courtesy.

'Who are you?' Katherine demanded.

'I thought it would be easier if we sat in here,' Valentine said, nodding pleasantly to a young couple sitting two tables away.

'Your friends, are they?' Katherine asked sarcastically.

'Former colleagues,' said Valentine, choosing his words carefully. 'That is why I suggested your flat, I thought it would save them the trouble.'

Understanding dawned on Katherine.

'My flat is bugged?' she said.

'Of course,' said Valentine placidly.

'What gives you people the right to do that?'

'National security, of course,' he said.

'Am I on file?' Katherine ventured.

'Of course you are. Surely you all know you are?' Valentine spoke as if he could not believe her naïvety. 'You spend enough time muttering your jeremiads about the secret state. I mean to say, if you're not a legitimate target I really don't know who is.'

Katherine swallowed hard. This all seemed like a bad dream.

'You wanted to say something to me,' she said, 'and presumably to your former friends.'

'First of all,' said Valentine, 'a few facts about myself, to counterbalance the disinformation.'

Katherine suddenly realized who the man was.

'You're him!' she exclaimed, laughing. 'So *you're* what Michael Crowe thinks of as charismatic.'

Valentine gave her a wry smile.

'Yes,' he said modestly. 'I've been an MI5 officer since coming down from Oxford in 1957. I spent eight years as head of F branch, domestic subversion. For the past three years I've led, charismatically or otherwise, a special unit whose existence will never be admitted to in any circumstances by my superiors or their political masters.'

Katherine felt disgust. But at the same time, he did have a certain presence.

'One of my duties was to assist an operation across a dusty concern. Desert Song is the supply of arms to terrorist bases in Gadaffi's Libya. It's primarily a cover CIA operation. Our American cousins bring the weaponry into Heathrow and we supervise the police moving it across London to Stanstead, from where it's flown on to Libya.'

Katherine now understood why she had seen Russian arms in a British police van.

'What is in it for Commander Fine?' asked Katherine, remembering John's conviction that the man responsible for the police involvement could only be Fine.

'Purely money,' said Valentine. 'Buckets full of it. He's a greedy, greedy man.'

'Why guns to Libya?' asked Katherine, puzzled.

'Theoretically, the rationale is that by getting someone like Katz into terrorist bases in Libya, western intelligence can monitor who's being trained to do what. The thought that those weapons might reappear in European cities to murder young policewomen apparently doesn't matter.'

Katherine saw why Valentine had refused to go along with the scheme.

'Michael Crowe says you're crackers,' Katherine remarked boldly.

For a moment or two, the pair of them stared out of the window as the boat chugged past County Hall. Katherine thought of the few heady years of Red Ken's time in power. Valentine evidently had other things on his mind.

'I have received psychiatric counsel for a number of years,' he said, 'for normal stresses and strains. I'm not unstable. However, I expect to be charged within a day or two.'

'With what?' Katherine was all attention.

'I don't know,' said Valentine, as if this were of no significance. 'If the Prime Minister's feeling brave, section 2. Like you, I'm becoming devoted to the idea of openness, freedom of information. As a token of goodwill, I've sent some information on Desert Song to your journalist friend. I've also sent something to Mr Bingham which he may find helpful.'

'Why do you need our goodwill?'

'I'm going to need good lawyers,' smirked Valentine. 'I know you and Cartwright are good. All your mail intercepts came across my desk for eight years.'

He finished drinking his tea. She wanted to puncture his bland superiority.

'Aren't you going to offer me some kind of explanation?' she asked.

Valentine glanced at her bruised face.

'Oh, that,' he said dismissively. 'What explanation do you need?'

'It wasn't Santiago. This is England. It was in the middle of the English countryside.'

The boat came into dock at Westminster pier and Valentine rose to leave.

'Yes, it is England, isn't it,' he said ruefully.

He clicked his heels together and bowed to Katherine.

'Au revoir,' he said in a jaunty manner, as he turned and walked away.

Katherine watched the two from the nearby table follow him. Her nightmare had grown in dimensions, but now at least she felt that she understood a small part of it. She hastily rose and left the boat before it set off on another trip.

She rang Frank from a public phone box, to ask if she could stay at his house for a while. Then she hailed a taxi to take her to Notting Hill. As far as she could tell, nobody was following her.

Back in her flat, Katherine packed. She threw a selection of her clothes into two suitcases, and a number of files and books into her briefcase. She hated herself for feeling so vulnerable, but her own flat seemed to have been invaded by invisible enemies. She scowled at the telephone sitting blandly by her bedside.

'You won't get away with driving me out!' she shouted. 'I'll be back!'

CHAPTER SIX

That evening, James asked himself round to Frank's basement kitchen, for a discussion with Frank and Katherine. James carried a thick dossier which had been sent to him anonymously. Katherine explained who had sent it.

'Valentine said it was a token of goodwill for the radical Bar,' Katherine explained. 'But he was really talking to his ex-colleagues, saying "If you make me the scapegoat I will not go quietly."'

Frank looked up from the documents which James had brought round.

'So there is another Bill Turner,' Frank observed.

'What sort of a country is it where they would just throw away this man's life like this?' fumed James. 'And they lied to my father!'

Katherine burst into laughter and choked on her wine. James turned to her with an aggrieved look on her face.

'Something funny, Katherine?'

'I'm sorry, James,' Katherine apologized through her giggles.

'No, please, share the joke,' James insisted.

'Well, it's just that these people piss all over Bill Turner and me — in my case literally — and you get aerated about the fact that they lied to your father. I think he got off lightly. I wish I'd been wearing the right school tie! Maybe I'd have got off with being slipped a couple of white lies instead of being beaten up and thrown in the shit.'

'I'm afraid I find class prejudice hard to stomach even in these circumstances,' asserted James.

'Class prejudice?' questioned Katherine, incredulously.

'Just because he's my father and doesn't happen to live in a tenant house in Salford doesn't mean his feelings don't matter.'

'I just think it's ridiculous, but ridiculously, wonderfully eloquent about *you*, James, that the first time I've ever clapped eyes on you being angry it's caused by some petty piece of public-school bad form. "They lied to my father." I mean, what does that make your father? I mean, for God's sake, it's exactly the knowledge that the country is run by a sacred club of overgrown schoolboys that drives me round the bend.'

'Oh, that's what drives you round the bend? I thought it might be the strain of being such a rude, opinionated, bigoted hypocrite!' shouted James.

'I'm a hypocrite as well, am I?' Katherine shouted back.

'Yes, you are. I'm a life member of this club, I suppose?' James asked ironically.

'Yes, you are, because you were born into your class and there's nothing you can do to get out of it.'

'*You* seem to have managed!' James retorted.

They both sat back in silence, stunned by what they had said to each other.

'Well,' said Frank, 'now that's all finally out in the open, maybe the two of you can come to some sort of a working relationship?'

He raised his glass of wine and toasted his two friends. Katherine caught the look of fury on James's face, and couldn't help laughing. After a moment or two, James joined in.

*

The next day, James drove down to Essex with Helen Robinson, Bill Turner's new solicitor, and picked Bill up from the sordid bedsitting-room in which he was now living. Bill had insisted on making the journey with them, and was almost besides himself with glee at the thought of meeting the man for whom he had been mistaken.

'The same name, virtually the same national insurance number, but a real subversive! It's like coming face to face with your doppelgänger!' Bill prattled, as James drove through the suburbs of Chelmsford. 'Doctor Jekyll is about to meet Mr Hyde!'

James shot a glance at the other occupant of the car. Helen Robinson was a small, tough woman with fair hair and metal-rimmed spectacles, renowned for her opposition to the Official Secrets Act. James knew she had taken an instant and unsurprising dislike to Bill Turner, and that she had severe doubts about her client's mental health. Turner's babbling could only be adding to those doubts.

James finally pulled the BMW up outside a small, suburban semi-detached with an overgrown garden. Bill Turner ran up the short garden path to ring the doorbell. Chimes sounded, and the door was opened by a gangly, genial man in a dog collar.

'Hello, come in,' the Reverend Bill Turner welcomed them warmly. 'Welcome to the hub of my network of subversion: Bill Turner, I presume?'

The vicar thrust a large paw out at James, who shook

his head and pointed to his client. Bill Turner was looking round his namesake's hall with a mixture of horror and distaste. Peace movement posters all but covered the peeling floral wallpaper.

'As you can see,' said the subversive Bill Turner, 'I'm active in the peace movement. Funnily enough, I've always been a bit annoyed that nobody ever tampered with my mail. I mean a lot of my friends have had their phones tapped and I never have, you know. I was beginning to wonder if it was a plot to make me look like an informer, or to make me look even more insignificant than I already am. Thank goodness there's an explanation at last. The security services are completely incompetent!'

James and Helen laughed. They had both taken a liking to the big, amiable clergyman. Their client, however, had not.

'I don't think your activities are funny, I'm afraid, Reverend,' he said, gesticulating somewhat wildly at the walls. 'I've paid the price for all this.'

'Actually, I do little more than lick stamps,' said the Reverend apologetically.

'Someone obviously thinks there's more to it than that,' said Bill Turner aggressively.

James tried to cover this insult by handing over a file to the Reverend Turner.

'This belongs to you, rightfully,' said James. 'We haven't made a copy. But we would like you to consider giving evidence.'

'Of course, of course,' the clergyman agreed, looking at the file with obvious delight. 'Oh, how wonderful! My very own MI5 file! It's just like Eamonn Andrews!'

'Just a minute, that's my evidence! That's my liberty you're handing over!' Bill Turner tried to wrench the file back out of the clergyman's hands.

It was only through the intervention of a horrified Helen Robinson that a brawl was averted. James and Helen refused the vicar's offer of tea, and bundled Bill Turner back into the BMW as soon as they decently could.

CHAPTER SEVEN

The inhabitants of Fetter Court looked on in amazement as members of the security services vetted the Chambers. Hugh ostentatiously read a copy of *Spycatcher*. A large safe, the size of an industrial fridge, was hauled up the stairs and located next to Frank's desk. Two men, supervised by a man who introduced himself as Tyler, were electronically sweeping the area for bugs.

The reason for all this was that David Valentine had been charged, as he suspected he might be, under section 2 of the Official Secrets Act. He had rejected the solicitor which MI5 had offered to provide for him. Instead, Valentine had demanded the radical solicitor George Viner, with Katherine and Frank as his two briefs.

'Which area will be used for case conferences?' enquired Tyler, as his men went up the stairs to the gallery.

'We have three conference rooms,' replied Frank.

'You'll have to undertake to use only one,' said Tyler. 'It's a lot simpler that way.'

'For whom?' Katherine asked sarcastically.

Tyler ignored her.

'Now you must understand,' he said as though they

were small children who had to be taught how to behave, 'all documents relating to the case have to be kept under lock and key at all times when not actually being worked from. You cannot take any papers away from the Chambers, and no other members of the Chambers can be allowed to see any of the documents.'

He looked at Katherine and Frank with obvious distaste, exacerbated by the fact they were finding it difficult to keep a straight face.

'Now, I'd like to speak to you in private,' Tyler continued, indicating that they should follow him into one of the conference rooms.

Frank, Katherine and Viner followed Tyler upstairs. Tyler firmly shut the door and then produced three documents from his briefcase.

'I'd like you all to read and sign this,' said Tyler, distributing the sheets of paper.

'What is it?' asked Frank.

'It's a copy of the relevant part of the Official Secrets Act,' replied Tyler.

The lawyers all looked at each other and nodded in agreement. Viner spoke for them all.

'We're already bound by the Official Secrets Act, in the same way as we're bound by the Road Traffic Act or the Historic Monuments Act,' he pointed out. 'Why not ask us to sign those?'

'Are you refusing to sign?' asked Tyler.

'This is straightforward intimidation,' said Viner. 'Can I drink after time because I haven't signed a copy of the Licensing Act?'

Tyler turned to Katherine.

'You are required to sign this by law,' said Tyler.

'I know what the law is,' said Katherine.

'All right,' snapped Tyler. 'Not my problem. We'll go back out now and I'll tap in the combination number.'

'Why?' asked Frank.

'So you can use the safe,' Tyler explained, as if to a retarded child.

'Why do *you* need to know the combination? Whose safe is it anyway?' Frank persisted.

'Ours,' said Tyler.

Katherine stared at Tyler.

'Well, take it back with you,' she said. 'We didn't ask for it.'

Though plainly infuriated by their attitude, Tyler handed them a sheaf of instructions. Once downstairs again, he seemed only too pleased to get out of the place. He signalled to his sweepers and safe men, waiting for him by the sliding door, that they could go. As he walked towards the exit, past the clerks' desks, Tyler tapped Hugh's book.

'Fantasy,' Tyler murmured.

He left the Chambers briskly, as though they were in some way contaminated.

Silence fell over the room as the door clanged, only to be followed almost immediately by nervous laughter.

*

Everybody else had left the Chambers as Frank and Katherine waited for Viner to return, this time with Valentine. Valentine's first act was to look curiously around the large room.

'Have they been?' he asked.

'They claimed to be sweeping the entire place for bugs,' replied Frank.

'And did they pronounce any room in particular to be more free of eavesdropping devices than the rest?' asked Valentine, drily.

'The conference room up there seems safest, they thought.'

They all chuckled.

'Good, let's use it,' said Valentine. 'I want them to be in no doubt about what I intend to make known.'

Katherine led the way up the stairs to the conference room. Valentine had evidently been drinking heavily, but expounded his argument with great clarity.

'I'm afraid I can't oblige you with a nice "right to know" defence à la Ponting, for the simple reason that I don't believe people *do* have a right to know,' began Valentine. 'My defence is as follows. I'm charged with retaining and/or communicating information contained in three batches of documents. I have copies here.'

He opened his briefcase and passed a file from it across to Frank.

'The first batch,' said Valentine, 'was the file on the second Mr Turner. If they wish to run an official secrets case against me on that, they'll make themselves look even bigger fools than they really are. The second batch refers to Desert Song.'

Valentine looked shrewdly at Katherine, and then at Frank.

'Frank,' Valentine asked, 'have you been indoctrinated into Desert Song?'

Frank nodded; but Valentine clearly wanted to make sure he really understood. Or perhaps Valentine just wanted his old employers to understand the man they were up against.

'Desert Song is a straightforward money-making scam,' said Valentine, 'being run by people who are little better than animals, in my humble opinion. I am referring here to our senior partners in the intelligence community, the Americans, whose every bidding we are obliged to do every time they come up with some idiotic scheme.'

Frank posed a question.

'But I thought the purpose of Desert Song is to infiltrate CIA agents into terrorist training camps in Libya?'

'The purpose of Desert Song,' riposted Valentine, 'is to make a lot of money. This is my point. They cannot accuse me of prejudicing the national interest by disclosing the operation, when the operation is straightforward private enterprise. Don't you think it's beautifully ironic that we're now colonized by barbarians?'

'I don't understand,' said Frank. 'If Desert Song is private enterprise, where does all the money go, and why did you go on helping it?'

'Because I was ordered to do so,' stated Valentine. 'Where the money went is the biggest question of all. At first, weapons for the Contras, weapons for the Mujihadeen, for their own terrorist training camps in America. But after that: homes, swimming pools, hotel bills and all the paraphernalia of bribery and corruption.'

Katherine was impatient with Valentine's rhetoric.

'There's a third batch of documents, you said. There's more to this than guns to Libya?'

Valentine snapped his briefcase shut.

'I think that's enough for today,' he announced to everybody's surprise. 'It doesn't do to over-egg the pudding, does it?'

He stood up and shot one final glance round the room before leaving.

As Frank was depositing the Desert Song file in the safe, Valentine asked Katherine whether anyone from the security services had given a name.

'Tyler,' she replied.

Valentine nodded, in his usual superior manner.

'It's a racing certainty that Tyler was behind the attack on you,' he said airily. 'Of course, he'd have put it out to tender.'

Katherine felt sick at Valentine's callousness. At the

same time, she felt a certain admiration for his lack of concern for his own safety.

'Ta ta for now,' Valentine said breezily. He left the room walking in a jaunty fashion, as if pleased with a good evening's work.

Katherine walked over to the safe, where George Viner and Frank were talking.

'George here is worried about you being on the defence team,' said Frank as she joined the two men.

'We should face the fact that the Bar Council might take issue with you doing it, given that you have made some public utterances on all this,' explained Viner.

Katherine was having none of this.

'No, I haven't. I've spoken about something I saw in the street. What's that got to do with Valentine blowing the whistle?'

'If the prosecution wanted to be nasty, they might say there's a risk you have evidence which might, just might, have to be used in the case.'

'They can call Hugh,' countered Katherine. 'They can call the woman who leaked information to my journalist friend. How many witnesses do they need? I'm doing this case and I'm not going to let some manoeuvre dressed up as etiquette stop me.'

Frank and Viner looked at each other.

'OK,' said Frank with a smile. 'We're all in it.'

*

Katherine was not totally surprised when Valentine's legal team was summoned to the office of the Director of Public Prosecutions. As she was kept waiting in the wood-panelled ante-room with Frank and Viner, Katherine felt unusually on edge.

Part of the problem was simply lack of sleep. She hated taking sleeping pills, because she had seen too many people who had become dependent on them. Even when she finally got to sleep, she was cursed with terrible nightmares about the attack on her, and by day she was haunted by memories of the men in balaclava helmets.

After the trio of lawyers had all been kept waiting for the statutory amount of time, they were shown into the DPP's office. A suave, distinguished, elderly man rose from behind his desk and shook them all by the hand.

'Thank you for coming,' the DPP said, indicating that they should sit down. 'Now clearly we all have an enormous problem.'

He looked towards his visitors for a reaction which did not come, and then coughed before continuing.

'The problem is how to ensure that your client has the fairest possible trial without national security being prejudiced at all. I understand that you've refused as yet to sign a copy of the Act. I have to say that that refusal is certain to be detrimental to your client. You see, the prosecution will prove its case by establishing that Valentine has a wealth of potentially damaging information which he must be prevented from disclosing.'

Frank spoke for the three lawyers.

'Politically damaging to the security services and to the government, maybe, but not to national security. That's not an issue.'

The DPP shook his head.

'You simply aren't in a position to know that. We can't give you the documentary evidence which proves that, unless you give a solemn and binding undertaking never to disclose it afterwards. The case itself of course will be heard in camera.'

'That's for the judge to decide,' said Katherine, irritated by the DPP's blandness.

The DPP smiled patronizingly.

'I think we can all assume that.'

'Are you telling me we can't see the evidence against our client?' asked Viner.

Frank and Katherine exchanged glances.

'Are you going to blindfold us when it's produced in court?' Frank added caustically. 'Or do you intend to hold the trial not only in the absence of the press and the public, but in the absence of the defence lawyers too?'

'Very democratic,' Katherine mumbled.

'The jury is made up of members of the public,' retorted the DPP.

'Will the jury be allowed to see and hear everything?' asked Viner.

'Well, that again will be for the judge to decide.'

'Will the jury be allowed to see and hear anything?' asked Katherine sarcastically.

Frank interposed quickly.

'Sir, I will undertake here and now not to disclose anything likely to be prejudicial to the security of the nation, and if I ever do so the Attorney-General can have me charged under the Act. But I will not undertake to help keep secret the facts about so-called intelligence operations which are clearly politically or commercially motivated. And in case you have any doubt, let me tell you precisely: our client's defence is exactly that.'

Frank looked at his two colleagues, and they rose together to take their leave. Both sides knew there was little point in talking any further.

Outside, dusk was falling. Katherine shivered, and was glad that she was not having to return to her flat. Frank and she refused Viner's invitation to a drink, and set off together for Islington.

*

Even though Katherine felt relatively secure in Frank's home, there were still times when she felt frightened for no apparent reason. She was washing lettuce in the basement kitchen one evening when suddenly she remembered her attack in every appalling detail. She stood utterly rigid, grasping the edge of the sink in panic.

Fortunately, she had pulled herself together by the time John and Peter came charging down the stairs and threw themselves at her. They had both proved remarkably resilient to their mother's death. Most of their daily care was now dealt with by a young Scottish nanny who had the right combination of common sense and fun needed to rub along in the Cartwright household.

Tonight was one of the nanny's nights off; and Katherine was pleasantly surprised at how much she enjoyed the company of the children. The East Anglian nightmare had to be forgotten as Katherine attended to them.

'Katherine!' yelled John. 'Peter's hurting me!'

John was given the task of waving the salad shaker, which sent out sprays of water, much to his delight. Peter was given the chore of setting the table for the evening meal.

'It's not salad for supper again,' moaned Alethea as she came in.

'I thought you were worried about getting fat,' retorted Katherine.

Alethea let out a long-suffering sigh, with the world-weariness of a woman of fifty. Katherine smiled. Of all the children, Alethea seemed to have suffered most as a result of her mother's death. Katherine recognized in her some of the same feelings she had experienced when her own mother had died.

Alethea had suddenly grown up very fast. She reminded Katherine frighteningly of Annie, as she had been at nineteen, and sometimes she wondered how Frank could cope with the similarity.

The boys rushed upstairs when they heard the front

door open. Frank staggered down to the kitchen basement with a case of wine from one of the local wine warehouses, the boys dancing attendance.

Supper was followed by a game of Trivial Pursuit, during which Frank showed off appallingly. Katherine as usual was baffled by any question which had anything to do with Sport or Science, and was secretly delighted when Alethea won.

'Bloody hell,' said Frank, who still had one segment to go.

John and Peter (who had one segment each) duly burst into tears and were dispatched to their bedrooms. Alethea announced her intention of watching a mindless Australian soap on television.

'It'll rot your mind,' warned Frank.

'I would remind you,' said Alethea haughtily, 'that I have just beaten you in a contest of general knowledge.'

Katherine sat down to work on her brief for the following day. She had taken to using the large kitchen table as her desk, and was so deep in thought that she did not notice Frank come down the stairs and sit opposite her at the table.

'Fancy a nightcap?' he asked, unscrewing a bottle of whisky.

Katherine looked up with a start.

'Is that the time? Good heavens! I had no idea it was so late,' she said. 'Yes please.'

Frank pushed a glass towards her.

'I've been thinking about our non-Trivial Pursuit,' said Frank. 'I don't think it'll stop with the DPP, somehow.'

'No?'

'No,' said Frank.

He looked old and worried.

'How on earth can Valentine get a fair trial?' he asked after a pause.

'He can't,' said Katherine.

'That's what I was thinking.'

'It's a wonderful system of justice where only the judge can see the evidence, isn't it?'

Katherine put her papers away in her briefcase and got up. She ruffled Frank's hair as she walked past, and gave him a little kiss on the top of his head.

'See you in the morning, Frank.'

'Yeah,' said Frank. 'And Katherine . . .'

'Mm?' she asked, pausing on the stairs.

'I wanted to say . . . It's good, having you here,' said Frank. 'The kids like it. I like it.'

'I like it too,' said Katherine.

There was an awkward pause. For the first time in their relationship, Katherine felt that Frank and she were both lost for words.

'Hey ho,' said Katherine, yawning. 'I'm in court tomorrow with my flying pickets. I don't give them much chance either.'

Frank smiled, with an absent-minded expression which told Katherine that for the last few moments he had been thinking of Annie.

'Ah well,' said Frank, draining his glass. 'I suppose we should know better than to think there's really any justice in the world.'

'Sleep well, Frank.'

'And you.'

*

'Cartwright,' said the Attorney-General pleasantly, 'may I get you a drink?'

Frank looked around him at the faded grandeur of the Garrick Club. Unlike James, Frank never felt at home in such surroundings; and he felt even more uneasy that the Attorney-General himself wanted to see him here.

'No, thank you,' said Frank politely, as he sat.

'Congratulations on your silk,' said the Attorney-General. 'Long overdue. Absurd that an advocate of your distinction spent so long as junior counsel.'

'Well, being junior counsel has its advantages,' said Frank.

'Yes, well . . .' said the older man, impatiently. 'Now then, this business. We really have to get it sorted out. We can't go into court on this basis.'

Frank waited.

'As you know,' said the Attorney-General, 'it wasn't my idea to prosecute the fellow, but prosecuted he will be. Make no mistake about it. The government won't run away from this.'

He paused, as if waiting for a reply.

'Fine,' said Frank.

'What I need from you,' said the Attorney-General, 'I mean to hell with all this rubbish about solemn undertakings. There *are* people in Westminster who regard the radical Bar as agents of the Kremlin, but you know me and I know you. I know you're a professional barrister. So all we need is a gentleman's agreement.'

'About what?' asked Frank, genuinely puzzled.

'Cartwright, even I won't be allowed to see absolutely everything that's relevant to the case.'

'You mean,' said Frank, 'you're going to prosecute Valentine without seeing all of the evidence?'

'The fact is,' said the Attorney-General, shifting uncomfortably in his chair, 'it's not really *you* who poses the problem. But Katherine Hughes is a different matter.'

Frank stared at the Attorney-General.

'She's a splendid advocate,' added the older man, hurriedly. 'But politically . . . emotionally, volatile.'

Frank nodded.

'We would need to know that you were able to guarantee her discretion too,' said the Attorney-General.

'Ah, I see,' said Frank 'I see. Yes.'

'Good,' said the other man, relieved. 'Can I then rely on you to be decent about this?'

Frank thought for a moment.

'No,' said Frank. 'You can't.'

The Attorney-General's avuncular smile faded rapidly.

'Well, you're a bloody fool, Cartwright. Bad show.'

CHAPTER EIGHT

Valentine staged his second case conference at Fetter Court with evident enjoyment. As they all sat round the conference table, with the early evening sunshine striking Valentine's pate like a spotlight, the man reminded Katherine of a rather bad ham actor. Valentine enjoyed playing to the hidden gallery of his old employers, just as he enjoyed shocking his left-wing lawyers with the secret workings of the state. Katherine was unsure in her own mind of Valentine's motives. The one thing of which she was positive was that he was telling the truth.

Valentine opened his briefcase and produced his third batch of secret documents. He then attempted to give the assembly what was obviously intended to be a background résumé.

'The year 1974,' Valentine lectured them, 'was a turning point for the country. With the Heath government being humiliated by the mineworkers for the second time in two years, and Wilson winning two successive elections on a policy of naked appeasement towards militant workers, many of us became convinced that the rot had to be stopped. The measures that were taken are now more or less common knowledge, thanks to Massiter and Wright. Three years ago, the service was reorganized so that there would be no more whistle-blowing. The third batch of documents is called Wheatsheaf.'

'Wheatsheaf?' asked Frank.

'It is about the workings of a secret team. In fact we're known as the Safe Team. The only objective of the Safe Team was to continue to ensure that no left-leaning party would ever again be returned to power in this nation. To prepare the ground for action against it if it ever happened. To encourage and forge strong links with those on the political scene who would wish to move the Conservative Party permanently to the right.'

Valentine spoke with absolute moral certainty.

'What about parliamentary democracy?' asked Katherine.

'We care as much about parliamentary democracy as you do, Miss Hughes,' smirked Valentine. 'Like you, we regard it as necessary window-dressing. We've sorted out the unions for good, we've sorted out the Labour Party, we've sorted out CND and other such riff-raff. We did what the country wanted.'

'So what went wrong?' asked Frank sourly.

'When the Americans came along with Desert Song, I was opposed to Safe Team participation. I was, however, overruled. When I was subsequently able to establish to my superiors what Desert Song really was, I was again overruled. I was instructed that this was the opportunity we'd been looking for, a chance to achieve private capital funding. I was to receive a cut of the money the American team were making. Our operations could now be funded by participatory profits in arms and drug smuggling.'

Katherine could hardly believe what she was hearing, as Valentine continued.

'The publicity surrounding the death of the child meant that a scapegoat was required.'

Valentine turned to stare accusingly at Katherine. Katherine looked intently back at him.

'Why you?' she asked.

'Just because I'm an anachronism,' Valentine said. 'It became apparent that the Safe Team, or should I say Tyler and I, no longer shared the same values. I think his loyalty is not primarily to this country, though he disputes that, but to absolutes of power and secrecy.'

Valentine seemed satisfied that he had told them and his ex-employers enough. Again, he allowed no more questions and bustled out.

*

Over the next few days, everything seemed to be going Valentine's way. Suddenly, the Attorney-General dropped the charges against him; but Frank and Katherine realized that Valentine was after more than that. He wanted the Safe Team disbanded. Once again, Valentine invited James, Helen Robinson and Bill Turner to meet him at Fetter Court.

By this time, Valentine was acting as if the bugged conference room at Fetter Court were his new office. He plainly enjoyed taking his revenge on Tyler, and had even tracked down the two microphones in the conference room, so that he could position himself to best advantage when speaking.

'Bill,' said James, 'Mr Valentine wants to give evidence for the defence in your case. He was once head of the division which took wrongful action against you.'

'Mr Turner,' said Valentine magnanimously, 'I can't undo all the harm that we did you, but I can tell the court how and why you have been the victim of appalling injustice. I hope you'll forgive me.'

Valentine offered his hand to be shaken. Bill Turner

pumped it, as if the man who had ruined his life was now doing him an enormous favour. James could hardly bring himself to watch.

Outside Fetter Court, James was surprised at how quickly a black cab with a yellow light appeared to take Valentine away. Why didn't they do that when he wanted one? Bill Turner was still waving and saying thank you, as the cab drove off.

CHAPTER NINE

The next day, James and Helen Robinson arrived at Bill Turner's bedsit, to discover that he had put on a special spread for them: tea with sandwiches, scones and jam. He must have noticed James's surprise.

'You said you liked cream teas,' Bill explained.

'Yes, Bill, the thing is,' said James uncomfortably, 'Helen and I have to . . .'

'Let me just brew the tea. Helen, would you like to . . .? Can you get your knees in there, James?'

Turner busied himself with brewing the tea as James and Helen squeezed themselves round the table. James noticed two photographs pinned on the wall: one of Bill's former home, the other of his ex-Volvo.

'I built it myself,' explained Bill.

'I didn't realize,' said James, wondering if he meant the Volvo.

'Yes. Not a bad little house. Nothing like yours though, James.'

James looked puzzled.

'Couldn't resist, I'm afraid,' said Bill. 'I didn't make a nuisance of myself. I just drove past a couple of times. Shall I be mother?'

Bill poured out the tea.

'Sort of place you secretly dream about really, not that I'm complaining,' Bill rambled cheerily. 'I was happy in my niche, my place on the ladder – not as far up as you, but that's how it should be. Do you mind if I ask how much it is worth?'

'Erm. Well,' James thought for a moment, 'about one point two.'

'Christ! What's the mortgage repayment on that?'

'Well, my wife was left it,' admitted James, wishing that Helen Robinson was not there to hear all this.

'Ah,' said Bill Turner, without acrimony. 'Of course, I had to work for every brick of mine.'

'Yes, yes,' muttered James, 'it's an unfair system.'

Bill Turner seemed not to go along with this analysis.

'Well, presumably your wife's father worked for his money?'

'Not really,' said James.

'Well, somebody must have earned it at some point,' said Bill. 'You don't get owt for nowt, as we say.'

James decided it was safer not to continue on this topic. In any case, Helen and he had some rather unpleasant news to impart.

'The thing is, Bill . . .' James tried to get down to business.

Bill, however, was still musing about real estate.

'The sort of place – you know, you think "one day" . . . Well. Who knows? I'm only forty-four. I can start again. That's the thing about this country. What with you and Helen and the Vicar and Mr Valentine all working on my behalf.'

James and Helen exchanged looks. James tried again.

'The thing is . . .'

This time Bill caught the tone of urgency in James's voice.

'Bad news?'

'David Valentine,' said James, 'has disappeared. Vanished.'

A scone halted in mid-air, on its way to Bill's mouth.

'But he's my witness. I'm relying on him.'

'Of course,' continued James, 'it doesn't mean we won't win the day. It just means . . . we're back where we were.'

'Oh.' Bill was struggling to hold back the tears. 'Mr Valentine's left me in the lurch, sort of thing. Right?'

*

Katherine was surprised at how upset James was by the news that Bill Turner had killed himself. That same evening after they'd left him, Turner had managed to rig up a system with a timer, so that when the clock struck twelve, he was electrocuted where he lay, in bed.

Katherine even found herself feeling a bit sorry for Valentine, who had vanished without trace. Neither Katherine nor Frank seriously believed that the man would still be alive. He was far too much of an embarrassment to the authorities.

As a small gesture of defiance, Frank still refused to give Tyler the combination of the safe at Fetter Court. Nevertheless, Frank, James and Katherine could only watch as Tyler's men cut open the safe, and extracted Valentine's secret documents.

Katherine thought – perhaps fancifully – that she recognized two of the men who had assaulted her in the farmyard. Still, she knew she could do nothing about bringing them to justice.

She looked at Frank on one side of her and James on the other side of her, and realized that over the past few weeks all three of them had changed. Accepting the implications of what they now knew to be true about the secret state had meant crossing an invisible but important line. All three of them had crossed it; and not one of them – not even James – was any longer part of the cosy, seamless consensus of 'sensible' political thought.

Now they were in a world where you can't trust the earth under your feet, where it's more important than ever not to lose your grip on reality, but harder than ever to believe what you know to be true.

Tyler and his men left with the documents. Maybe, thought Katherine, we've forgotten the meaning of liberty. That's why we don't care about justice any more.

*

Frank drove Katherine back to Islington, and they did not speak for a long time. Finally, Katherine broke the silence.

'Do you think Valentine was a scapegoat?'

'I *was* sure he was doing it for revenge, or for his pension to be reinstated,' said Frank slowly, 'or because they probably told him once that he'd get a knighthood and he wanted them to keep their promise. But no, I think he'd actually realized it's out of control. Not just his team of high-tech thugs but the whole idea of an England decked out in permanent blue. In a sense, you know, he was an English dissenter, a defector even.'

Katherine looked at Frank, thoughtfully.

'The thing I really hated about him,' she said, 'was that he thought we were so naïve.'

Frank did not speak for some seconds.

'Weren't we?' he asked.

They subsided back into silence. Katherine looked out of the car window as Frank drove up the New North Road towards the comfort of N1.

'Frank, it's been wonderful,' she said. 'But I think it's time I slept at home again.'

Frank laughed.

'Why?' he said. 'Are you worried about your reputation?'

There was another silence.

'Your flat's still bugged,' he said.

'And your home isn't?' asked Katherine.

'We don't know, do we?' asked Frank.

Oh come off it, thought Katherine. She wondered if Frank was trying to say that he would miss her, if she went.

'Do you think this car is bugged?' she asked.

Frank looked startled for a moment.

'Why?'

They drew up outside Frank's house. Katherine's voice became very serious.

'Because I have something very important to say to you.'

'What?' asked Frank, who sounded worried.

Katherine smiled radiantly, and put a hand on his thigh.

'Just that . . . I'm really glad you set up Fetter Court.'

They turned to see the boys opening the front door, and Alethea watching them from the front window. Alethea gave her a welcoming smile. Katherine looked at Frank.

'You wouldn't mind,' said Katherine, 'if I changed my mind and stayed a little longer?'

FOR THE BEST IN PAPERBACKS, LOOK FOR THE

In every corner of the world, on every subject under the sun, Penguin represents quality and variety – the very best in publishing today.

For complete information about books available from Penguin – including Pelicans, Puffins, Peregrines and Penguin Classics – and how to order them, write to us at the appropriate address below. Please note that for copyright reasons the selection of books varies from country to country.

In the United Kingdom: For a complete list of books available from Penguin in the U.K., please write to *Dept E.P., Penguin Books Ltd, Harmondsworth, Middlesex, UB7 0DA*

In the United States: For a complete list of books available from Penguin in the U.S., please write to *Dept BA, Penguin, 299 Murray Hill Parkway, East Rutherford, New Jersey 07073*

In Canada: For a complete list of books available from Penguin in Canada, please write to *Penguin Books Canada Ltd, 2801 John Street, Markham, Ontario L3R 1B4*

In Australia: For a complete list of books available from Penguin in Australia, please write to the *Marketing Department, Penguin Books Australia Ltd, P.O. Box 257, Ringwood, Victoria 3134*

In New Zealand: For a complete list of books available from Penguin in New Zealand, please write to the *Marketing Department, Penguin Books (NZ) Ltd, Private Bag, Takapuna, Auckland 9*

In India: For a complete list of books available from Penguin, please write to *Penguin Overseas Ltd, 706 Eros Apartments, 56 Nehru Place, New Delhi, 110019*

In Holland: For a complete list of books available from Penguin in Holland, please write to *Penguin Books Nederland B.V., Postbus 195, NL–1380AD Weesp, Netherlands*

In Germany: For a complete list of books available from Penguin, please write to *Penguin Books Ltd, Friedrichstrasse 10 – 12, D–6000 Frankfurt Main 1, Federal Republic of Germany*

In Spain: For a complete list of books available from Penguin in Spain, please write to *Longman Penguin España, Calle San Nicolas 15, E–28013 Madrid, Spain*

FOR THE BEST IN PAPERBACKS, LOOK FOR THE

PENGUIN BESTSELLERS

Is That It?   Bob Geldof with Paul Vallely

The autobiography of one of today's most controversial figures. 'He has become a folk hero whom politicians cannot afford to ignore. And he has shown that simple moral outrage can be a force for good' – *Daily Telegraph*. 'It's terrific . . . everyone over thirteen should read it' – *Standard*

Niccolò Rising   Dorothy Dunnett

The first of a new series of historical novels by the author of the world-famous *Lymond* series. Adventure, high romance and the dangerous glitter of fifteenth-century Europe abound in this magnificent story of the House of Charetty and the disarming, mysterious genius who exploits all its members.

The World, the Flesh and the Devil   Reay Tannahill

'A bewitching blend of history and passion. A MUST' – *Daily Mail*. A superb novel in a great tradition. 'Excellent' – *The Times*

Perfume: The Story of a Murderer   Patrick Süskind

It was after his first murder that Grenouille knew he was a genius. He was to become the greatest perfumer of all time, for he possessed the power to distil the very essence of love itself. 'Witty, stylish and ferociously absorbing . . . menace conveyed with all the power of the writer's elegant unease' – *Observer*

The Old Devils   Kingsley Amis

Winner of the 1986 Booker Prize
'Vintage Kingsley Amis, 50 per cent pure alcohol with splashes of sad savagery' – *The Times*. The highly comic novel about Alun Weaver and his wife's return to their Celtic roots. 'Crackling with marvellous Taff comedy . . . this is probably Mr Amis's best book since *Lucky Jim*' – *Guardian*